Ple

tel

Noi

ww

THE
BIRTHDAY

By Julie Highmore and available from Headline Review

Country Loving
Pure Fiction
Play It Again?
Sleeping Around
Kiss Me Quick
Your Place or Mine?
Beautiful Strangers
The Message
The Birthday

THE
BIRTHDAY

JULIE HIGHMORE

headline
review

First published in Great Britain in 2010
by HEADLINE REVIEW
An imprint of HEADLINE PUBLISHING GROUP

1

Cataloguing in Publication Data is available from the British Library

ISBN 978 0 7553 4302 7

Typeset in Adobe Garamond by
Palimpsest Book Production Limited, Falkirk, Stirlingshire

Printed and bound in Great Britain by Clays Ltd, St Ives plc

HEADLINE PUBLISHING GROUP
An Hachette UK Company
338 Euston Road
London NW1 3BH

www.headline.co.uk
www.hachette.co.uk

For John

PART ONE

ONE

3 November 2008

The only light came from a laptop, the only sound too. It was the usual – Middle Eastern mixed with R and B. His thing. There was a heady aroma of fruit, garlic, incense, along with the damp. Everything was bathed in red from the curtains, giving the impression of warmth, when in fact the room was cold.

'Hey,' came a voice from the bed. Not a real bed, just one mattress on another, with Egyptian cotton sheets and a beautiful cover. There were big soft cushions, lots of them, dark and silky and inviting.

'Hey,' she said back, out of breath, throwing down the keys to her other life. She began unbuttoning her top, but her fingers were icy and she fumbled and laughed. Long brown arms appeared in the gloom and stretched out for her.

'Let me,' he said, and so she kneeled and crawled towards him;

towards the face that became clearer and more attractive, even, than the last time. Friday. Three days ago. Saturday and Sunday had flown by, thank God, or she'd have gone crazy with wondering. What he was doing. Who with. As soon as she was with him again, like this, it no longer mattered.

She nodded towards the music. 'Is that you?'

'I wish.'

'How was your week—'

His finger was on her lips. 'No. Don't.'

She knew about not discussing their time apart. It had been her rule, after all. Now she wanted to break it – end it, even. Tell him about Martha in the park, cycling without stabilisers. About Alex being offered a transfer.

'You look pretty,' he said, unbuttoning her now, as she sat astride him. He'd pulled the cover over her shoulders to warm her. 'Pretty Emily.' He always called her that; to everyone else she was Em. His voice was soft and deep with an early morning rasp. His eyes, so brown and so white in the light of the laptop, were fixed on hers. He smelled of maleness, in a nice just-woken-up way. She stroked his smooth cheek with the back of a finger, loving the soft sheen of his dark skin. Hers was so pale against him, but he liked the contrast, he'd said; found it erotic.

On the wall above the bed was a framed Persian proverb, once his grandfather's. Hadi had translated the Farsi: *The blind man is laughing at the bald head.* 'You understand?' he'd asked. She'd nodded, although she hadn't been sure. Count your blessings. Nobody's perfect. Or did it mean people have unfounded prejudices? Hadi was clever, with his Ph.D.; she should have got him to explain.

Sometimes, when out shopping, she'd see a bald head, which

would remind her of this proverb in its small carved frame, and that would make her think of Hadi and sex, and her tummy would tighten, her legs lose strength, and she'd stop and grip the buggy handles until the moment passed.

'Hadi,' she whispered. She loved saying his name – Haardi. The way he said it, but not quite. 'I can't stay long. George has a bug and couldn't go to nursery. A friend offered—'

'Shh,' he said, sliding her shirt down her arms and kissing her shoulder, her neck.

Em was back in Putney by ten forty, scooping up her son and apologising.

'After I dropped Martha off, the traffic was a nightmare, then I stopped for some things. Juice for George, more Calpol.' Too many excuses, she thought, too many lies. Did she look as though she'd had sex, or smell of it? One day she'd be punished. Not yet, though, please God. 'There was such a queue in the chemist's. Always the way, when you're in a hurry!'

She laughed and hugged her hot, floppy son, kissing the top of his head and wondering how she could feel so euphoric and so lousy at the same time. Elation mixed with guilt. Hope mixed with dread. Hope for what, she didn't know. For Alex to take that job in Paris? Obviously, they wouldn't uproot the family. Martha loved her school, and they couldn't just plonk her in a French one. He'd have to commute, weekly or fortnightly, by train or plane. How free she'd be.

'OK,' she said, feeling in her pocket for keys; the keys she'd taken a while to find in the dark, while Hadi had slept again. 'Let's get you home, sweetie.'

In a little cotton pouch, tucked inside a tissue-packet holder, in a pocket of her handbag, sat Em's second mobile. It was tiny, pay as you go, always on silent, and only one person had the number. Sometimes he'd text and sometimes there'd be a 'missed call', which meant she was to ring him back. In the car, with George all pink and sniffly, strapped in his seat, Em took the phone out and found a message. *Love loving you, love H.* She heard herself make a noise, then turned it into a cough, then another, for George's sake.

'Mummy poorly?' he asked behind her.

'Mummy's fine. I just had a frog in my throat.'

'Why?'

'Well, because that sometimes happens.'

'Why?'

'It's gone now. Look.' She turned and opened her mouth wide, then closed it and smiled. 'He must have jumped out of the window when we weren't looking.'

'Why did he jump out the window?'

Here we go, she thought. George and his 'Why?'. 'To go back to his family in the pond, I expect.'

'Why?'

'Because they were missing him.'

'I missed *you*, Mummy.'

'And I missed you too, sweetie. But there were things Mummy had to do.'

'Why? Why did you have to do them?'

'Because . . .' Em groped in the door pocket for a CD. She found it and ejected the Duffy that had churned her up ten minutes ago.

'Maybe it was a Mummy frog.'

'Shall we listen to Peter Rabbit?'

'And her little boy frog was missing her and crying.'

'Well, she's back now. Sorry that she left her little frog. I expect they're sitting on a leaf together, eating tasty insects.'

She turned the mellifluous tones of the narrator up before George could ask why, then reread Hadi's message. She put the phone away, switched the engine on and pulled out. Hadi would have to wait for a reply. If she did it now, full of self-loathing, she'd end the affair. She'd count her blessings and be normal. For once in her life, she'd settle for normal.

TWO

3 November 2008

She was there again, the ponytailed woman with a face like her cat had died, the one who'd asked what he needed it for. That had caught him off guard and, not thinking, he'd said, 'Headaches.'

'Brucofen can cause headaches,' she'd told him, like he didn't know; like he wasn't an expert on the stuff. He'd sensed her suspicion; that she wanted to add, 'In those who are dependent.' Instead, she asked if he'd taken it before.

'Some time ago,' Ben told her, attempting a smile. 'I found it really helped.'

'Oh, yes?' She'd given him a look, then having no option, reached for twelve Brucofen.

'A large box,' he'd said, suddenly feeling in charge. It was an over-the-counter drug and perfectly legal. 'Please.'

She'd asked for his loyalty card and he'd lied about not having one. He'd handed her cash and she'd sneered. Cash payment, no loyalty card – there'd be no record of his secret vice. Bitch, he'd thought. She should try some herself and loosen up.

Today she was one of three on the pharmacy tills, and as he moved forward one place, Ben prayed he wouldn't get her again. If he did, he'd ask for something else. It would be a pain in the arse because then he'd have to go to the next chemist on his list. Rotation was the best plan. That way he wouldn't be recognised as a frequent buyer. Could they refuse to sell, if they thought he was taking too much? Like a pub turning a drunk away? Ben thought not, but still, no one wants others thinking badly of them. He'd been here in this queue three days ago, having come full circle on his list of pharmacies. He hadn't got through the pills, he just liked to stock up, hiding them in a laptop case, on the shelf at the back of his makeshift wardrobe.

'Next, please!' she cried, just as he reached first in line.

He hesitated, hoping one of the others would shout out. But they didn't, so he made his way to her till and asked for cough mixture. Soon she was back with stuff he'd never use in a box he'd never open, wanting three ninety-five.

'Ah,' he said, suddenly feeling brave. He got the impression she hadn't remembered him. The other day he'd worn his snug black hat, which could explain why she'd treated him like a criminal. 'Do you have Brucofen?'

'Yes, we do.' She pointed at them. 'Which size?'

Ben squinted and leaned forward, tapping his bottom lip. 'Um . . . oh, let me see. The largest? Thirty-two? Looks like the best value.' He straightened up with a groan and a hand in the small of his back.

She took the box from the shelf, scanned it and placed it on the counter. 'Have you taken it before?'

He frowned, pretending to think back. Maybe she had that face-blindness thing. 'I'm not sure. A friend said it was good for backache?' He'd done this so many times he should get an Equity card.

'Are you taking any other medication?'

'No.'

'Don't take more than six a day.'

Yada, yada. They'd all learned the same script. 'OK,' he said. *And don't take them for more than three days.*

'And don't take them for more than three days.'

'Right.'

'The codeine can be addictive.'

He always thought they shouldn't be telling people that. Advertising its potency, letting them know it makes you feel so good people are getting hooked. 'OK.'

'Would you like anything else?'

'No, thanks.'

'That's ten twenty-eight, please.'

Jesus. He could change his mind about the expectorant but that might be obvious, and besides, didn't it make you high and help you sleep? He took out a twenty and handed it over. It wasn't cheap, being a codeine junkie. Not that he was, because it was under control. One day last week he'd gone down to half doses. For the afternoon, anyway.

The woman opened the till, then stopped and stared at him, making his insides freeze. 'Do you have a Supasave card?' she asked.

'No.'

'Can I interest—'

'No, thanks.' He smiled and she smiled, she gave him his change and receipt, and he moved off to her shrill, 'Next, please!' They must serve so many people. He shouldn't get so paranoid.

Before leaving the shop, Ben conjured up saliva, then popped two white capsules out of their strip and into his mouth. The woman with the ponytail had made him edgy and he needed to calm down. It had been only three hours, rather than four, since the last dose, but what the hell. And anyway, it was more like three and a quarter.

In a café he got a coffee to help the tablets down, then sat with a newspaper and read about the credit crunch, the housing slump and rising unemployment. His wasn't the only life that had crashed, but that didn't make him feel better. In fact, the daily bad news just added to his sense of hopelessness. He'd lost his job and couldn't get another. He was stuck in a negative-equity flat with his ex. And nothing in the news made him think either situation would change soon. Everything sucked at the moment, totally. While he read, his free hand made its way to the box in his pocket and popped a tablet out. He washed it down with his cooling coffee and closed the paper.

He felt resentful, and he had a right to. The last-in-first-to-go policy had chucked out hard-working geniuses like himself and left close-to-retirement Peter the Pillock still in place, haemorrhaging the bank on a daily basis. Peter had one A level, in history. Peter should *be* history – not him, with an MBA he'd sweated blood to get. 'MBA – your passport to progress in the world of business.' It had nearly killed him and it was all bollocks.

Ben drained his cup and thought about getting another. But two coffees would come to . . . a lot. On top of the tablets, etc. He got up, went over to the milk-sugar-spoon corner and poured himself a cup of water, then back in his seat flicked to the business pages. Friday's FTSE dive, some big takeover. How very boring it was when you were no longer there, in that world. He went back to the front page, where it was all Obama, Obama. They were predicting a win, but who knew with those crazy Americans? A black president, not that much older than himself; little black girls living in the White House. How cool that would be. Ben tried not to dwell on a McCain/Palin win, since he was down enough already. His rooting for Obama was, he knew, partly for selfish reasons. He had faith in the Democrats to turn the US economy around, and that would have a knock-on effect in the UK, and then he'd get another job.

In the meantime, he'd go to the library. It was modern and light, but cosy and welcoming. And it was warm. If he went home he couldn't put the heating on, and that would make the bed – if you could call it one – tempting. Since the split, he'd slept in the study on a sofabed he had to make up each day because Julia spent her evenings and weekends on the PC, working. 'Remember work?' she'd once said, when he'd asked if he could sleep.

The other week, she'd found him napping during her lunch break and had a meltdown. He'd been out all morning job hunting, arrived home depressed, taken Brucofen, opened the bed and fallen into a nice fuzzy state under the duvet. A waste of space, she'd called him. Not very original, but that was Julia.

The library, then. Ben felt happy at the prospect. He'd find some engrossing book: crime fiction, a political thriller. How lucky he was, really, not having to go to an office full of investment bankers. He wondered how much he'd actually enjoyed it, working all hours and having no time for the gym or a pint. Some aspects had been good, like the pay and the bonuses. Obviously. They'd got him a pretty decent flat overlooking the Thames. It was a view that did nothing for him now, except remind him of a lifestyle he couldn't afford. Perhaps they'd have to sell and take a loss. Money wasn't everything. There was contentment, love, friendship.

Ben tried to imagine what it would be like, not living with someone who didn't speak to him; not living with someone who thought he was a self-obsessed arrogant-wanker loser. Julia's exact words. He could move out and maybe pitch up at his sister's, or even his parents' . . . but since he was thirty-seven, almost, Julia would add 'sad git' to her list, and rightly.

As was often the way in relationships, the aspects of Julia he now feared and detested were those he'd loved initially. That sharp lawyerly mind, her drive and ambition, the dark tailored suits. He no longer found business suits hot, especially if they were topped by a retroussé nose and bobbed blonde straightened-to-death hair. Julia was cute, almost childlike in appearance, and she had a high voice to match. There was no denying he'd fallen for her looks, then at some point he'd noticed her towering intellect. How she'd follow some heavy discussion at a dinner party, one that had lost him early on, throwing in her own informed, well-crafted opinions. 'That's a valid point,' someone would say. 'You may be right, Julia.'

Although he'd told himself they were patronising her because she was a woman, he'd known all along she was frighteningly clever. Ben could give the impression he was clever, but once Julia realised he wasn't her intellectual equal, and once he'd lost his impressive-sounding job along with any chance of finding another, and once the funds began diminishing, she'd turned on him. Or turned quiet. Lost interest, basically. Lost the little bit of respect she'd had because he was handsome, charming, worked for a top bank and spent hour upon hour trying to please her in bed. 'Trying' being the operative word. Thank God for her Rampant Rabbit, he used to think, when she'd finally groan in an unerotic way, push him off and reach to her bedside drawer. For the past six months it had been just Julia and R.R., which was fine by him, snuggled up with a book on the sofabed. Would he miss anything about her? Probably not. 'She's like an arctic roll,' his mum had once said. 'A thin coating of sweet, but mostly ice.' Inevitably, Julia was proving to be an ace lawyer.

Leaving the café, Ben felt the familiar high. Life was good. Not working was good. He had the whole day to do as he pleased, albeit on a budget. God, he was lucky. He patted the box in his pocket and set off on his bike, his helmet still clipped to the handlebars. He felt positive and he felt invincible. No bendy bus would veer him headfirst into a passing lamppost. Not today.

At half one he was parking by the library when his mobile went. 'Hi,' he said, seeing it was Em.

'Hang on, Ben. No, George, you can't watch *CBeebies*. Here, draw a cat, or Daddy. Hi, you still there?'

'Yep.'

'I read that too much TV makes them autistic.'

'Jesus.'

Ben thought having kids must be like having a long nervous breakdown. In recent years, his sister had gone from hardcore party girl to neurotic care giver. Alex had calmed her down, of course, initially. He'd made her easier to connect with again, more likeable, more settled. Before the kids, she'd had the odd badly paid, arts-connected job in galleries and suchlike, and she'd done up the first flat she and Alex bought, and then the Putney terrace they were in now. His sister turned out to be surprisingly house-proud, once she'd finally grown up. Contented too.

But then little Martha came along and slowly drained away her mother's energy and spirit. With George it happened more quickly. They'd both been bad sleepers, which couldn't have helped, and Alex had had to do more and more, on top of his job. 'I want to go travelling again,' Em had once told Ben, stony-faced, baby at her breast. 'Back to India.' He'd got the impression she meant alone, but hadn't dare ask. Now the kids were no longer babies, she was a lot better, if a tad bossy and humourless.

'It's just a quickie about tomorrow,' she said, while he clicked his bike lock. 'Alex and I thought we'd take a couple of bottles of bubbly. I wanted to check you hadn't bought some before we spent a fortune. You know Alex, only the best.'

Ben tried to work out what his sister was on about. He said, 'Tomorrow?' and was met with one of Em's silences. They usually came with a sigh. So often he'd wanted to swap his little sister for a brother.

Finally she spoke and it was in her mummy voice. 'Ben, you *can't* have forgotten. You really are . . . *No*, George, not on the wall. God, you wouldn't believe how ill he was this morning. Now he's— Hang on, Ben.'

15

It came to him, slowly, foggily. His mother's birthday. Em, the perpetual organiser, had organised something that, yes, he'd forgotten about. She was back with a, 'Still there?'

'Of course I haven't forgotten Mum's birthday.' He laughed and fell back against the wall. 'Do you think I've lost it, just because I'm unemployed?'

'Are you all right, Ben? You sound a bit weird.'

'I'm fine. I'm very, very fine. And no, I haven't bought champagne, although I thought I might.'

'Let's take a bottle each, yeah? I'll text Alex to pick one up. I don't want to leave everything till the last minute.'

'No,' Ben said. Heaven forbid.

'What have you got Mum? Not something for the kitchen, I hope. This *is* her sixtieth.'

'No, no. Nothing for the kitchen.' Nothing, in fact. 'What have you got her?'

There was a pause. 'The country-house mini-break?' Em said, or rather asked.

'Oh?'

'I *told* you, Ben. You said, rather oddly I thought, why not just give her a three-day coma.'

'Did I? That was quite funny.'

'You think? Listen, I'd better go. I have to shop before I pick up Martha. See you tomorrow. Oh, is Julia coming?'

'Uh, she hasn't said. I mean, we're not exactly together any more.'

'She knows she's welcome.'

'I'll tell her,' he lied.

'Tomorrow at seven, then.'

'At Mum and Dad's?' he asked, just to be sure, but she'd gone.

Ben heaved himself away from the wall and unlocked his bike. This was going to be hard, finding something for his mother that wasn't a kitchen item, or smelly stuff that might or might not be nice. Did she still like all that old music? Whatsisname . . . the skinny guy with the guitar. He could look through the folk CDs until he found him. But what if she had it all? Something classical? A scarf, that was an idea. In a colour that matched her eyes. He tried to recall what that was. Sort of hazel, he thought. Or light brown. Or he could surprise her with something quirky, like a personalised T-shirt – 'I'm sixty, you know!'

Maybe not. Ben yawned and pinched the bridge of his nose. It was good to have a challenge, a sense of purpose, but his head felt like mush. He wove his way into the traffic with no destination in mind. Normally, he liked the numbness, the lovely soft blanket between him and the world, but not today, not when he had to think. He'd go home for a rest, he decided. Have a kip. Then he'd be fine.

The overhead light went on, like it was six a.m. in a prison. Julia pushed past him with a swish of tights and a whiff of day-long perfume. The computer fired up and another light went on, while Ben rubbed his eyes and slowly sat up. Then she was in front of him, her Jaffa-cake knees – the only chubby part of her – level with his eyes.

'I want you to move out,' she said calmly. 'Preferably by the weekend. You're not contributing in any way, shape or form, and your very presence irks me.'

Ben looked up. 'Why don't you say what you really mean?'

17

'Oh, you're so hilarious.' She stepped across to the wardrobe, opened it and reached to the top shelf. 'And take your stupid brain-numbing pills with you.' The laptop case flew his way. It bounced off his leg and on to the floor, spilling silver strips galore. Was it time to take more, he wondered, and he began counting backwards. Five o'clock, four o'clock . . .

'You fucking *addict*,' she added, not quite so calmly.

Three o'clock, two . . . He checked the time on the screen – yes! – and picked up a beautiful strip. Sometimes Brucofen felt like his very best friend, or even his only one.

THREE

3 November 2008

Em arranged the flowers Alex had bought her, wishing he hadn't, wishing he wouldn't be so thoughtful. She had friends who were never given flowers; whose partners came home too late to see their children, let alone cook for them, as Alex was doing now, or bath them and read them a bedtime story. You're so lucky, she was always hearing.

As he chopped onions and peppers, Alex listened to his daughter recite lines for her class assembly. Em already knew it by heart, and even George joined in. The theme was helping others and Martha was playing an old lady, complete with wobbly voice, stoop and a hand on her back. A natural, everyone said.

Alex stopped chopping and laughed at his quite brilliant daughter, the love of his life. One of them, anyway. A family man, he was never happier than when at home: playing, soothing, teaching, feeding. Em watched him now, with his nice face and nice eyes and nice light brown hair, and saw again what a catch he was. He'd filled out since she met him, but he wasn't fat. Just tall and solid, broad-shouldered. Her head said he was perfect, while her heart longed for a man she barely knew.

She'd loved him once, this husband of hers. Been in love, that was. Back then, when they'd been squashed into a double room in an interesting, shambolic shared house, finishing their art history Masters. Then travelling. Nepal and India on a shoestring. She'd been so in love, with India and with Alex, but once home he'd changed. She was sure it was Alex who'd changed and not her.

He'd started looking for a proper job and talking about marriage and finding a permanent base, and how they weren't getting any younger. That was when she should have bailed out and gone in search of a real kindred spirit, not the fake or temporary one Alex turned out to be. He did find a proper job, with a company of fine French food importers, where he could use his degree-level French. The art history had become redundant, but they liked the idea of employing a post-grad. Alex found a decent but cheap flat, where he and Em could start saving up to buy a place of their own. Em had panicked. She not only felt let down, but scared as well. Alex had always been up for a good time, only there'd been something solid there too. And she'd needed that, after her 'wayward spell', as her dad referred to it, making it sound like ten months not ten years.

So, although Alex had revealed his true self, or more likely had just grown up, Em stuck with him, because life without him would be frightening. Faced with a choice between boredom and insecurity, she'd chosen boredom. In many ways it had been a good decision – the main one being that if she had wandered off at that point, she'd never have produced these little people in front of her now. Little people she didn't deserve.

Alex wiped his hands so he could hug his little girl, angelic Martha. The image of her beautiful mum, he was always saying, but again she'd rather he didn't. She wanted him to cool it; become distant and neglectful, like a normal man who'd been in a relationship ten years. Why did nothing about her irritate him? She could be moody and grumpy and a perfectionist. Obviously, they had things in common – shared interests – but they were quite different too.

Strangely, considering some of the cruddy places she'd lived, Em liked order and routine in the home. The only place she wasn't keen on it was the bedroom, which, sadly, was where the usually messy Alex became orderly and routine driven. In the old days they'd done it everywhere and at any time of day – parks, toilets for the handicapped, the car – urgently, excitedly. Now lovemaking was what happened after ten, after teeth were cleaned, the children were checked and, just in case someone appeared, the lights were off. It took up fifteen or twenty minutes of their time, two or three nights a week, and followed a tried-and-tested format that worked every time for Alex, but less frequently for her. In fact, since meeting Hadi, it hadn't worked at all.

As tempted as she'd been to conjure up her lover while having sex with her husband, Em had resisted. Aside from the guilt she'd feel, she liked to keep the other thing separate and magical. It was when she was alone, Alex at work and the children at their schools, that she fantasised. When she should have been cleaning and tidying, she'd lie down and indulge in a 'Hadi' fest. She'd tried to feel bad about it, about everything, and often did. But then she always came back to the same question, the same conclusion. How could being so physically pampered by a beautiful man, and being made so happy by it, be sinful and wrong? And she *was* happy, except for when she wasn't; when she felt guilty and a freak, often at the school gates amongst the proper mummies.

Alex had gone back to the peppers, humming as he chopped, then popping some in his mouth. Happy as Larry, she thought, watching him chew, hum, chop, his shoes surrounded by bits he'd dropped. Her husband was a lot like her father at that age. Alex wasn't as classically good-looking, but he was as kind and unflappable as she remembered her dad being. Which was no doubt why she'd gone for him.

'Who wants sweetcorn with theirs?' Alex asked, and the children cried, 'Me! Me!' Em would have just cooked it and presented it, which was what made her an OK parent, and Alex a great one.

They ate together at six fifteen, a ridiculously uncool time to be having dinner, but Alex considered family meals important. He'd ask the kids about their day, and maybe relate something relevant from his own childhood, that would have them asking questions, or begging him to *please* tell them again. And he knew stuff, about animals and mountains and the planets. Or he made it up. The meal would fly by in a way it never did when he wasn't there entertaining them. The children didn't bicker, all the food got eaten – mealtimes were definitely more civilised when Daddy was present.

While Em filled the dishwasher, he carried Martha and George up the stairs, where they yelled and splashed for half an hour.

When Em bathed them, she'd tell them over and over not to flood the bathroom, constantly mopping the floor with a towel. Alex never did, and he'd often be soaked himself when Martha and George padded back down all pink-cheeked and ready for their hot milk.

On the sitting-room sofa, under a spotty fleece blanket each, the children listened first to George's choice of book, and then Martha's. Alex would act while he read, giving the characters different accents, adding gestures and facial expressions that made Martha and George giggle or squeal. Em had tried that, but sensing the kids thought she was rubbish, she now just read.

'One more book?' Alex asked, as if he needed to. 'This time I'll choose.'

Around eight, with the children asleep and the kitchen cleared, he poured two glasses of wine. 'Anything on TV?' he asked.

'I don't know. Why don't you go and check? I've got a couple of emails to send, then I'll be with you.'

Out of the blue, he kissed her cheek. 'You look wonderful, you know.' He was stroking her hair, tenderly, the way Hadi did.

'Do I?' she asked, staring at the floor she'd just mopped.

'You always have.' He seemed nervous. 'Listen, I—'

'Thanks,' she said, not wanting him to carry on. Wanting him to go. Into the sitting room. Anywhere.

'You do love me?' he asked.

'Of course I do.' Just not enough, or in the right way. 'Don't be silly.'

'We are in it for the long haul,' he said. 'Aren't we? I'd never do anything to hurt you, Em. You know that?'

23

'Yes,' she said, worried now. This wasn't like Alex, not at all. He tended to avoid serious, and was generally upbeat. 'I know you wouldn't.'

'Not deliberately. Only if I thought it was in your interest, our interest.'

'What do you mean?' What was he talking about – the job offer, perhaps?

'Nothing,' he said. 'It's nothing.'

Em looked in his eyes and tried not to see the love there. She should give him a hug, she knew, but she stepped back and then around him. 'I'll join you in a bit.'

In the study area, at the end of the landing by a small window, Em answered a couple of emails, sent one to her brother reminding him about the champagne, and then, with a glance over her shoulder, took the mobile from her bag. No messages. No missed calls. She went back with a smile to one he'd sent late morning, when she'd got home with sick George. *I love the little sounds you make when I kiss you, there. It's become my favourite place in the world. H*

She heard the stairs creak and quickly dropped the phone in her bag. Delete. Remember to delete.

'Nothing on telly,' Alex whispered through the banisters. 'Shall I order us a film for fifteen minutes' time?'

'Sounds good.'

'Anything you fancy?' His eyes wandered to her handbag, then back to her.

'Oh, you choose,' she said. 'I'm happy with anything.'

'Right,' he said, and again he looked at her bag. 'How about *The Hours*? You know, Virginia Woolf.'

'Great.'

'Here.' His arm shot through the rails and made her jump. 'Pass me your glass and I'll top it up.'

She stood and handed him the glass, then turning back saw the blue glow of the mobile screen at the top of her bag. Had he seen it too? Surely, he'd been at the wrong height. God, she was getting careless. *Delete*, she told herself again, but when she sat down and reread Hadi's words – words that knotted her stomach and made her close her eyes and remember – she just couldn't.

When the film finished and Alex was switching back to TV for the news, Em slipped away. Upstairs, in the bathroom, she took out her phone and found nothing. At lunchtime she'd sent a text in response to his, then another asking if she could come tomorrow morning. Why hadn't he answered? Hadi was always so responsive.

She'd give him a quick whispered call, she thought, pressing the button. 'Calling' it said, as she sat on the edge of the bath, nervous, biting her lip. It rang and rang, and then she heard his husky voice, telling her he couldn't answer right now, asking her to leave a message.

She stood and went over to the wash basin, leaning on it for support, staring at her face in the mirror. Why no texts? Why couldn't he answer right now? Why was he so busy at ten o'clock at night? A gig, maybe, but then he usually told her when he had a gig; one of the few things he did tell her. Why did it matter to her, anyway – where he was, what he was doing – when it was only about sex? And if it was only about sex, why did she feel so bereft?

'Why?' she asked out loud, sounding like her son.

'Em?' she heard, followed by tapping. 'Are you all right?'

Go away. 'Fine!' she called out, and she flushed the loo and put her phone back and opened the door.

'I was getting worried. You were ages.'

'Was I?'

'Let's go to bed,' he said, and he slipped an arm around her waist and pulled her towards him. He was giving her no choice but to kiss him, and it felt odd and forced, as she clung to her bag wedged between them. They never kissed out of bed, not like that. He stopped and took her hand. 'Come on.'

She could see lights on downstairs, and no one had checked the kids, 'But what about—'

'Later,' he said.

FOUR

London, 1971

At Waterloo, Susie got off the train and made her way to the Tube, which would take her to Bank station, one exit of which, apparently, was right beside London Star Insurance. It sounded easy, and it turned out to be, because when she emerged from the underground, there, she guessed, was the building – tall and imposing and rounded, right on the corner. All about her, people walked fast and purposefully. The men were in suits; lots with briefcases, some in bowler hats. The women and girls were more casually dressed, but not in jeans or hotpants or anything.

After a month of temping in the West End, Susie now had a permanent job in the heart of the City, all thanks to the agency. No interview necessary, they'd said, not with her background. It had been frightful temping, always being the new girl and not knowing where the carbon paper was, or the bogs, or where to go for a sandwich. *Always* having to ask. She was a hopeless self-taught typist, which hadn't helped. At least there'd be no typing involved at London Star. The Life Department, that was what she had to find. Report to Mr Strong in Quotations.

The entrance was on Lombard Street, and while she walked along looking for the door, a young chap in a pinstripe suit wolf-whistled as he overtook, then gave her the once-over and said, 'Nice legs, darlin'.' He swaggered off and Susie looked down, and then around at the other women office workers.

Was her skirt too short? Too white? She'd chosen it because it was her smartest, and because it matched her white ankle-strapped, cork-wedge sandals. At least it covered her derrière, not like some girls', and at least her legs were fabulously tanned from all the lying in the sun swotting. For all the good that had done her.

She tugged the skirt down, and pulled her lacy low-cut T-shirt up, and decided that if they didn't like the way she was dressed there'd be stacks of other jobs around, especially for girls like her, even ones who'd spectacularly failed their exams.

She found the entrance and went in. At a small wooden desk that matched the floors, the staircase and the wood-panelled walls, a man of around ninety, with military hair and the same suit as everyone else, gestured to a nearby door and said, 'Second floor, and mind you close the concertina when you gets out.'

Susie thanked him and on opening the door found a tiny old-fashioned grille-type pull-across lift, similar to the one in Aunt Phyl's mansion block. 'I think I'll take the stairs,' she told the doorman, or receptionist, or whatever he was, then felt his eyes on her rear as she made her way up and round a bend. The skirt was all wrong, she knew now. OK for Oxford Street, wrong for the City. It wouldn't have bothered her a year, or even two months ago; in fact, she'd have revelled in the attention. But not getting a single pass in her three As had dented her confidence – not hugely, but enough to make her feel a disappointment to her parents, and, well, pretty dense.

The second floor was a large open-plan office with tall windows, where people were either whirring away on calculator handles, speaking on the phone, or writing things down. Some were doing all three. In a corner, a lone middle-aged typist clicked furiously. It was the usual story: far more women than men. Four weeks of temping had taught Susie that in an office environment she gelled better with men, unable as she was to talk makeup, boyfriend, hubby or telly – none of which she wore, had or watched. Her main love was reading. She'd read anything, so long as it was fiction, from Mills and Boon to the classics. If she'd read less and swotted more, she might not have found herself standing there in a sea of clerks, wondering what in the world she was doing, and about to retreat.

But then a good-looking – *really* good-looking – young man, not much older than Susie, jumped up and came over.

'Can I help you?' he asked. He gave her a warm smile that showed off neat white teeth. He was about five eleven, Susie guessed, the same as her father. Nice nose, she thought, knowing she should say something but, for once in her life, stuck for words. His hair was dark and thick and a little bit wavy, half covering his sideburns and curling over his big collar. His eyes were bright blue with long dark lashes, and his face tanned, as though he'd just come back from somewhere fabulous. Without the biros clipped on his pocket, he'd have passed for a pop star.

'I'm here to see Mr Strong?' she said, looking around the room.

'Ah, the new girl.'

'Yes.'

'Eddie!' the handsome boy called out, and an older man on the phone held up his free hand and beckoned. 'Why don't you go over? He shouldn't be long. There's a chair by his desk.'

'OK. Thanks.'

As she moved off, he smiled again and held out a hand. 'I'm Duncan, by the way. Senior life clerk.' There was a trace of the north in his vowels. Dooncan. Like poor Fiona when she'd started at Benenden, aged eleven. In less than a term, and after much ribbing, she'd sounded like the others.

'I'm Susie,' she said, taking his hand and thinking she was going to rather like Dooncan.

By the coffee break, which was a cup of something and a biscuit delivered to each desk, Susie's head was spinning. Whole life, endowments, decreasing term assurance. And what on earth was an annuity? With profits, without profits, mortgage protection. She believed a mortgage was something to do with houses, but didn't bother asking when there was so much she couldn't follow.

'I hear you went to public school,' Eddie had said, 'so you'll no doubt pick it up quick.'

How could she tell him one didn't necessarily follow the other? And then there'd been Duncan distracting her, as he'd walked around the room looking completely gorgeous. Once or twice he'd glanced her way and caught her staring.

Eddie was very round with a big head and a halo of tight blond curls. He perspired constantly and kept glancing at her bare thighs. Tomorrow she'd wear something longer, or at least put tights on, like absolutely every girl in the office had today. Eddie's butcher's fingers worked deftly on one of the electronic calculators. 'Everyone'll have one soon,' he'd told her, patting the keys on the neat, book-sized machine and coming up with something called a premium.

'What's a premium?' she'd asked bravely, and he'd laughed and shaken his big head, as though she'd asked what a kettle was.

'It's what the suckers have to pay. Monthly, quarterly or annual. Sometimes, it might be a one-off, like in an annuity.'

'And what's an—'

Eddie had picked up his ringing phone. 'Quotations!' he'd announced, awfully gruffly, she felt. 'Can I help you?'

If only she could be a model, Susie thought, dunking her biscuit and flicking through the fat black book she was to work out premiums with. Pages and pages of columns of numbers. Male, female, age next birthday, term, maturity . . . It was so dreadfully boring that she yearned to be back in Oxford Street in last week's accounts department, and that was saying something. She yawned, turned another page and dunked again.

Not long after getting her results, she'd taken photos of herself to a modelling agency, only to be told that curves were 'still out', sorry. One woman suggested she approach the *Sun*, saying they'd snap her up.

After initially feeling insulted, Susie began thinking it might almost be exciting and glamorous, being a page-three girl. She had no qualms about taking her bra off – she rarely wore one anyway – and nobody she knew read the *Sun*. But then it occurred to her that some of the airmen would, and other civilian chaps who worked on her father's station. He was no saint, but seeing his daughter's boobs in the press would devastate him. He might even get demoted or chucked out – like the flying officer who'd passed a bad cheque – and then he'd never speak to his daughter again, and she'd be homeless, unloved and destitute.

Susie looked around at her fellow clerks. Girls with feather cuts and neat fitted blouses, chatting quietly over their coffees. The men generally got on with their work while they drank; tapping, whirring, answering the phone with tedium in their eyes. How had this happened? How had she ended up here? It was astonishing that a person's life and ambitions could have altered so much and so rapidly. She'd aimed to become a doctor, which now felt such an embarrassing goal.

The end of her biscuit fell in her tea, swirled a bit and sank. Susie was trying not to see that as a metaphor – or was it an allegory? – for her current situation, when Duncan appeared. 'Want me to show you around?' he asked.

'Super,' she said, grabbing her only proper handbag in the world. Perhaps he'd tell her what an annuity was.

At lunchtime, Duncan put his jacket on and took Susie to a pub where the London Star inspectors drank. He explained on the way that an inspector was like a salesman, 'Drumming up business, liaising and, er, stuff.' *Stoof.* Susie got the impression Duncan didn't know exactly what inspectors did, but that he had aspirations in that direction. He walked quickly on his long legs and, determined perhaps to get to the pub, seemed unaware of the looks he was getting from girls.

The Birthday

It was called The Anchor and it was packed, mainly with men. Some had taken their jackets off, while others sweltered in the hot dark room. Duncan kept his on, perhaps to look older and more serious.

'What are you having?' he asked.

'Oh, a lemonade, please.'

'You what? Come on, have a lager or some wine. Vodka and tonic?'

'Um . . .' Susie looked around. Every single person was holding a beer or wine glass, even the handful of women. If she had a drink would insurance be interesting? 'Perhaps a cider,' she said. She liked cider because it was fizzy and tasted like pop, especially with blackcurrant – only she couldn't ask for blackcurrant 'Do they have sandwiches? I don't want to get sloshed and sleep all afternoon.'

Duncan laughed and waved an arm at the crowd. 'I think that's the general idea.'

'Really?' Perhaps working in the City wouldn't be so bad. Duncan wandered off and left her propping up a wall. All around there was much jostling and guffawing and patting of backs. Tall men and short ones, old and young. Some even younger than Duncan.

After a while a man sidled up to her, thrust his head towards her neck and breathed on it. 'And what, my little blonde beauty, might your name be?' He slid an arm around her waist and held it there loosely. He reeked of spirits and was at least forty. His eyes were bloodshot and as saggy as his chins. He could even have been fifty.

'Susie,' she told him, and she smiled sweetly because for all she knew he was chief manager or chairman or something of London Star Insurance.

'Sweet Susie, hmm?' His hand casually slid down to her buttock, stayed on her white skirt for three seconds, then went to his jacket pocket. 'Rodney,' he said, swaying. 'Rodney Gill-Blackmore, stockbroker.' He took a pen out and held it unsteadily over the other hand. 'Now, where can I get hold of you, my lovely?'

'Oh!' Susie said, spotting Duncan with the drinks. 'Here comes my boyfriend.'

'What? Ah. Pity. But still, a girl's entitled to a little extracurricular, *n'est-ce pas*? With a real man, eh? Not a boy, know what I mean?'

Susie felt ill at the thought, or perhaps it was the alcohol fumes; then Duncan was there, handing her a pint of cider and Rodney double-barrelled winked and meandered off.

Duncan tutted. 'These dirty old men. Think they get the pick of the young women.' He sneered at Rodney's broad back. 'I'm really sorry about that.'

'It's hardly your fault!' she said, rubbing his arm. Duncan was very sweet, she decided, as well as a dish.

As the place filled up even more, they had to shout to be heard, taking it in turns to lean towards the other's ear. Susie told Duncan that she was living with her parents, who'd just bought their first house, some way from the RAF station her father commanded.

'It feels terribly small,' she said, 'after the CO's quarters.' She had to explain what a CO was and what a quarter was, and then Duncan put his mouth by her ear and told her he was from Boston, and that his dad worked in a bank and his mum was a school teacher. She could smell beer on his breath and rather liked it.

34

'You don't sound American!'

'Boston, Lincs,' he shouted back. 'As in Lincolnshire.'

'Oh, I see. I lived in Lincolnshire when I was little. RAF Coningsby?'

'Oh, aye,' Duncan nodded. Someone pushed past and they were suddenly much closer. 'We used to go to their dances. Saturday nights at the Castle Club.'

'I was five or six. Started school while I was there.'

'On the camp?'

Susie laughed, rather loudly, she realised. She was almost through her pint and had only had a biscuit since getting up. 'Prep school, I'm afraid. Where do you live now?'

'Essex,' he said. 'The only place I could afford to buy.'

'Golly, a house owner!'

It went through her mind that he might like a lodger to help pay for it. Anything would be better than living at home, in a house her mother loathed and her father was hardly ever in. It was obvious her mother missed life on the station: the status, the parties, all the officers' mess pomp and festivities. Susie suspected she'd been depressed since returning from Germany and being forced into life on a modern estate.

'You're terribly young to buy a house,' she said.

'I'm twenty-nine.'

'No!' She found that hard to believe, but then she'd never had much to do with twenty-nine year olds. One or two pilots and navigators, but perhaps Forces chaps looked more mature, with their short hair and uniforms and hats.

'The in-laws helped with the deposit,' Duncan was saying. 'A loan, like.'

It was then, as Duncan raised his pint glass in the six inches separating them, that Susie spotted the gold band on his wedding finger. Not only was she as dense as mud, but unobservant with it.

'What's your wife's name?' she asked, trying to sound breezy and unbothered. Surely he couldn't be married. How terribly unfair.

'Frances. Well, Fran.' He looked at his watch. 'I suppose we should head back. Don't want Willard giving us detention.'

'Who?' It didn't feel like they'd been out an hour.

Duncan took her empty glass and put it beside his on a ledge. 'Mr Willard, Head of Life.'

Susie followed him, thinking surely God, not Mr Willard, was head of life? She giggled at her silly idea; then, out on the street in the bright sunshine, it dawned on her that she was squiffy.

'I ought to eat something,' she told Duncan, hurrying on her cork wedges to keep up with him. People and buildings passed by in a strange swirly manner, but she felt ridiculously happy. And all from one glass of cider. It was pathetic, really. Her mother could drink gin for days and not be drunk. She'd just have to get more practice in.

'Here we are,' Duncan said, grabbing her hand and steering her into a door she'd passed.

She looked up and read 'London Star Insurance' on the gold plate. 'Oops.' She giggled again and waved at the old receptionist, and before she knew it was chest to chest with Duncan in the lift.

'Going up,' he said, pressing a button, then lowering his eyes. 'If you get my drift.' He put a hand on the back of her head and kissed her until they jerked to a halt, then they got out on a floor she didn't recognise.

'I think we've—'

'Shh.' Again she was being steered, this time by the hand on her back. When a woman came out of a room that said 'Claims', Susie tried to appear sober, even though her legs were rubbery and her head spun.

'In here,' Duncan said, once they'd turned a corner. He looked over both shoulders and led her by the hand into what appeared to be a stationery room. He let go of her and moved a box against the door, and before she knew it she was on the floor watching a fancy Victorian ceiling spin round and round. Then, in place of the ceiling was Duncan's lovely face saying how pretty she was.

'So are you,' she told him, and next thing they were kissing and fondling.

There had been boys before, but no one this attractive, and no one she'd wanted to go all the way with. She was about to lose her virginity and she didn't care because it seemed so right, and adorable Duncan was so completely and absolutely the person to lose it with. Or was he? He was married and that didn't seem right, but, on the other hand, what he was doing felt very right. While she stroked his soft hair and moaned as his hand went up her skirt, she could feel his biros digging in her boob. Perhaps he'd married terribly young. He'd fall in love with her and leave thingamajig . . . whatever her name was. She'd go and live in Essex with him. Essex sounded wild and exciting . . . maybe because it had 'sex' in its name. 'Ohh,' she groaned, while his hands explored.

'Mm, you like that, do you?'

'Yes,' she sighed. They should stop, they really should.

'And did you like the cider?' Duncan whispered. 'Or should I say double vodka and cider?' He chuckled in her ear; such an attractive chuckle.

Suddenly she felt wonderfully wicked. Getting drunk at lunchtime, having it off in the office with a married man. 'Yes, I did. It was very . . .' Vodka, she thought she'd heard. What had he said? Something about vodka? Susie felt the dreaminess and happiness draining away. 'Did you put vod—' He was kissing her again and she wanted to wallow in it, enjoy it, and she almost did, but she realised he was trying to shut her up. Somehow she found the strength to stop. She didn't want to but the part of her that was cross won, and she pushed him off. 'Vodka?' she asked, and when he smiled and shrugged, she sat up and swept her hair back with one hand. 'You pig,' she said. 'You absolute pig!'

He laughed again, perhaps thinking she was joking, and when he came for her, she hauled herself off the floor, straightened her clothes, picked up her bag, went and pushed the not-very-heavy box away from the door – anybody could have walked in! – and left the little room. She didn't look back and she didn't return to the quotes department. Instead, after finding a ladies and splashing water over her face, she flew – or so it felt – down endless flights of stairs and out of the building.

Standing on the pavement, she felt dirty and sullied in the sun's glare, and both sick and hungry at the same time. She put a hand over her eyes. The road opposite looked as though it might have shops and cafés, and she negotiated several streams of traffic on her spongy cork soles that felt more like bouncy rubber, just like her legs. Where was her bag? Yikes, not still in that room? She found it on her shoulder and tucked a hand in to check for her purse. She needed money for something . . . what was it . . . A taxi hooted and someone said, 'Watch out!' and grabbed her arm, and her bag spun round with her hand still in it. 'Sorry,' she said to the man's back. 'Thank you. Sorry.'

Cheapside, it said, when she got there, and she thought how apt, because she was feeling so cheap herself. A coffee, that would sober her up. And food. She had to have food. Just something to get her head back into the real world. She laughed out loud at the ridiculousness of what had just happened, and on her very first day. If that was insurance, they could jolly well keep it. People were staring, she knew, but then they often did.

On passing a newspaper stand, Susie doubled back and scanned the rows. 'May I have the *Sun*?' she asked the man beside her. Her voice sounded peculiar, like someone else's.

'You certainly may,' he said, picking one up and half folding it before handing it to her, as though selling something he shouldn't.

'*There* you are,' Duncan said, plonking himself on the opposite seat. She could hear he was out of breath. 'I'm so sorry.' His hand went to cover hers but she quickly moved it. 'That wasn't on, I know.'

Susie bit into her egg and cress sandwich and tried not to look at him. Her head had cleared while she'd queued, just a bit. Once the sandwich was inside her she'd be normal again, then she could look at him, talk to him, across the table. It was a very basic café, with mugs of tea that came with too much milk. For energy, she'd poured in masses of sugar from a bottle.

39

'I'm sorry, Susie.'

'So you said.'

'You must have a terrible impression of me, and I'd really hate that. I don't know what came over me, honest. Only you are dead stunning, you know. Not that that's an excuse for—'

'Spiking my drink?' Susie continued staring at the *Sun*. It was a story about a footballer she'd never heard of, and how he'd cheated on his pregnant wife. The words jumped around but she'd got the gist.

'I only did it to relax you,' Duncan said. 'I could tell you weren't much taken with London Star. That you were finding it a bit confusing, as we all did at first. If it's any consolation, I had a double vodka myself. At the bar, like. I suppose it must have gone to my head, and, well, then you rubbed my arm and kept pressing up against me—'

'I did not! Gosh, not deliberately.'

'I suppose it felt like a bit of a come-on, and, I dunno, I thought you liked me.'

'I did. Past tense.' Susie finally looked up and wished she hadn't. Why did he have to be so handsome? Why did he have to have eyelashes she'd kill for and a mouth you'd want to kiss all night if you were his wife? She remembered her name: Frances. I'm sobering up, she thought. Thank the Lord, and the sandwich too. Frances, that was his wife. It was a pretty name, but not pretty-pretty. Frances was probably dark and interesting and everything Susie wasn't. This was silly. Why was he bothering with her when he was married to the lovely Frances?

'Please don't be like that.' He looked devastated and as though he might cry.

'Shouldn't you be at your desk?' she asked. She sounded hard and unlike herself, but he really shouldn't like her, this married man.

Duncan took an anxious look at his watch, then stared into her eyes with a long, please-forgive-me puppy-dog stare. 'I'll wait for you.'

'There's no need,' she told him, but she willed him not to leave. Was it the alcohol that had made her so furious in the stationery room? Was she like those perfectly sweet officers who got sloshed in the mess, then punched someone's lights out? She couldn't think clearly enough to know if she'd overreacted. Whether she had really led him on. Whether his was perfectly acceptable behaviour in these liberated times, and she was just a sheltered and naïve boarding-school girl. He'd been tiddly himself, after all, and he hadn't been forceful, or hurt her or anything.

'I'm sorry,' he was saying again. 'It was unforgivable. It's just that . . . maybe I shouldn't tell you, but Fran's pregnant, you see, with our first child, and she doesn't want to take any risks, and that means no you-know-what for a while.'

'No what?'

'Nooky,' he whispered.

'Oh, I see.' She looked at Duncan and then at the footballer. He was good-looking too, with a lovely smile that would make you think he'd be a terribly nice person if you met him. Like Duncan. There were things about men she really didn't get.

'So, I expect I'm feeling a bit . . . er . . .'

'Sexually frustrated?'

He laughed. 'Randy, I was going to say, only you have a much nicer way with words. But it's not that, not really. In fact, not at all.

41

When you walked in the office I couldn't believe my eyes. You were so pretty. *Are* so pretty. And lovely with it.'

Something was happening, she realised, that was nothing to do with being tipsy. Something was filling her up – not anger, but a much nicer, more warm and exhilarating sensation. Should she tell him she'd had the same reaction on seeing him? No, no, she shouldn't, not in her current state. She guessed she was halfway between drunk and sober now. The feeling had come back in her legs and one ankle hurt. She must have twisted it somewhere . . . on the stairs, or when she was beneath Duncan. It really had been nice lying under him. The kissing, the caressing . . .

'Am I forgiven?' he asked.

'I'm not sure.' This time she let him cup her hand on the table and she even smiled at him, wishing she hadn't been so cross, knowing she was partly to blame.

'You've got cress on your tooth,' he told her, and before she could do anything, Duncan had leaned so far forward, his face was an inch from hers. 'Let me,' he said, and once again they were kissing, his tongue just inside her mouth.

When a waitress cleared her throat, Duncan flopped back in his seat and looked dreamily at Susie, still holding her hand. 'Do you believe in love at first sight?'

She squeezed his upturned palm, not knowing if it was love she was filled with, or desire, or excitement, or all three. 'Maybe,' she said, smiling again and not giving a fig about cress on her teeth. Suddenly, she felt like her old self – confident, happy. 'May I ask you something, Duncan?'

'Anything you like,' he said, running a finger along her bare arm.

'What's an annuity?'

'It's like a pension.'

'Ah.'

They both laughed and then he sighed and tilted his head. 'What am I going to do?'

'I don't know,' she said, and this time, because she was still a bit drunk and because he looked like Warren Beatty in *Bonnie and Clyde*, only with more hair, and because she couldn't help it, she leaned across the table and kissed him.

FIVE

4 November 2008

Sixty! How was that possible when turning forty had been so recent? They say time speeds up as you get older, but this was ridiculous. Perhaps if she stayed here, under the duvet, the day would pass painlessly. She'd pretend to be ill, then no one would make a big deal of it. By no one she meant Em.

Fran reached for her glasses and slipped them on. Everything sharpened up, her husband included. She still liked to watch him sleep. The salt-and-pepper hair that's attractive on a man but not a woman; ditto the high forehead and grey temples, and the leathery skin from hundreds of European and long-haul business trips, dozens of foreign holidays. Duncan had sailed through his sixtieth, six years ago. They'd gone out with the Goodwins for a curry. The kids had popped in with presents and cards, and treated

44

it as just another birthday. It was so easy for men, this ageing business. Less significant.

'*Mum*, it's your sixtieth,' Em had said, 'and it'll be Bonfire Night. Well, almost. And election night. You can't *not* have a party.'

'Election?' she'd asked, for it had been some time ago, before Obamania had reached the Chilterns. More recently, of course, November the fourth had been talked about feverishly, endlessly; a constant, dispiriting reminder of her birthday.

Duncan's breathing was deep and wheezy, his face baggy and lined and beginning to need a shave. It was still a handsome face, though, and so familiar. More familiar than her own. But then, she thought, we rarely see our own features: three or four times a day in a mirror, straight on, eyebrows raised, chin up. That's why we're shocked and appalled by photos of ourselves, or in her case, the video Ben had taken and emailed last Christmas. 'Hi Mum and Dad, thought you might like this.' No, actually, she hadn't.

Her husband made a funny grumbling sound, then his big hand moved to her thigh and rested there. For some time now he'd taken a tablet each night. It saw him through eight or nine hours of sleep, but he could be groggy as anything the next morning, and increasingly, now, throughout the day. Fran told him to go back to the GP and ask for something milder, and Duncan said he would but never did.

He'd put his post-retirement insomnia down to the lack of activity and stimulation that had always left him drained at the end of a working day. It was true, Duncan had never had a sleep problem until a year ago, and then it became Fran's problem too. He'd padded around the house in the early hours, switching on the TV or booting up the PC in the study beneath their bedroom. He'd make tea with the inevitable clatter of crockery. More times than not, she'd joined him on the sofa, and in the dull dead of night they'd watch something about volcanoes or whales. How relieved she'd been when he'd come home with 'something to tide me over the transition period'. These days he was asleep in minutes.

His fingers twitched on her thigh. They could make love, she thought. What better way to start your seventh decade? Something debauched, perhaps, to mark the occasion. She'd wear that scratchy bustier he'd bought her in the eighties. Would it still fit? Where was it? For decades, Duncan had tried spicing up their sex life; not just the lingerie, but other stuff, like attaching her to the bedknobs with two of his ties. She recalled the discomfort and gave one wrist a rub, looking back with relief at the new solid headboard.

No. They were so out of practice, and besides, there was a lot to do. It was all very well Em insisting on a party, but someone had to produce clean floors and a Gordon Ramsay chicken stroganoff. Hopefully, Duncan would cook. He liked that role, but he was a chaotic, use-every-pan cook, so there'd be mess to clear up before the family arrived. No friends, she'd decided, and Em had agreed.

Fran eased her leg out from under the hand, and got up as quietly as she could. She found her slippers and put on the chunky robe that made her look fat, then crept past the en suite and over lime-washed floorboards. To postpone her birthday a bit longer, she'd let Duncan sleep. The longer he slept, the less groggy he'd be. She knew that from some of her clients, many of whom had to knock themselves out at night.

On passing the full-length free-standing mirror, Fran closed her eyes. In the bathroom, once more, she avoided her reflection. She'd wait till she'd had coffee and a ciggie before looking at her sixty-year-old self. It's the new forty, people kept telling her. Young, patronising people. No one in their sixties would say it.

But then she caught herself in the glass and nothing had changed: same thick, ash-blonde, well-cut, just-above-shoulder hair. Fran was naturally dark, but in recent months her trusty ageing hairdresser, Stan, had finally talked her into a pale blonde, rather than the supermarket 'rich chocolate' she'd slapped on for years. He'd called her Morticia Addams once too often and she'd given in.

She liked being blonde, and she liked the new sweeping, fringe-less style he'd given her. 'Classy,' Duncan had said. 'Very whats her name, the actress. You know . . . oh, the blonde.' She'd started going through the alphabet with him, and at 'h' he'd cried, 'Helen! Mirren!' hands clapping. And then he'd yawned and flopped back in his chair, as though the thinking and the clapping had worn him out. He did a lot of yawning and flopping these days. 'Old age,' he'd say, his eyes slowly closing.

Fran lifted her glasses and leaned closer. Her eyes had their morning puffiness, but that would go by ten. What wouldn't go, not without Botox, were the pucker lines around her mouth. She'd been shocked to see those in the video. It was the ciggies, of course. She grinned and they were gone. Great. She could carry on smoking and just smile a lot.

47

Still, she decided, there'd be absolutely no filming this evening. With a bit of luck, unemployed Ben had been forced to flog his camera. That was a mean thought, she knew, but he hadn't asked permission to film them. What if she was on YouTube, all wrinkles and jowls, reading out a cracker joke? It was so intrusive, all this being on view: people snapping away with their phones, CCTV every ten yards.

Fran lifted her head and stroked away the chins she was sure she'd see in profile. Her husband said she was sexier now than at twenty-five, not realising he'd hurt her feelings a bit. Had he not fancied her at twenty-five? Could he even remember her then? Duncan's memory wasn't what it was. He not only forgot names, but constantly mislaid his keys, glasses, mobile. We all do that, Fran kept telling herself, but there were other things too. Small, simple operations often threw him. Filling in a form, filling up with petrol. And last weekend, on their way back from Em and Alex's, he'd taken a wrong turn, close to home in the village. Suddenly he was driving along the road two down from theirs, blissfully unaware until Fran told him.

'Oh Lord, I was miles away,' he'd said, forcing a laugh, then yawning as he three-point turned.

Fran might have forced a laugh too, if he hadn't had the longest face throughout lunch and barely said a word. He'd told one anecdote that he later repeated. It was a story they'd all known, anyway, about a beggar he'd taken for a Big Mac, and there'd been lots of darting eyes when he'd begun it the second time. Em – it had to be Em – stopped him.

'Dad, you told us that earlier.'

'Did I?' Duncan had asked, frowning at his pie and ice cream,

48

as though wondering how it had got there and what he should do with it.

Downstairs, Fran made coffee. Several colourful envelopes had trickled in over the past week and lay on the table unopened. The postman might bring more, so she'd wait and get it over in one go. The card from her brother had been airmailed from New Zealand. Patrick was a lecturer, sixty-two and yearning to retire and come home. Fran thought she'd detected a badge on the card. She pictured '60' in bubble writing, or something equally silly and demeaning. Would people start treating her like a child, she wondered. Or worse, after this big eventful day, stop seeing her at all? She'd become one of the invisible, indistinguishable elderly – unless, of course, she took up something extreme: sky-diving or whatever. Old ladies who sky-dived got attention, got into the local paper. It was a thought, she decided, opening her ciggie box and heading outdoors.

In the scruffy late-autumn garden, Fran lit up. It was here that smokers smoked these days, since George's asthma attack following a visit to his grandparents. Fran was convinced Em had made that up, as she'd heard no more about George's affliction. In the meantime, she'd got used to the exile, and even quite liked the bracing air, first thing, last thing, and at those times when Duncan – 'I know I put it somewhere' – made her want to scream.

She'd wrapped a cream throw around her shoulders but her feet were cold in the flimsy slippers. She'd get her warm fluffy pair out today and find thick socks. This would be her first winter of smoking in the garden and she ought to prepare for it. Get some sort of shelter attached to the back wall and a patio heater.

And something more comfortable than an upturned tub to sit on. Gradually, a conservatory took shape in her head. But that would cost, and since property values had plummeted, they'd never get it back if they sold. Not that they would sell, not now. They had talked occasionally of a more remote spot – Cornwall or Wales, near the coast. France, even. But not recently. She missed that more than anything, the making of plans together, even if they'd known, deep down, that they wouldn't move again.

She could hear Duncan in the kitchen. He'd be getting out the marmalade and the spread that's good for your heart, and putting them on the far end of the long pine table they'd had for ever. He might be adding a card and present to the existing pile. This year she hadn't dropped any hints because she couldn't, truthfully, think of anything she wanted. A holiday, perhaps, but she'd seen so many places. What she'd have liked really, in truth, was her old husband back.

It was quiet, and she turned and saw him watching the toaster. Just staring, deep in thought, trying to wake up. And she could see through the glass door that the table hadn't been laid.

From her tub, she called out, 'Morning, love!'

'Morning!' he said loudly, in his deep, increasingly gravelly voice. He looked up and gave her a wave.

Fran stubbed out the cigarette and finished the coffee that had cooled too quickly. The butt went in the terracotta ashtray she emptied at night, and Fran went in the kitchen. 'Gosh, it's chilly,' she said.

'What happened to that really good toaster?' Duncan asked. 'The silver one?'

'I don't know. We've had lots of toasters.'

'This one takes ages.'

'Does it?' She hadn't noticed.

Her eyes scanned the room and saw no prettily wrapped gift, no card. She waited for her first, 'Happy Birthday!' but perhaps Duncan had a surprise in store for her; something he was saving until they were properly awake. She looked at him now, his robed back to her; one pyjama leg riding higher than the other, bare feet on the cold tiled floor, head resting on a cupboard. *Turn around. Speak to me. Wish me happy birthday with a big smile.* He'd put on a little weight recently – a fact that clothes could disguise but a towelling robe couldn't. It was the inactivity, along with the tablets. Most days the stairs were his only exercise. If they hadn't decided against a ground-floor toilet, he'd be even lazier. Fran took a long calming breath, and then another, and decided to keep busy. It usually helped.

The phone rang while she was laying the table. Em, probably, making a quick dutiful call before flying off to school and nursery.

'Shall I get it?' Duncan asked.

'No, no. I expect it's for me.' *It being my birthday.*

Fran went through to the hall where the receiver stood in its charger, but she deliberately walked slowly. She couldn't talk to her daughter, not now, and certainly not cheerfully.

By the time she got there the ringing had stopped. She gave it a minute or so, then listened to Em's message, wishing her a happy birthday, saying she had a frantically busy day ahead, but that they'd be over earlier, at five thirty, and would it be possible to make up the bed and cot, as the overnight sitter had let them down.

Fran liked the idea of Martha and George coming. Children

51

diffuse things, tension and so on, with their noise and their demands. For the first time, she began to look forward to the evening. Her evening. She saved the message and returned to the kitchen, where Duncan was just as she'd left him, yawning noisily.

'It *is* taking a long time,' she said, going over to his side and looking, with him, at two slices of bread protruding from their slots.

Duncan's hand landed on her shoulder and he squeezed her and kissed the top of her head. 'Bloody thing,' he said.

'Me or the toaster?' she asked, trying to laugh but wanting to cry. Not on your birthday, a voice said. Her mother's. Or you'll cry every day for a year.

'It was good,' said her husband, 'that big chunky silver one.'

Fran sometimes wondered if it was more than 'old age', all the forgetfulness, the lack of energy, the occasional out-of-character snappishness. But at sixty-six, Duncan was too young, surely, for dementia to be creeping in, and as far as she knew there was no family history. Something was wrong, though. She'd get him to have a full medical examination; call the surgery herself if necessary.

She leaned across and pushed down the lever on the side of the toaster. 'There,' she told him. She put an arm around him and squeezed him back. 'Shouldn't be long now.'

Duncan shook his head. 'What a plonker I am.'

She laughed. 'You said it.'

He looked down at her with his sad and sleepy eyes. 'Happy Birthday, my love.'

'Thank you.'

SIX

Florence, 1974

She asked an American couple if they'd take a photo.

'Sure,' the woman said.

'Thank you.' It was their first holiday abroad and she wanted to capture the significant moments.

'Say "cheese",' the woman shouted, stepping back to get both them and the Duomo in. 'Terrific!' She gave the camera to Duncan and said, 'What a beautiful couple you make,' and Duncan smiled uncomfortably and thanked her.

Susie prodded him and laughed. Duncan wasn't happy about photographs, but she'd put her foot down and promised never to sell them to the *News of the World*. Not that they'd want them. Duncan was hardly George Best. He was a sales rep for a bathroom manufacturer, albeit a rapidly expanding one with overseas interests.

It was their second day, and apart from the photo business, he'd been a total joy. Spouting the few bits of Italian he knew to shopkeepers and waiters, and being terribly romantic in the balmy atmosphere of their first evening. He must have felt guilt and remorse, but being Duncan he'd never let it show and ruin her holiday. And, besides, they always had such fun together.

He'd bought tickets for the opera, claiming he'd never been to one. 'What better place than Florence to start,' he said, and Susie hadn't mentioned she wasn't keen, having been dragged to too many as a child. She liked James Taylor and Carly Simon, not the classical stuff she'd been forced to play on her clarinet. And she loved to dance to the Stones and The Who and Free, and music that made her feel alive. She knew Duncan did too, because on their clandestine weekends they'd gone to discos and let their hair down.

But Duncan was trying to better himself, which was why he'd left London Star for a higher salary and improved prospects. And travel. It was the travel that sold it to him. Hotels all over the world needed up-to-date and reliable bathroom fittings; so did offices and airports. The list was endless and Duncan's company was cashing in. 'You'll be able to come with me, or at least meet me,' he'd told her, in his slowly changing accent. 'It's the perfect solution, don't you see?'

What Duncan hadn't seen was that Susie had rather a lot on, herself. She was working part time and retaking her A levels, after a three-year gap. And if all went well, she'd soon be studying medicine – intensively, all hours – and she had no idea how they'd work things out then. In the meantime, he'd tagged four days on to a business trip to Rome, and here they were, a beautiful couple in beautiful Florence.

Susie was having a ball, and she loved Duncan so much; every-thing about him. She loved him for phoning home in front of her, during their first afternoon. He'd sat on the edge of the bed, doing baby talk to Ben, and she lain to his side, not touching him, especially when he was talking to Fran, pretending to be in Rome still. He could have sneaked off somewhere and phoned, but he'd asked her and she'd said yes, and somehow that made her love and trust him even more. He couldn't live without her, he often claimed, and she believed him. But he couldn't leave his wife and little boy, either. And she wouldn't want him to. That was what she told him, and what she told herself.

He'd hung his head for a while after the call home; a little bit of shame, homesickness, perhaps. He didn't say, and Susie didn't ask, because before long he was lying beside her, holding her hand and asking what she'd like to do that evening.

Several photos and a good deal of walking later, they were back at the hotel, showering and changing before heading out for lunch.

'This is heaven compared to Greg's house,' Susie said.

The house, which Greg shared with two equally untidy people – both girls – was in Chiswick. Greg, a friend from London Star and the only hippie there, had given them a spare key each, and told them the place was empty during the day. 'Best to get out before five,' he'd said. 'Although Pauline and Brenda are pretty laid-back.'

In exchange, Duncan treated Greg to the odd drink and the occasional football match. Greg, a former public-school boy, was the type of hippie who looked the part and took lots of drugs, but whose ideology didn't quite square with the wider movement.

He worked for the large insurance company as an actuary, he drove the new Porsche his parents had given him for his twenty-first, and as far as Susie could tell, he'd never been to a sit-in, or marched, or demonstrated. At home he ate lentil bakes, but only because the girls he shared with were the real thing. Most weekends found him home on the estate, shooting and suchlike, or in London, drinking, smoking things and watching his latest passion, Chelsea, play.

Duncan was a Manchester United fan, but gradually he mentioned them less and less. He'd started having golf lessons, and claimed he was almost good enough to play clients and potential clients. Susie, who'd overdosed on competitive sports at school, failed to see the attraction of golf. These days, she simply loved to swim. If Florence had been on the coast, it would have been even more perfect.

She'd wondered if next time Duncan might take her to the sea. Not that he'd paid for her Florence trip. Her parents had, thinking she'd come to study hard with an old school friend who'd done brilliantly in physics and biology. She'd hated lying but couldn't possibly have missed out on four days in Florence with Duncan. She'd brought all her books and notes with her for credibility, and if she found herself with an hour to spare she might well look through them. The exams were less than a month away, and she had to pass, absolutely had to. Six months at London Star and a series of clerical jobs, most of which involved hours on end of filing, made her realise what she really wanted in life. One of the things, that was. The other was to have Duncan to herself, full time, and not to have to be so furtive. But that wasn't likely to happen, so she'd grab her chances when they came.

Susie had tried not to let Greg's room depress her, with its over-flowing ashtrays, piles of clothes and dirty plates. The only time she'd been in the kitchen it had made her want to retch, and she'd found it hard to believe two girls lived there. But Greg's place was better than nothing, and it was kind of him to let them use it. She still lived at home in Oxfordshire, and neither she nor Duncan could afford hotel rooms. The second time they'd gone to Chiswick, she'd taken two single sheets, which they rolled up and popped in carrier bags after each encounter, then tucked away in a corner of the room, in amongst the mess. It was all rather thrilling, and on leaving the house, she always felt high. Duncan said he did too, and they'd laugh about it being the residue of drugs in the air.

But then, back at home, in her apricot-walled bedroom, when she pictured Duncan having a dinner with his wife or playing with Ben, she'd often feel lonely and cheated. What she could do with was a husband of her own. She'd carry on seeing Duncan on the side and things would be nicely balanced. There was no chance of that, though. Since meeting Duncan, she hadn't seen a solitary attractive chap. Sadly for her, she was a one-man woman.

'Spaghetti Bolognese,' she decided, closing the menu and putting it down.

'Really? Don't you want to try something a bit different? I'm going to have the fish, I think.'

'Spaghetti Bolognese,' she insisted. They'd had it at school a million times, but she wanted to try the real thing. 'Definitely.'

They ordered, the food came, and Susie eulogised over her dish. The meat was tender, rather than gravelly. The Parmesan complemented the sauce in a way grated Cheddar couldn't. It was like no Bolognese she'd ever had, and she ordered it again when they went out for dinner, and again the following evening. No matter where they ate, it was too delicious for words.

'We'll have to find us a good Italian restaurant in London,' Duncan said the last time, when she was twirling yet more spaghetti around her fork. He smiled and wiped sauce from her chin with his napkin. 'Or I'll learn to make it for you.'

'In Greg's kitchen?' she asked, and they laughed and pretended to gag at the idea.

On their final night they went to *The Barber of Seville*. Duncan wore a suit and no tie and looked almost his age. Susie was in a long silver sleeveless dress that she'd last worn to an officers' mess summer ball, and had brought, just in case, along with her cream shawl with matching sandals. At the last minute she put some mascara and lipstick on. Duncan did a mock swoon when he saw her, then she swooned over him in his suit, and it was as much as they could do not to forget the opera and fall into bed.

Later, they did fall into bed, or rather on it. *The Barber of Seville* had been surprisingly wonderful, and they'd had some wine before and during, and some more wine after, and back at the hotel at midnight, they'd made fantastic dreamy love, with the windows open and the street sounds filling the room. Afterwards, lying in Duncan's arms, Susie knew she'd never been so happy.

But being happy had made her forgetful, she realised, when she went to use the toilet. On the shelf above the basin sat her pink plastic Dutch-cap case, and in the case sat her cap.

SEVEN

The key was on a piece of frayed string, which Em pulled through the letter box, very slowly and carefully, trying not to make any noise. She opened the door, wove the string and key back and hesitated, tempted to leave again. Hadi wasn't expecting her. Whenever she'd been here before it had been prearranged, but he hadn't answered his phone again this morning. She'd tried over and over, feeling more anxious and annoyed each time she heard his voicemail message.

Foolish or brave – she couldn't decide. She hoped he'd see her as spontaneous and daring, turning up unexpectedly, waking him, perhaps. What a lovely surprise, she heard him say, still half asleep, slurring his words. He'd tell her he'd left his phone somewhere, sorry, then he'd take her in his warm bare arms and stroke her long, freshly washed hair as he slowly came round.

The place was silent. His housemate, Nigel, left for work in a school at seven each morning. Teachers didn't take days off in term time, so he was more or less guaranteed not to be there. The only noise Em heard was her heart, pounding in her ears. How would he really react? Once, only once, she'd seen Hadi lose his temper. It had been soon after they'd met, the previous March, at Cat's cousin's gig, before they'd got physical and into their current arrangement. A girls' night out, she'd told Alex, for Cat's birthday. It was almost true.

Hadi knew Cat's cousin and the following day got Em's number, on the pretext of wanting to buy Alex's guitar. Em had told him, at the bar and as they'd flirted and danced, about her life, her family, her husband's foray into guitar lessons, only to discover he had no aptitude. When Hadi rang, she hadn't been that surprised. For a while, he feigned an interest in the guitar, saying it would be handy as a spare for his pupils. 'I'm not sure it's what I'm really after,' he said, and he'd laughed infectiously, deliciously. 'I think it's you I want.'

George had to be picked up at one fifteen, so they'd arranged an early lunch at a pub in Putney. It was one she'd never been to and it was down towards the river, a safe distance from her home. Approaching it, Em felt nervous, but also so very alive. She'd just about forgotten how that felt.

When Hadi bought the first drink, the barman short-changed him but failed to apologise. Hadi called him racist – forcefully and angrily, and loud enough to make some customers turn. By the time he got back to Em, he was perfectly calm; asking if she'd found anything good on the menu. Later, she'd quizzed him about it, and he said it happened so often it could only be his skin colour. The incident had made Em count her change for a while, and twice in one week, she'd found it short. 'It could only be because I'm a woman,' she told Hadi, and he'd laughed and wrestled her on his sumptuous bed.

She didn't hang her coat in the hall this time, but wrapped it tightly around her as she climbed the stairs and walked along the landing towards the big, cosy, bay-windowed bedroom she'd grown to love. Today it scared her, though. The house felt alien and unwelcoming. She hadn't been invited, after all. And it really was quiet. The bedroom door stood half open, and by now she'd be hearing music or the deep heavy breathing of Hadi asleep.

She stopped, her courage waning. What if he was with someone, doing the things he did with her, to her . . . ? Or they were just curled up together, asleep, naked, intimate. She could never ask if he had another woman or other women. That would have been against the rules, obviously, even though the subject ate away at her when they were apart. She knew so little about him, considering how familiar she'd become with his body over the past eight months.

She did know he was born in Britain, shortly after both the Shah and his parents fled Iran. He was a guitarist, working very occasionally as a studio musician, but most of his income came from private lessons, mainly to teenage boys, after school and at weekends. He'd once told her, quite unembarrassed, that his parents resented him wasting his education but still paid his rent.

Hadi was in a couple of bands, one of which played a mix of East and West. In the corner of his room was a small guitar-like instrument, called a tar, he said, a Persian tar. He'd played her something on it one morning, and the Middle Eastern sound had come as a shock. For the first time, perhaps, she saw the Iranian in him, as he worked the strings with a metal plectrum and ran his fingers up and down the long neck. The culture was in his blood, clearly, but he wasn't a practising Muslim. He drank, he had sex with a married, agnostic woman.

Eight months of wonderful clandestine sex, and here she was glued to the spot outside his door, unable to go in but unwilling to turn back. Petrified. He may have heard her creaking along. How silly she'd feel if he caught her retreating.

This was wrong, all wrong. Sordid and wrong, and not, after all, that good for her soul. Fear and distaste had taken the place of the yearning, and even if he were there, waiting and smiling, she no longer felt she wanted him. Beam me up, she pleaded, take me home. Let me clear cereal bowls, hoover, listen to *Woman's Hour*. She took a deep silent breath. She'd go in the room and tell him it was over, in as kind and friendly a way as she could. Her legs were weak but they got her to Hadi's door, and she peeked around it.

Her first thought was, where's the Persian tar? The red curtains were there, closed as usual, and the wardrobe and chest and a chair. But they had nothing on them or in them. The open wardrobe door showed empty shelves, and there was a nail in the wall where the proverb had hung. More shocking than anything were the two mattresses, bare and ugly and so unlike his beautiful bed.

Another room, she thought, turning back, legs still weak. He must have moved to another room. She knocked on the first closed door she came to. It was Nigel's room, but perhaps Nigel had moved into . . . where? It was a two-bedroomed house.

She opened up and was met with PCs and wires and beer bottles and clothes, and an acrid and unfamiliar smell.

Em found herself checking the bathroom, then the front and back room downstairs – rooms she'd barely spent time in, but which felt emptier, definitely. It was the kitchen that was really empty. 'Nigel never cooks,' she remembered Hadi saying. There were two beer cans in the fridge, along with ketchup, white rolls and a pack of butter. In a cupboard, on almost empty shelves, were coffee and a box of Cup-a-Soups, along with trails of the spices that once stood there.

Em leaned against the back door, taking it all in, or trying to. She pulled the little mobile from its pocket and checked for messages. Nothing. With a shaky hand, she called his number and got voicemail. He'd gone. Hadi had gone. It was crazy. Who sends an erotic text message, then disappears? He's in trouble, was all she could think. That must be it.

Nigel. Nigel would know something. She went out to her car and tore a sheet from a drawing pad and found a felt tip. '*I'm trying to contact Hadi regarding a guitar lesson. Could someone give me a call or text, please? It's urgent.*' She put her secret mobile number. If Nigel phoned, she'd be able to call him back. '*Many thanks!*' she finished, with no name.

Em let herself out. She closed the familiar door with its peeling black paint, pushed her note through the letter box, then stood on the pavement looking up at the top bay, as she'd often done when leaving. Sometimes he'd been watching and she'd blown a kiss. Occasionally, very occasionally, they'd left together and gone to a café. But that had happened less and less recently. They'd exhausted their childhoods and couldn't talk about the present, which left little to discuss over panini and coffee. Their comfort zone had been the bed, but, along with her lover, it had gone. Just two scruffy mattresses, one lying crookedly on the other.

She put Duffy on and played 'Mercy' over and over again. She didn't cry or even feel upset. He'd let her know what had happened and where he was. He had to. They were so close. What they had was so special. She wouldn't have ended it, not really.

EIGHT

London 1974

Susie moved out of her parents' house and into Greg's, shortly before she began to show. Duncan took the afternoon off to help, but first her mother drove her and her pitifully few possessions there.

She thought her mother would faint when she saw the Chiswick house, but needn't have worried. So relieved was she to hand her pregnant daughter over to other people that she bravely ignored the littered and filthy hall carpet, stair carpet and landing carpet, and said, 'Oh, what a lovely room,' when they reached the dirty middle bedroom.

Particles of dust floated in the orange light, filtered by the makeshift curtain. On the floor were cotton wool and tissues and plastic bottles, and an ashtray, and everywhere were the ends of joss sticks. The walls were covered in drawing pins and the vague outlines of where posters had been.

'I'll put your suitcase here by the wardrobe,' said her mother. She placed the bag containing two ironed sheets, a blanket and two pillowcases on a bed with no pillow. I'll leave you to settle in, darling. I expect the others will help.'

She'd told her parents she'd be sharing with a boy and another girl, but since it was a weekday neither was there to greet her, which was something of a relief. Susie hadn't met Brenda yet, but knew from Greg that she wore eccentric clothes and made biscuits that got him high.

On the doorstep, she and her mother kissed but didn't hug, and Susie couldn't tell if either of them was upset. What might have been an emotional leaving-home moment for many girls felt like just another drop-off, since her entire teens had been spent being either delivered to or picked up from school. What *was* upsetting, although unsurprising, was that through the entire hour and a half in the car, no mention had been made of the pregnancy.

Duncan must have been lurking nearby because as soon as her mother drove off with a royal wave, he was there giving Susie a cuddle and making her feel safe again.

Pauline had gone to Africa to do VSO, and when he saw the room she'd left, Duncan swore and said maybe she should have done some voluntary work at home first. Then he set about airing the room and sweeping it, and finally – after rummaging in Greg's shed, and after Susie had taken every drawing pin out with a knife – painting it. The only tin with enough paint in was a pale yellow, and as she watched Duncan in only his tight little underpants, with the one decent brush he'd found, the room became more cheerful and clean-looking, and began to feel like somewhere you could, if you were desperate, and if he or she wasn't too noisy, keep a baby.

But Greg had said this was to be a temporary arrangement, because if the 'capitalist bastard landlord' saw she was pregnant, he'd flip and kick them all out. Mr Wilson called in unexpectedly several times a year, and once she got big, Susie was to hide under blankets if he came. Duncan said he'd help her pay for a proper flat, but how he'd do that with a mortgage on the new house in Chelmsford and a wife and son to keep, she had no idea.

At the back of her mind, sort of as a last resort should her parents stop coughing up, Susie had her great-aunt. Phyllis, a widow, was terribly wealthy, having been married to a shipping magnate. When young, Susie had, to much hilarity, asked her parents how you married a magnet. They still laughed about it now. Well, perhaps not now. Perhaps now they failed to find anything about their daughter amusing.

Aunt Phyllis, her father's father's sister, had a three-bedroomed luxury apartment in a mansion block in Belsize Park. She'd always been fond of Susie, saying she reminded her of herself as a 'young gel'. In her early twenties, she'd been part of a Bohemian set, and would tell Susie stories of her decadent youth that she'd had to promise never to repeat. Aunt Phyl had been an artist's model before marrying the wealthy businessman, and had alluded to an affair with a 'noted and notorious' married painter.

As far as she knew, her parents hadn't told Great-aunt Phyl the news; after all, they'd barely spoken about it themselves. Duncan thought they'd probably come round to accepting the baby and turn into doting grandparents, but Susie wasn't so sure. She wouldn't reveal who the father was, which was adding to the friction.

'You can't sleep here tonight,' Duncan was saying, down on his knees in the corner. 'Not with all the fumes, especially from the gloss. When I've finished this skirting board we'll go and find you a hotel or a bed and breakfast. I'll need a shower, that's for sure. Can't go home looking and ponging like a navvy.'

Susie laughed but felt the familiar stab. A night on her own in a hotel didn't bother her, and she knew Duncan couldn't stay, but still . . . how nice it would be to have him there, all night.

'Won't it be terribly expensive?' she asked. Her father had put three months' rent in her Post Office account and she still had savings from her last part-time job, but not a huge amount. For the first time ever she'd have to watch the pennies.

'Don't you worry about it,' Duncan said. He bashed the paint lid back on, then joined Susie on the single bed in the middle of the room and admired his handiwork: lemon walls and white wood.

'It's lovely,' she told him, kissing his splattered cheek. 'Thanks awfully.'

Pauline had left a stripy yellow and orange piece of material up at the window, which Susie would put back when the paint dried because she liked the way the light came through. And there was a darling little fireplace that someone had painted lilac, and a Victorian pine wardrobe with a mirror on the front and three drawers and a rail inside. It was all she needed for now, but she tried picturing a cot and nappies and all the paraphernalia babies need, and, luckily perhaps, couldn't quite see where it would go.

'Come on, then,' Duncan said, putting his shirt back on and then his suit trousers. 'Before you start feeling pukey again.'

'Oh, that's all over,' she said, 'thank goodness.' The last place you'd want morning sickness was Greg's house.

It didn't take long to find a cheapish hotel. The room reeked of cigarettes, but it had a small, neat, clean-looking bed and its own bathroom, and was perfectly good for one night. Duncan immediately ran a bath, and after he got in Susie joined him and soaped his back and made sure all traces of paint were off his face and arms and chest.

'My baby,' he said, placing the palm of his hand over her flat tummy.

'Yes.'

Sometimes she wondered if this was actually going to happen, that a complete person with legs and ears and things was going to come out of her. At the ante-natal clinic, when she and another first-time mum had been saying just that, an enormously pregnant woman nearby scoffed and said, 'Wait till it's your fourth, sweethearts, and you'll know for sure it's a bloody baby.' Susie couldn't imagine saying 'bloody' about her child, who, when it did seem real, she already completely loved.

While they were drying, Duncan used the phone by the bed to ring his wife and say the boss had called a meeting and he'd be a bit late. He asked about Ben's conjunctivitis, and whether the gas man had been to service the boiler, and it all seemed a million miles from Chiswick, and a million miles from her and Duncan and her new room and their baby. She often wondered how Duncan split himself up and whether one day he'd have a mental breakdown.

And because she loved and cared about him so much, she

sometimes thought about leaving him and having the baby on her own, so he could concentrate on Fran and Ben, and on golf and his career. But the one time she'd suggested it, Duncan had virtually begged her never to do that, vowing that if she left him he'd leave Fran, so there'd be no point. 'How could I stay with her, knowing she'd made me lose you?' Duncan had a way of making you believe him, and not counting the fact that he told his wife fibs, he seemed to Susie to be a man of his word.

The next day she unpacked her things and arranged the little room the way she liked it. She put photos of herself with school-friends on the mantelpiece, and one of her parents too, taken in the back garden in Germany. They were in deck chairs and laughing into the camera. They'd been so much happier then, and probably wished they could roll the clock back two years to a time of cheap plonk and parties and a daughter who was tucked away in a boarding school and not pregnant.

Susie had a box, just a small one, full of little ornaments and souvenirs and other knick-knacks she'd accumulated during her years at Benenden, along with letters and postcards from her parents, great-aunt and friends. She dipped into some of them. 'Good luck with the exams' . . . 'Daddy and I will be in Berlin for a week' . . . 'Here's ten shillings, darling. Do buy something frivolous'. The ten shillings had been from Great-aunt Phyllis – just one of many contributions that had gone towards records, chocolates, bubble bath. She must visit her, Susie decided, and break the news.

She put the contents back and slid the box under her bed, then in order to shake off the sadness and nostalgia that had crept in, decided to take a walk around Chiswick. Because they'd always been pushed for time, she and Duncan had never seen much of the area.

It was lovely, she discovered, with its wide streets and cafés and trees. How fab it would be to spend your entire life somewhere like this, and in London too, which she'd grown to adore, and not only because of its association with Duncan. She'd never lived in a city, or even a town, only on RAF stations and then in a rural school. London excited her; just going on the underground with its whoosh of wind when a train approached, or suddenly seeing Big Ben in the distance, gave her a thrill. She didn't even mind the grottiness and litter and things, because the grandness of the buildings and the super parks and all the different coloured faces somehow made up for the dirtiness.

She'd been stuck in Oxfordshire for the past year, studying for her retakes, working part-time in the office of a builders' merchants, and only coming to meet Duncan at Greg's house once a week. She'd missed working in London, but now she was actually living here, which meant she'd get to see more of Duncan too. No wonder she was happy, despite the odd dip when she found herself low and tearful. That would be her hormones, Duncan had explained. 'Fran was crabby as hell.'

After buying a sandwich and some crisps and a bottle of Coke, she took them back to the room that only smelled faintly of paint now. There, she ate on her bed, smiling at the bits of wall Duncan hadn't quite covered and missing him terribly.

After lunch, she tried to nap but couldn't, not without a pillow, so went down to the kitchen with the aim of clearing away the clutter and washing the stack of plates and pans. But on seeing and feeling the sun pour through the kitchen window, she unlocked the back door and took her first steps into the garden. It was bigger than it looked from her window, with an apple tree in the centre and a red-brick wall all the way around. The grass was long and tickled her calves as she made her way to the far end and a small square vegetable patch.

What fun it must be, growing your own vegetables. Her parents hadn't much bothered with gardening, never seeing the point of nurturing and tending plants they'd shortly be saying goodbye to. Their new garden was mainly a neat lawn and a patio, all laid by the builders. A man came in and tidied it up, but it never took him long.

Here, runner beans had wound their way up bamboo sticks, and a row of knee-high plants had actual tomatoes on them. Nature was so incredible, the way it made beans and tomatoes and babies grow.

She picked a sprig of something that smelled powerful but nice, and then broke off a leaf that smelled different again, then another. They were herbs, but she had no idea of the names. She did recognise half a dozen lettuces, but couldn't make out the big pretty plants at the back, with no flowers or vegetables on. Knowing Greg, she guessed it was marijuana. She stepped over the lettuces to sniff them, but was none the wiser.

A long thin blanket lay on a flattened area of grass, half in the shade of the apple tree. There was a pillow – her pillow? – sunglasses, an empty mug, a plate and a spread-eagled book, as though someone had just upped and gone off to work but would return to the spot later. It looked so tempting that Susie gave up on her plan to tidy the kitchen, and on her other plan to ring Duncan at work from a call box. There was a phone by the front door but the dial had a lock on it. All that could wait, she thought, settling herself down and picking up the book.

She'd heard about *Jonathan Livingston Seagull* and wanted to read it, but not being in the mood, lay it down again and thought about Duncan, and what he'd say about the way she'd arranged the room. A spider plant would look nice, she thought, on the mantelpiece, beside the photos and her little swivel mirror. Perhaps she'd splash out on one later, one with little dangly babies.

Susie wished her mother could see the room too; see how much nicer it looked now. She'd like both of her parents to come and visit and wondered if they ever would. She'd have to vacuum the stairs beforehand, and clean the crusty cooker and sweep up brown rice and onion peel. And she'd open the windows to let the smell of pot and garlic and joss sticks out. But her parents would never drop in, and she'd been given the impression they'd rather she didn't visit them, not now they'd got to know the nicer neighbours, and had even had them round for a cheese and wine party.

Having got her photos out and reread some letters, Susie thought about writing to best-friend Caroline with her news, or Fiona, her second best. The trouble was, they were both studying – Fiona at Cambridge and Caroline at Sussex – and the times she'd visited them, they'd talked of nothing but essays and the societies they'd joined and the parties they'd been to. Caroline had a boyfriend who was studying politics and she'd become quite political herself, rabbiting on endlessly about 'feminism', which meant 'women being equal to men in all spheres', especially the workplace. Susie hadn't been sure how that would work, all the time women had babies, but Caroline assured her it would because educated women were going to establish careers before starting a family, and enlightened fathers would do fifty per cent of the parenting so their wives could work.

No, she wouldn't write to Sussex with her news. Caroline would see her as letting the side down. Fiona she'd write to, though. Or she might just surprise her by turning up in Cambridge in the early spring with a bundle in her arms. 'Hello, Fiona. Meet baby . . .' Baby what?

Susie watched the sun dancing around in the leaves above her and, not for the first time, pondered baby names. It was early days, obviously, but there was a boy's name she kept coming back too. One she'd liked since she was fourteen, when on a school skiing trip to Aviemore she'd had her first real kiss at the disco, with a boy in another school party from Inverness. He'd been watching her for days, he said, and because he was going home the next day had plucked up the courage to come and dance beside her, then with her. When a slow record came on, he manoeuvred her into a dark corner and kissed her for at least five minutes before Miss Fuller, gym teacher and chaperone, prised them apart. 'What's your name?' Susie had called out to the boy, whose long curly hair was probably red, but looked blond in the dark. 'Alex,' he shouted, looking both happy and sad as Susie was ushered away. 'I'm Susie,' she said, and then she never saw him again.

Sunglasses on, she heard herself breathing deeply and began to think she could manage a doze now. You were supposed to take an afternoon nap, they'd said at the clinic, if possible. The woman on her fourth 'bloody' baby probably couldn't. No wonder she was irritable. Four would be too many. In fact, one might be enough. She was an only child herself and couldn't honestly say she'd missed having brothers and sisters. Not until now.

Alex, she thought, liking it more and more. 'Hello, Fiona. Meet baby Alex.' If you were going to have only one child, you'd want to get the name right.

She woke up refreshed but hot and thirsty, and rather than drink her housemates' funny-looking juice, she went out again and bought a bottle of Ribena and a big bottle of Coke. She loved coca-cola again, after all those weeks of not liking the taste. Pregnancy did the most peculiar things to a person, like making contact lenses no longer fit, or clearing up acne. Susie didn't have lenses or acne, she'd just been sick, sick, sick, which had made it a trifle difficult for her parents to ignore the problem; to sweep it under the carpet in that stiff-upper-lip way that made her, rather uncharacteristically, want to slap them. Did pregnancy make women want to slap people?

On the way back, she phoned Duncan, or tried to. 'I'm afraid he's in a meeting,' she was told. 'Is that Fran?'

'No.'

'Oh, sorry. May I ask who's calling and take a message?'

'No,' Susie said again. 'No, it's all right. I'll try again another time.'

Back at home and fighting off glumness, she wrote Duncan a letter, thanking him for his hard work and for putting her up in a hotel. She described the room now, and how pretty Chiswick was and how she'd had a peaceful snooze in the long grass. And she talked about the spider plant she wanted. Silly things, she told herself. Things a busy man couldn't possibly be interested in. Finishing off with a 'Miss you', she signed it and put one large kiss beside her name.

For the third time that day, she left the house and wandered up the road; this time only as far as the post box. He'd receive her letter at work tomorrow, and he'd be bound to write back. Susie loved receiving letters almost more than anything. She supposed it was to do with having been a boarder, waiting for precious words from home, or from a friend she'd met during the hols. Duncan's letters were short and affectionate, but frequent. Previously sent from his place of work to hers. Because she'd only been part time, she'd had to pop into the office when off duty, to see if one had come.

Susie kissed the envelope, double-checked the address and posted it, with a 'There'.

After letting herself back in the house, she jumped at the sight of a large girl at the far end of the hallway. The person wore a huge tent of a black dress, lots of gold jewellery and some kind of African-type headdress.

'Who the heck bought this?' she asked Susie, sounding quite northern and holding up the Coke bottle. She came towards her, almost the width of the passage. 'Brenda,' she said. 'I'm guessing you're posh Susie? That's what Greg calls you, only I'm not sure he's one to talk. Pots and kettles and all that. You don't eat meat, do you? We only tend to eat animals that have had a nice life, not that you can ask them once they're dead, or even before. Anyway, we all eat together and it's vegetable crumble tonight.'

'Sounds super,' Susie said, while Brenda squeezed past her,

opened the front door and placed the bottle of Coke on the front garden wall.

'Some idiot will take it,' she said. On seeing Susie's face on her way back in, she stopped and embraced her. Brenda smelled just like the house, but more concentrated. 'You'll learn, posh Susie. Now come and try my fig and gooseberry cordial.'

NINE

They were at the ticket machine, where Duncan was trying to tap in the car registration. While his fingers hovered over the buttons, Fran wanted to say, 'Here, let me.' Instead, she willed him to remember; to just do it, as he had dozens of times before, far faster than she'd ever managed.

'N . . .' he was saying. 'Um, F . . . zero . . . oh, what is it . . . zero, four.'

'Zero six, Duncan, not four. Here, let's press cancel and—'

'Oh, you do it,' he said, 'if you're so bloody clever.' He walked off, heading for the shops rather than the car, where they'd need to put the ticket on the dashboard, gather the shopping bags and lock up with the key he had in his hand.

'Duncan!' Fran called after him, in as gentle a tone as she could manage, and with a queue now forming. 'I need the car key, love!'

Her husband stopped, opened both palms, saw the key in one

and lobbed it her way. It landed at the feet of the young man behind Fran, who picked it up and gave it to her.

'Thank you,' she said, a catch in her voice. *Don't cry. Birthday.* 'Sorry. I'm so sorry.'

The entire morning had lacked birthday jollity. Duncan had presented her with theatre tickets he'd hidden in the car – a David Hare play at the Cottesloe – along with a spectacular bouquet of flowers. He'd made an effort and Fran was grateful, but within half an hour he'd been asleep on the sofa; reading glasses halfway down his nose, mouth open, newspaper on his lap. When it was time to go shopping and she'd gently tapped his shoulder, he'd come round grumpily and resentfully, and she'd had to ply him with strong coffee to lift his mood.

Fran now regretted having left this day client free, and longed to be in her little room at the centre, listening to anxious Pat and OCD Colin. Sandy on reception would have organised cakes for the staff in Fran's honour, or even a proper birthday cake. They'd have toasted her with their mugs of coffee or redbush tea. How preferable that would have been to this. Still, too late now. It was a decision made months ago, when Duncan had been quieter and more lethargic than usual, but still pretty much Duncan.

He was back by her side at the ticket machine. 'I'm sorry, love. Just not feeling myself today, and on your birthday too. Sorry.' He kissed her on the forehead and took the ticket and key. 'I'll do it.'

'Let's have spag bol,' Duncan said, halfway round, when their trolley was filling with stroganoff ingredients.

'I don't know. I mean, we've already—'

'It's your favourite, isn't it? Ever since Florence? Let's do your favourite meal for your birthday.'

He sounded so pleased with his idea and was already heading for the meat counter, that Fran decided not to resist, and not to remind him that they usually bought meat at the butcher's. Martha and George would have to have theirs chopped up, but they'd probably like spaghetti Bolognese. Fran herself was indifferent; she and Duncan must have eaten it only a dozen times in forty years.

'Three pounds of your very best mince,' he was asking the young assistant, who probably had no idea what a pound was. 'No, make it four.'

They'd holidayed in Rome and loved it, despite the hordes of tourists. It had been mid-March and they'd thought, foolishly, that it would be quiet. They'd done Umbria, Sicily and Naples, and they'd stayed in a friend-of-a-friend's villa on Capri. They'd never been to Florence, though, only talked about how they must try and get there. And Fran much preferred pizza to pasta . . . always had.

'What do you think?' Duncan asked, pointing at the boy weighed down with mince. 'Enough?'

'Plenty,' said Fran. She could always freeze some.

'Now. Tomatoes, bacon, onions, celery . . . *and* our special secret ingredient. Which is . . . ?' He was grinning, eyes wide, waiting for an answer.

What was he talking about? 'Mixed herbs?' she asked.

'Oh *really*, love. You're becoming very forgetful, you know.' He put an arm around her as he steered with one hand. '*Valpolicella*, silly. Let's go and find some.'

'OK,' Fran said, fixing a smile, stressed, wishing it was tomorrow. If the wine had a screw top, she'd sneak a few swigs behind the car.

They'd turned into the booze aisle when Duncan stopped dead and stared ahead. He made a strange noise, and Fran immediately grabbed his arm, thinking he might be about to fall.

'I meant Rome,' he said, turning his white face her way.

'Ah,' she said, nodding. As though it all made sense now.

Duncan suggested they put it all away later. 'Let's have a coffee and a sit down first. Watch a bit of news. Big day today.'

'Yes,' she agreed. It was a big day, but since most of America was still asleep there'd hardly be anything happening. What Duncan meant was that he was knackered.

While her husband mustered the energy to make coffee, Fran put the choc ices she'd got the children into the freezer and picked up phone messages. Ben was shouting in traffic, her cousin Linda said a card was in the post, and two colleagues sang 'Happy Birthday' and told her not to feel too old, since sixty is the new forty. She laughed and played the last one again. How she wished she'd been there today. All the more so, when, after putting perishables in the fridge, she found her husband flat out on the sofa, head on one arm, feet up on the other. Two full mugs stood on the coffee table, and she so wanted to pour one over his slack sleeping face.

Fran took her mug into the garden and lit up. Just keep busy, she told herself. She could sweep up leaves. Sweep the patio for this evening, even though she'd be the only smoker on it. Was it worth running the Hoover around, if the grandchildren were coming? There was the cot and little bed to make up, of course. Yes, she'd go and do that, once the rest of the food was away.

She went back in and emptied the bags, slowly, one by one. Several times she looked at the clock; watching it move from quarter to one to ten to. She'd make the two of them something. Soup, perhaps, and a roll. How nice it would have been if Duncan had suggested lunch somewhere. Old Duncan would have booked a table, days in advance. Still, she appreciated the flowers and theatre tickets. Considering the effort that must have taken, for someone in his state, she should be extra appreciative. But then again, she couldn't help suspecting her daughter's helping hand.

TEN

Kent, 1975

Susie settled on the same name but with an 'a' on the end. All along she'd been talking to the little person inside her and calling it Alex, so when a big and beautiful nine-pound girl appeared at five a.m. on a cold January morning, she became Alexa.

Brenda had been there throughout, breathing deeply or puffing with Susie, rubbing her back, holding her hand and wiping her with a damp flannel. All the things Duncan should have been doing, but couldn't. Susie had decided in advance that it would be too big a burden for Duncan – to experience the birth, then go home to Fran – and she'd asked Brenda to be with her instead. And what a great support she was proving. When Alexa finally slid out, Brenda kissed red sweaty mum and said, 'Well done, my lovely.'

Susie could tell the midwives thought they were lesbians, even though she wore her cheap gold ring and said several times how her husband was away on business. Brenda was a warm and demonstrative woman from Yorkshire, and as could be seen by her outfits, didn't give a damn what anyone thought. Over the past six months, since they'd moved from London to Kent, Susie had grown really fond of her. For extra cash she had helped out in Brenda's shop and on the Sunday market stall, and had even begun wearing some of the larger smock-type vintage stuff that came in. She loved the brocades and organzas and all the elaborate embroidery. Worn over or under jumpers, they'd kept her warm through the cold months.

To match the clothes, Brenda would give Susie's long blonde wet locks dozens of tight plaits, and then, when dry and unwound, her hair would be wild and kinky until the next wash. Often, she'd wear a headband or bandanna. Duncan had said he loved her new look, but that she might have to tone it down once she became a doctor. 'Fat chance of that,' she'd told him, smiling and stroking her velvet-covered bump. Somehow – divine intervention, or something – she'd achieved three As in her A level retakes.

'Look at me blubbing,' said Brenda, while someone weighed and wiped the baby, and another bound her tightly in assorted white things, then handed her over to 'Mum'. 'She's a right whopper, eh?' Brenda added. She took a lace handkerchief from a bejewelled bag and blew into it.

'You've a small tear,' the nicest of the midwives told Susie. 'The doctor will be here soon to pop a couple of stitches in.'

'Oh, no,' Susie groaned. She'd forgotten about tears and stitches, having read about it all so long ago.

'Don't worry, dear. After what you've been through, it'll be nothing.'

When the doctor came, Alexa was placed in her plastic cot on wheels, while Brenda went off to phone Susie's parents, and Susie suffered the humiliation of a gorgeous young man working on her doo-da with a needle and thread.

It was like the first time she saw Duncan, love at first sight. They were alone at last and the baby sucked away at her, quite miraculously, as though she'd been having lessons. Susie couldn't stop unwrapping bits of her and checking everything was there, and wished so much that Duncan would walk through the door and hold his daughter and cry and say how totally superb she was. But Duncan had been through this before and would no doubt be blasé. Well, she'd find out tomorrow – or today. After Brenda phoned him at work with the news, he'd come up with some vital meeting he had to go to. Or, better still, an illness, then he could spend all day with them. His new family, kind of.

He'd left in such a hurry that he'd forgotten his coat, and was shaking with cold rather than emotion, as he held little Alexa for the first time. Susie was exhausted but incredibly happy to see Duncan at last, and to show off their little girl and let him know how clever they'd been to produce something so wonderful.

'She looks like Gandhi,' he said, disappointingly, although she could see what he meant. 'But don't worry, they all do. Either Gandhi or Churchill.'

Duncan the expert, thought Susie. 'She's been really good so far. Just sleeping and feeding.'

Duncan smiled at his daughter and then at Susie. 'You'll be a brilliant mother, I know.'

'Luckily for you,' she said, not meaning to sound bitter, but that was how it came out.

Duncan's face fell, and Susie felt like crying because the situation was hardly Duncan's fault. She could have had an abortion, but thank goodness she hadn't. It hadn't even been discussed.

'I'll do all I can,' he said. 'You know that?'

'Yes, I know.'

But it would be her, and Brenda and the others in the farmhouse, who'd be kept awake at night and have to live with nappies drying and sterilising units. They'd all said it would be a gas, having a baby around, and that this might be the start of the commune they'd talked about in the Chiswick garden. Brenda, Greg, Susie, Rick the out-of-work carpenter, and Tamara. Tamara wasn't really Tamara, she just didn't think Yvonne suited her now she did tarot for a living. Well, not quite a living. Everyone in the Kent farmhouse was on the dole, except for Greg, who still caught the train to London Star each day, then came home to a pot of bean and veg stew, served on the floor, surrounded by everyone on cushions. When Susie could no longer do the cushion thing, Greg had returned from home one Sunday evening with an elegant old rocking chair – Queen Anne or something. 'My folks'll never miss it,' he'd said.

'We'll be fine,' Susie told Duncan. 'Honestly.'

'She won't grow up on strange beans and fungusy sprouty stuff?'

Susie laughed, although she couldn't see the harm in that. They'd had visitors whose toddlers ate nothing but pulses and vegetables and had never seen a fish finger. They were full of energy, had rosy cheeks and spoke like mini adults.

'Duncan, don't be a nitwit.'

Now he was laughing. 'Nobody says "nitwit".'

'I do.'

'I know, and that's why I love you. You and your "super" and "jolly well" and "awfully".' He bent down, still with Alexa in his arms, and kissed her forehead. Susie had managed a shower and hair wash this morning and was almost relieved Duncan hadn't seen her during the birth, all red and sweaty. She wondered how Fran's labour with Ben had gone, and whether actually being there through all the grunting and yelling and sweating might put you off a person. How pleased, in fact, she was to be able to present herself and her baby all cleaned up and fresh, even if one of them did look like Gandhi.

'I'll tell Fran I have to be somewhere next week, so I can come and help. Up north, perhaps.'

'Would you?'

'I'd like to, if it's all right with you?'

All right with her? This was so unexpected, and a glorious surprise. She'd be able to cancel her mother, who'd only volunteered because that was what mothers did. Her parents had in fact been terribly good, once they'd accepted the situation. Her mother had taken her shopping for a cot and pram, and all the other things Susie hadn't even begun to think of, like a baby bath and a changing mat, and lots of white, cream or lemon-coloured clothes, and two little zip-up sleeping bag things, because the baby would be born in winter and be living in a place with not much heating.

'I'd love to have you at the farmhouse,' she told Duncan. 'All to myself. Well, *our*selves.' She'd read how important it was not to make the father feel abandoned or excluded, or even jealous.

87

That he should be allowed to bond with his child from the start. 'Are you sure you don't mind?'

'No, of course not. It'll be *spiffing.*'

Susie gave him a poke for mocking her, and they kissed over their baby's tiny sleeping head, and she wondered how long it would be before they could make love again. It wouldn't happen next week, she hoped Duncan knew that. Yes, of course he'd know. And he'd know how to put a nappy on and burp the baby. And he was patient too. Thank goodness, she thought. Thank goodness for Duncan.

The worst part was his leaving – for him too, she could tell. Duncan may have had his fill of bean rissoles but she got the impression he'd really enjoyed life in the messy farmhouse, with all the music and endless cooking and way-out friends of Rick's, and Tamara's clients calling in. And Alexa had been so good and so easy. She was terribly quiet most of the time, which Susie had found worrying until Duncan said she probably couldn't compete with the noise and chaos.

Nothing ruffled Duncan. He'd deal with green runny nappies, and he'd rub cream on Susie's sore cracked nipples. He'd scrub for half an hour at a burned saucepan, and never said a word when Greg played non-stop, full-volume King Crimson.

Until now – the point where he was actually having to leave – Duncan had only been less than happy and relaxed after ringing his wife from the phone in the hall. Each time he'd waited until Greg and Brenda were at work, Rick was quietly stoned and Tamara was either out or telling someone their future in her room. Susie would take Alexa off in her enormous old-fashioned pram to avoid background baby noise, then sit on the bench in the village and wait for Duncan, looking forlorn and guilty, to catch up. It had never taken him long to shake off the despondency, and in that way, Susie always felt, they were terribly alike.

But now both of them were in tears, standing on the platform, waiting for his train to come and take him out of their lives. He didn't know when he'd be able to stay again, but he'd 'bloody well' arrange something soon.

'I'll phone you every day,' he was saying, his voice cracking.

'That would be lovely. And I'll bring Alexa up to town as often as I can.'

'I'll send you the fare.'

'On top of everything else?' she asked. 'Are you sure you can afford it?'

Now there were actual tears trickling down his face. 'You're my family.'

'Well, Mummy and Daddy are helping, so don't worry if—'

'*Please*,' he said, hugging her.

The train approached, screeched to a halt and Duncan picked up his suitcase. He'd go home and talk about his week in Sheffield, and he'd play with young Ben and, worst of all, he'd make love with his wife. Susie was certain he'd do that, after all those frustrating nights beside her.

How funny, she thought, waving him off. It was the reverse situation that had got them together in the first place. But it wasn't funny at all.

Carrying her sleeping baby, she made her way back to the waiting taxi, feeling desperately alone and deserted. The tears were coming thick and fast, as they'd done a lot over the past week.

She was the one who was a drag now, while Fran and Ben were the fun ones to be with. Ben slept through the night and could talk and kick a football, and Fran wouldn't have sore nipples and hormones all over the place.

All of a sudden, the person she'd loved more than anything five minutes ago was the source of great misery, and Susie wondered if she'd ever again feel happy and secure and herself.

Beside the station was a phone box, and she handed Alexa over to the taxi driver, saying she just had to ring someone, if he wouldn't mind. She went in, and keeping a constant eye on her precious baby, dialled the number and waited for a voice before pushing the coin in.

'Aunt Phyl?' she said, and immediately started crying.

'Oh goodness, Susie. What is it? Not your darling baby, I hope?'

'No, she's fine, Aunt Phyl. In fact, she's perfect.'

'Thank heaven for that.'

Susie sniffed and sobbed into the phone. 'It's me. I'm the problem. I just don't know how to . . . oh, I don't know. It's all so hard.'

'Listen, darling.'

'Yes?'

'Are you able to phone for a taxi?'

Susie looked at the driver gently jiggling Alexa like an expert. 'Yes.'

'Then come straight to me, my dear. There's no need to bring anything. I have my son's cradle still and we'll mend and make do. Or is it the other way round?'

'Well . . .' Susie couldn't think of any reason not to just go. And the idea warmed her so much. 'OK.'

'Marvellous! I simply can't wait to see my new great-grandniece.'

Susie laughed. Who needed Duncan? 'I think you left out a "great",' she told Phyllis.

'Ah. Perhaps I'll just call her Alicia, then.'

'Alexa.'

Her aunt hooted down the phone. 'You'd better get here quickly, before I completely lose my marbles!'

ELEVEN

Julia was helping him: an unusual occurrence, but then there *was* something in it for her. In the study-cum-bedroom she was packing his clothes, while Ben handled things with wires.

'Look,' she'd said on arriving home unexpectedly at lunchtime, 'if you're going to move in with your parents and you're going there this evening anyway, why not take all your things? I'll bunk off work and drive you, if you like?'

'I'm sorry, are you offering me a lift?' Julia never did that. Ever. Not unless it was en route to somewhere she'd been going anyway. There must have been a man she wanted to get in the flat a.s.a.p. Poor guy. Ben squashed a jealous pang, deep down in his gut. The pills numbed him, but not always enough.

'Then I can say happy birthday to your mother.'

'Right. Well, OK. I'm sure she'll be pleased to see you.' He should have crossed his fingers while saying this, but they'd been slipping his old stereo into its battered box. He should flog it or

dump it, but it was the only thing he could play his old compi-
lation tapes on. Some had been made for his first girlfriend, Joanne,
but she'd thrown them back at him on leaving. The heartless,
final-stab act of an angry ex. There'd be no histrionics from Julia,
not now he'd agreed to go. Had he agreed? Ben couldn't remember,
but he was pretty certain he didn't want to stay.

'Could you put my name on your gift?' Julia was asking. 'What
did you get her?'

'Oh, a wok.'

She snorted. 'I'm sure she'll be thrilled.'

'It's red,' Ben told her. 'And nice. I liked it.' He wanted to slip
away for a couple of Brucofen but his stash was in the bottom
of the half-filled rucksack, right beside Julia. Bad planning. He
wondered if there were any in his coat pocket, out in the hall
cupboard.

'I'll really miss your mother,' she said.

'Oh, yes?' Julia's words had a hollow sound, but what did he
know? Perhaps she did have a heart beneath her Karen Millen
silk top. He watched her shove two pairs of his trousers in the
rucksack, followed by a shirt that she lifted to her little nose and
sniffed. 'You'll need to wash a lot of these.'

'OK.' Ben stopped winding cables, then casually stood up and
stretched. 'I'll go and get my stuff from the hall cupboard.'

'Need a hand?'

'No, thanks.' This was far more civilised than Ben had imagined. They'd spoken more in half an hour than in the past six
months.

In the narrow hall, he put his hands together in a prayer, then
delved into the cupboard and into first one coat pocket, then the

other. There, beneath a glove was a beautiful familiar strip – *yes*. Running his fingers along, he felt a solid capsule, which he pushed out, coughing to cover the noise. Then he found another and coughed again. The last two capsules, how lucky was that. He crossed to the kitchen and washed them down with tap water.

My plants, he remembered, and he took the peace lily from the kitchen windowsill and put it in the hall. Then he went to the living room and lifted the gorgeous palm he'd nurtured from a baby out of Julia's fancy pot, and stood its wet bottom on an old jacket by the peace lily.

He wondered if he should phone and tell his parents he was moving back in for a while, or if that would put his father in the doldrums, and ruin his mum's big day. Or, it could even make her day, knowing someone else would be around. His sister had mentioned several recent incidents, when their dad – their lovely, easy-going dad – had flown off the handle at some minor transgression by a grandchild. A biscuit dropped on the carpet, that sort of thing. On the phone, his mum had mentioned lethargy, a touch of agitation – casually, as though it were nothing to worry about. 'Grumpy-old-man syndrome,' she'd said with a ha-ha.

His dad had never been grumpy, or detached, or moody, or any of those typically male things. In fact, it was his mother who'd tended to lose it, blowing up over something he or his sister had said or done. Their father would step in, and smooth things over with his gentle humour. Although, often, he hadn't been there. Away on some business trip, making the money that bought skateboards and piano lessons and paid for the house and for his mum to get a psychology degree and train as a therapist. There were a lot of weekends without Dad, when he'd be at a trade fair or conference or something, but he'd always come back with presents, which sort of made up for it. And he'd kept up the pace right until retirement a year ago. It was funny, Ben thought, that he and his dad had lost their jobs within months of each other. In some ways, it had hit his father more than it had Ben. At least this wasn't the absolute end for him. Well, hopefully not.

No, it wasn't going to be a day at the beach living with a tricky parent, but what could he do? Keep to his room, maybe. Be out a lot, looking for a job. Did they have jobs in Aylesbury?

'Ben?' he heard.

'Yes?'

'Thinking about it, I'd rather you didn't put my name on the wok.'

'Oh, OK.' He went back in the cupboard and fished out shoes, wellies, jackets, hats, scarves and a pair of slippers he'd forgotten about.

'I'll send her something later. Something more personal.'

Not something for the kitchen, I hope, he heard his sister say, but somehow he hadn't seen a wok in that category. Not a lovely red one he'd rather like himself. He'd cook for his mum in it, as a bonus – the things he loved but Julia refused to eat, like meat and fish and all things remotely tasty. Not that he and Julia had done much eating together of late. Separate dinners at different times, but she still hadn't let him roast chicken or fry bacon. Living at home had to be easier than this. Julia was controlling, selfish, rude and an ingrate. Somehow his mother had spotted it before he had.

Ben filled a black bag with his things. One or two items were past their best but he couldn't be bothered to bin them.

He hesitated over the slippers before throwing them in too. Long Bellingham was a slippers kind of place.

'I'll just take a quick shower,' he called out. 'And clear out my bathroom things.'

'OK.'

Ben spent some time soaping himself, singing and rinsing. He wanted the tablets to kick in before he got trapped in a car with Julia, and he'd quite like it if she'd finished the packing in his absence.

After scooping his things off the shelves and out of the cabinet, Ben emerged clean, damp and dressed in a towel. He dumped the carrier bag of wash things by the door and didn't, at first, spot what was missing. He only knew something was.

'My plants,' he said, when it dawned on him.

There in the living room was his big dainty palm, back in Julia's pot. He didn't fancy an argument over plants, and since there was no way in the world she could claim it was hers, he just took it out and placed it back on the jacket in the hall. He then went to the kitchen for the peace lily, which he wasn't so attached to, but that wasn't the point.

By two thirty, the hall was rammed with his things, while the rest of the flat looked as though he'd never been there.

Julia jangled her keys impatiently. 'Got everything?' she asked. 'Your transformer collection? Athlete's foot cream?'

God, she was evil. 'Let me see. Nose hair trimmers . . . signed Shakin' Stevens record. Yep, think I'm there.'

TWELVE

Em couldn't move. She was on the sofa watching *Charlie and Lola*, George at her feet with a puzzle he couldn't do.

'In a minute, sweetie,' she said, her head filling again with Hadi's empty room, the empty kitchen shelves. 'I'll help you in a minute.'

She drank the tea she thought might comfort her, an eye on the clock on the mantelpiece. In thirty minutes she'd have to move. She'd have to put a 'car nappy' on George, get his coat on and drive to school.

'Mum*eeee*.'

'Let me finish my tea, George. Look, what's Lola doing now?'

She should be pleased her son would rather do a puzzle than watch TV. What a truly dreadful mother she'd become. Had she been good at it, at one time? Em thought perhaps she had, before Hadi started taking up her thoughts, and her time and energy. Passable, anyway, and maybe she'd become passable again, since he'd clearly buggered off.

The idea of him being in trouble no longer seemed plausible. He'd always appeared good and law-abiding. He'd shown no signs of a criminal personality, or of holding anti-Establishment political views. He wasn't a fundamentalist Muslim, he voted Green. No. He'd simply done a disappearing act. What more definitive way was there of ending a relationship?

When she did finally move, it was to reach for her secret phone. No messages, no missed calls. She went back through her inbox, reading them one by one. They were all about the sex, absolutely all of them. But then what else would they be about? It had all been about sex; a kind of addiction for her, and perhaps for him too. The lure of the illicit.

These words, his words, that had lifted her to unknown heights now, oddly, repulsed her. Without the actual person – real, loving, Hadi – in her life, they sounded crude, rather than intimate, and this unsettled her. Had she been taken in, somehow, or hypnotised by him. Used, then discarded. Had she just been a game for him? Was that all it had been to her? Maybe, but there were civilised, less cowardly ways to end these things. He might have gone off to get married, for all she knew. No wonder he wouldn't discuss his life. Bastard, she thought. It was tempting to chuck the phone in the wheelie bin, wrapped in carrier bags – the sim card, anyway.

'Mum*eeee*, where does this piece go?'

She wouldn't throw it away, not just yet. He might still get in touch with a reasonable explanation, or Nigel might phone. Em slipped it in her cardigan pocket and slid down to the floor. She'd never ached so much. Every limb, all of her, felt ridiculously heavy.

'OK, George.' She lifted a leaden arm and put it around her son. 'Let's see if we can make the dragon.'

She was getting her boots on when the landline rang.

'Hi,' said Alex.

'Hi.'

'Listen, I'll pick Martha up, if you like?'

'Er, yes. Great. If it's no problem.' Alex rarely went to the school, but must have finished early for her mother's birthday.

'Good. I'll see you in a little while, then. All ready for tonight?'

'Almost.' She'd given it no thought at all since first thing that morning. Now she had to pack cases, write her mum's card and arrange for the cat to be fed. It'll be good, she thought, being occupied, and to not be here this evening, waiting for a text that wouldn't come.

'Are you all right?' Alex asked. 'You sound tired.'

'I don't know. I could be coming down with something.' It was an ideal excuse, she realised.

'Vitamin C.'

'Yeah, yeah, I'll take some.' It was Alex's answer to all ailments. He swallowed two one-gram tablets a day and never caught colds.

'Take plenty.'

'I will.'

Em was incredibly pleased to see him walk in. It was like Alex was her prop, her pair of crutches; almost literally. While he rough-and-tumbled with George and got the kids choosing exactly two toys each to take to Grandma's, Em felt her limbs gradually strengthen. Then slowly, her mood lifted too. She filled a small suitcase for herself and Alex, and another for the children, and she popped next door to ask them to feed the cat, and she wrote warm words to her mother on a Tate Modern card. She folded the country house reservation confirmation and tucked it inside the envelope.

By four o'clock they'd loaded Em's car with cases, champagne, the badly wrapped presents for Grandma, which Alex had bought with the children, and a bouquet of flowers Em had picked up on the way to Hadi's. They had to use her car, despite the lack of space, because Alex's had recently been driven into, and his courtesy car, a little Citroën, was even smaller.

He insisted on driving. 'You're poorly. Try and nap on the way, yeah?'

She didn't nap, just sat quietly through the tiresome rush-hour traffic, arms around the bag on her lap. Inside the bag, in a pocket, in a little cotton pouch, tucked inside a tissue-packet holder, was her second mobile.

Em's heart was heavy but at the same time she knew she should be pleased. Everything was normal again, and safe. No more taking risks. She did love her husband and dreaded losing him. If she lost Alex, she'd lose the children. He'd fight for them and they'd want to be with him, and she'd give in and let him win because the three of them would be happy together, and because there was always a part of her that wanted freedom. Even now.

'"This Old Man"?' suggested Alex. They were crawling out of London at completely the wrong time of day. Not that they'd had much choice, fitting the birthday visit in between school and bedtime.

Martha began the singing and Alex joined in, while George

tried to. Em watched three young Asian men talking, laughing. There were lots of hand movements. Hadi would do that, gesticulate a lot.

"'This old man . . .'"

The car moved on and stopped by a betting shop. A middle-aged white man came out, scratching at his crotch. Hadi would never have done that, not in the street. He wouldn't bet, either.

"'This old man . . .'"

Where was he, Em wondered. Alex said they'd have to get petrol, so she'd check her mobile then. There'd be a message, she was sure. And if there wasn't, then she'd return to her old life and put him behind her. Easy.

Alex's hand moved to her knee and she jumped. 'You OK, Em?'

How many more times was he going to ask? 'Yes. Yes, I'm fine.'

She just wanted to be there now. At her parents' house, with food and drink and noise and laughter. Would there be laughter? Her father was hardly an end-of-the-pier act these days, and Ben's humour had taken a peculiar turn. Still, there were the children . . . and Alex would make an effort. Alex always made an effort.

THIRTEEN

London, 1980

At first she missed the farmhouse dreadfully: the crazy visitors, the smell of cooking, the constant music, the cats, Brenda and Greg's toddler twins, the garden and the countryside. And just having company. It felt too weird and far too quiet, just the two of them in the vast apartment with all her great-aunt's things.

Most of the large bits would stay, absolutely. Susie admired Phyl's taste in furniture, and never in a million years – or unless she became desperately hard up – would she sell the abstract paintings and gorgeous antique and art-deco ornaments, statues, vases and clocks. Not that she was likely to become hard up, having been the main beneficiary of a substantial estate, including the Belsize Park flat.

Along with Phyl's estranged son, Susie's father had received fifty thousand pounds. He'd seemed perfectly happy at first, and grateful that he wouldn't have to bother with 'the old girl's clutter'. But Susie had detected a coolness in recent weeks, when the final calculations had been sent to all beneficiaries. She'd done very well indeed, even after tax, as the receiver of the residue of the estate.

For the first few days in 'Number Ten', as it had always been known, Alexa complained about the lack of a garden to play in, and it was clear she missed the boys, so Susie cajoled Brenda and the twins into coming up for their first weekend. Greg would grab the chance to visit his folks. Brenda couldn't abide them and, apparently, the feeling was mutual.

Brenda and Greg hadn't meant to have twins, or even one baby. They hadn't even meant to have sex. But the isolation of the farmhouse – along with a good dose of ganja and barely any heating – had led the two of them to snuggle up in Brenda's bed one winter's night. Once she'd given birth, Brenda had put the clothes business on hold and become earth mother to Joe and Josh.

When they arrived at the flat, Alexa and the twins hared nonstop around the rooms and along the corridor. Later they all went out into the pretty tree-filled grounds for fresh air and a picnic. Alexa mothered the boys, making sure their beakers were full and they kept their sunhats on, and Susie could see she'd have to get her daughter some dolls to nurture and boss around. They weren't allowed pets, unfortunately.

On Sunday, the five of them tubed it to Hyde Park with the double buggy and ate by the Serpentine. By Monday afternoon, once Brenda and the twins had left, with promises to return *very* soon and a set date to visit the farmhouse, Alexa was much happier.

With Duncan's first visit in mind, she and Susie prettied up the smallest of the three large bedrooms, shopping for brand-new pink curtains with matching lampshade, and little-girl duvet sets and pink cushions and a princess rug. Things that would have been out of place in the farmhouse, and unaffordable, besides. For the past few years, Susie's parents' allowance had covered the basics, while Duncan's contribution and the money she made from garden produce had gone towards extras.

Alexa wasn't the only one missing a garden, but Susie was determined to focus on all the pluses of living back in London, living in style, and having a pile of money in the bank. They'd certainly get to see more of Duncan, currently on a long summer holiday in Florida – organised by Fran, he'd claimed – but due back in ten days' time. Alexa couldn't wait to show Daddy her new room, and Susie couldn't wait to see Daddy.

Surrounded by her belongings, Susie missed her great-aunt too, having spent many a half term in Belsize Park, when her parents were stationed abroad, and sometimes, by choice, when they weren't. Once Alexa arrived, she'd reconnected with Phyl again, coming to visit as often as she could and always leaving with a handful of train fare. With the added attraction of Alexa – a replica of herself at that age – Susie and her aunt had grown closer than ever. Even when two carers were taking it in turns to come in, and Phyl could barely see, they'd continued to make the journey, bringing raspberries from the garden and sleeping together in the big bed that had once dwarfed her.

She and Alexa had spent time with Duncan too; often a couple of nights in a London hotel. And he'd been down to the Kent farmhouse regularly, staying for as long as he could. And in the five and a half years since Alexa's birth, they'd managed two family holidays, one in Cornwall and one in the Italian lakes.

Duncan had kept up the effort, and Susie was grateful and tried to appreciate all he did, and to appear as happy and contented as she could in his presence. There was no point in being resentful, after all. Not even when he'd announced, shortly after Alexa was born, that Fran was pregnant with their second child. That had, in fact, caused a short-lived rift, while Susie came to terms with the fact that Duncan could hardly deny his wife sex or children. And, after all, the times he'd weakened and said he wanted to leave Fran and live with her, she'd been the one to insist he didn't.

Finally, Duncan came to see them in Belsize Park, and his expression was priceless as Susie led him from room to room. Part of it was relief, she could tell. He'd always made a sterling effort to cope with the farmhouse, but hippie had never been Duncan's thing.

'Wow,' he said again, running his hand along the Chesterfield, and his eyes along the deep red wall full of Man Ray-type photos and paintings of nudes. 'I can't believe you're actually living here, both of you. You've told me about your aunt's flat, but I had no idea it was so . . .'

'Opulent?'

'That's the word. And arty, and . . . God, this stuff must be worth a fortune.'

Me too, thought Susie, but she hadn't yet shared the extent of her inheritance with him. Until recently, she'd been unsure of the exact amount, but nevertheless decided to keep it to herself. Duncan, after all, kept the greater part of his life from her.

'Here she is.' Susie pointed at her great-aunt, reclining naked with a bunch of grapes.

'Hey, quite a looker. And a bit of a goer, you reckon?'

Susie laughed. 'Let's just say she lived life to the full.'

'Honestly, you could open this place to the public.'

'I could. Well, except for your daughter's garish room.' Alexa had gone off to tidy her princess collection. 'Come along, she's desperate for you to see it.'

It was late August and Alexa was due to start school in a week's time. She was looking forward to it, but Susie wasn't. Much to Duncan's distress, their daughter had never been to a playgroup or nursery. There hadn't been one nearby, and Susie couldn't drive, and besides, she'd enjoyed playing with her daughter herself, teaching her about growing things and birds and other wildlife, and later, how to read and do simple sums. But still, as advanced as Alexa might be, something as structured as a school could mean a huge adjustment for a little girl who'd already undergone a major one. Alexa was chatty, and she'd got on well with visiting children and the twins, but the thought of the poor mite being wrenched away from home and locked up for six hours a day, five days a week, made Susie fearful for her. Or, more likely – as dear, outspoken Brenda had pointed out – for herself. What on earth would she do all day with no one to talk to and no garden to tend?

Later, with Alexa asleep in her very pink room, Susie brought this up with Duncan. She'd cooked them salmon with new potatoes and salad, and they were at one end of a table the length of a ship.

'You could find a job,' Duncan said. 'But I don't suppose you'll need to work? What with the inheritance?'

'Er, no.' He was fishing, she could tell. 'Not really.'

'Not even part time?'

Susie shook her head and felt herself blush. She wasn't generally a blusher but her sudden wealth embarrassed her.

Duncan grinned, and nudged her with his knife arm. 'Go on, you can tell me.'

'Enough,' she said. She smiled back but decided to keep mum. 'Enough that you won't need to contribute now.'

Duncan pouted. 'But I like giving you money. And it seems right. Me huntergatherer-type thing.'

'More potatoes?' she asked, wanting to get off the subject and spooning some on to his plate. 'They're from the farmhouse garden. Brenda brought them up.'

'We do have potatoes in London.'

'Ha-ha.'

'Although I'm not sure about Belsize Park. I think you only have *pommes de terre.*'

Susie put the spoon down and tickled his ribs. 'No teasing, you beast.'

'Oooh, am I being beastly?'

He tickled her back and one tickle led to another and they found themselves on the floor, kissing with salmon on their breaths, then moving to the Chesterfield and making love.

'I wonder if your aunt the goer ever did this,' Duncan said afterwards, when they were covered with the tablecloth in case Alexa appeared. 'You know, on here.'

Susie giggled and pointed up at nude Phyllis on the wall behind them.

'Bloody hell,' he said, spotting the same Chesterfield. He looked down at the real thing and curled a lip. 'How tawdry.'

'Golly, you are a prude, Duncan. Come on, let's finish our dinner.'

They put their clothes back on and stood and had another cuddle before sitting down to cold salmon and potatoes. Duncan talked about what a busy first week back he'd had, and how tired he'd been, what with the long and energetic holiday. 'I'm so sorry I can only stay one night,' he added, perhaps realising his *faux pas* in bringing up his three weeks in Florida. 'Anything good on telly this evening?'

'Oh, there's no television.'

From the look on his face she might have said there was no running water. 'Even the farmhouse had a TV. What are we going to do all evening?'

'Aunt Phyl was into mah-jong. We could try that?'

His eyes darted to the painting and back. 'Some kinky sex game, I take it?'

'I'm sure she played those too.'

Duncan finished eating and took hold of her hand, staring as lovingly at her as he had the first day they met. 'A mansion block in Belsize Park. Mah-jong. French antiques. If you ask me, Susie, you've found your spiritual home.'

She laughed and kissed the end of his nose. 'Don't forget the *pommes de terre.*'

'Mummy,' came a little voice across the big room, 'may I have a drink of water?'

'Of course you may, darling.'

Susie got up, mimed 'Phew!' at Duncan and went over to her daughter. 'Let's get you some. Say night-night to Daddy.'

'Night-night, Daddy.'

'Night-night, Em – I mean . . . um.'

Susie watched Duncan struggle to remember, and all she could do was shake her head at him and lead her daughter out of the room.

'Night, Alexa!' he shouted, too late.

FOURTEEN

'Happy Birthday, Mum.' Ben handed her a box with a photo of a wok on it and a sticker saying 'Sale price £19.99'.

'Thank you.' Fran laughed and leaned over it to kiss him. 'I wonder what it could be.'

He was far too early. Duncan was taking his tenth nap of the day and nothing was ready. Beside Ben was a huge backpack thing, then Fran spotted Julia wheeling a case up the path. Her heart sank. How long were they planning on staying?

'Happy Birthday!' called out Julia. 'The wok isn't from me, by the way. I've got something else in mind for your present.'

'Oh, there's no need for—'

'Hey, love the new hair colour.'

'Thank you.'

'My mother just bleaches the grey away too. Ben's moving back in for a while, is that all right?'

What did she mean by 'back', wondered Fran, since Ben had never lived in this house.

Her son pulled a face and said, 'Sorry, Mum,' despite the fact that he didn't look particularly sorry, or remotely unhappy. They really were splitting up, then. It had been on the cards for months, and Fran had been secretly hoping Ben would extricate himself. She hadn't secretly been hoping he'd turn up on her doorstep, not with Duncan the way he was. And not with so much stuff. It had an air of permanence she wasn't sure she liked, and now Julia was back at her black Golf, lifting a box from the boot.

'Just a few more bits,' Ben said, then he too returned to the car and tugged two bin bags from the back seat. 'Don't forget my plants!' he shouted to Julia.

'Yes, sir!' she snapped back. They'd never been compatible, always bickering in company in that annoying way some couples do.

'Shall I put this in the hall?' Julia asked.

Fran stood aside, while her son's ex lowered a stereo box on to the flagstones. 'Is there anything I can—'

'Better dash,' Julia said, 'or I'll get stuck in rush-hour traffic. Have a lovely evening, Fran. Remember it's the new forty! Bye, Ben. I'll email you about those bills.'

'Oh, please do.' Ben waved her off, then hoisted the rucksack on to his back. 'Where do you want me?' he asked, but then he gasped, unhooked and dumped the bag and ran back down the path. 'My plants!' he yelled at the disappearing Golf.

Tulip House had once been Tulip Cottages, a couple of two-up-two-down seventeenth-century places, which, until the mid-seventies, had still had outside toilets. The owners before Fran and Duncan had knocked the cottages into one and extended backwards, sideways and upwards, although not all at the same time They'd been compelled by the relatively lax planners only to keep the small original front windows and at least one of the two front doors. Done more recently, and all in one go, the conversion might have created something charming and seamless, but Tulip House was a hodgepodge of old, new, and even newer. Duncan said he loved that about it, the fact that it was uncoordinated and yet pretty. Fran had wondered if that was a veiled reference to herself, since she'd never been able to dance well, or even clap in time.

Like a lot of old extended houses, the front of Tulip House had a very different feel from the back, and once you'd ducked to get through the front door – which Ben was doing now – the rooms gradually grew bigger, the ceilings higher and the windows larger, as you made your way through to the vast French-windowed kitchen. The family home, before the children left, had been a thirties semi in Chelmsford, and compared to that, and to their even smaller first home, this had always felt gloriously airy and spacious.

Fran often wished the children could have enjoyed a home this size when they were young, but whenever they'd contemplated moving, Em had wailed and sulked because her best friend was next door but one, and because she loved her attic bedroom with, first, blue sky and white clouds on the sloping ceiling, and then, as a teen, black sky and stars. And Duncan had always claimed he really liked the house, and queried whether they'd want the upheaval. They'd never been unhappy enough to move, that had been the problem, if it had been a problem.

'Can I leave this stuff in the hall?' Ben asked. 'For now? I'm exhausted.'

'Of course you can.'

'Got a few things to wash, though.'

'That's fine.' Was Duncan still dozing? How could he sleep through all this? 'Bring them through, and I'll put the kettle on.'

Fran stopped at the sitting-room door and saw her husband in his usual slack-jawed, hands-clasped position. With his head back like that, he tended to snore. Duncan could never look unattractive, but this was the closest he came.

In the kitchen, as she watched her son sniff clothes and put them in the washing machine, it occurred to Fran that her wish had come partly true. At least one child would enjoy the space of Tulip House, if only for a while. Hopefully, only for a while.

'Are you all right?' she asked.

'What do you mean?'

Was her son getting harder to talk to, she wondered. 'About Julia.'

'Oh, right.' He was opening all the wrong cupboards, looking for soap powder.

'Above the sink.'

He found the Ecover, then opened the washing-machine drawer. 'Which, er . . . thing . . . what's it called . . .'

'Compartment? Middle.'

Ben yawned. 'Christ, I'm knackered. Moving home is such hard work. How do I switch—'

'I'll do it.'

'Cheers.'

Ben wandered off to find his dad and Fran turned the dial to a hot wash and pushed the 'on' button. In front of the machine was Ben's backpack, and beside it was a pile of clothes too clean to wash, or were they to be washed later? She'd leave them there, she decided, and move the bag. But on grabbing a strap, it tipped the wrong way and dozens of strips of tablets rattled on to the floor.

'What on earth . . . ? Fran whispered. She pulled the bag upright and felt around inside. 'Oh my God.' There were more. Lots more. 'Brucofen' it said on the back of each strip. She'd never heard of it.

What was wrong with Ben that he'd need this much medication on him? Her little boy, ill. How awful! She'd have to bring it up somehow, but how? It could be an embarrassing illness he'd rather not discuss, or, God forbid, something serious. This wasn't right. She was sixty today, and perfectly healthy, while her son obviously wasn't. He'd just said he was knackered, and he couldn't remember the word 'compartment'. He hadn't answered her question about Julia, or even phoned ahead to ask if he could stay. His mind wasn't working properly. She thought back to their recent phone calls and realised it hadn't been working for a while. Very early dementia? No, not at thirty-seven; she'd even ruled it out for Duncan at sixty-six. A tumour? she wondered, going cold, completely cold.

After a calming cigarette in the cold, Fran found Ben in the sitting room, asleep in an armchair, not far from his father, still snoozing on the sofa. She picked up the TV remote and switched off *Deal or No Deal* and Duncan immediately woke up.

'Ben's here,' she whispered.

'Ah,' he said. 'The festivities have begun, then?' He hauled himself up and shuffled off, rubbing himself warm, yawning. 'Is the heating on? It's as cold as a witch's tit.'

Fran sighed and yearned for Em to arrive, so she could have a decent conversation. She sat on the sofa and looked at her poor son. He didn't look unwell, in fact he'd put on weight. Should she tap his knee and wake him up and have a quick whispered chat, or just let him sleep. There were things she ought to be getting on with. Duncan creating a spaghetti Bolognese for seven didn't seem feasible, but if she did a bit of preparation it might help.

Ben had let his hair grow and it suited him. His head had been practically shaved for quite a while, and although he was handsome, she'd never got used to it. He favoured Duncan in his looks, and in his temperament too. Ben had always been such a good boy, never rebelling or going off the rails the way Em had. Being out of work had hit him hard, though, and Fran wondered if she'd been supportive enough in the past few months. The trouble was she'd got so used to her son being self-reliant, even when young. Unlike his sister.

Em – dark-haired and pale-skinned, like Fran – had, from the age of thirteen until well into her twenties, been their problem child. Luckily, motherhood had changed her, hormonally, or whatever, and she was very settled now, and a caring wife and mother. Duncan used to say Em was an adrenalin junkie; someone who couldn't cope with the ordinary or the boring. And it was true. As soon as things were going smoothly she'd stir up trouble. It hadn't been easy being her parents, that was for sure, even after she left home. They'd bailed her out so many times when her money had gone on drugs, alcohol, clothes. They'd paid off maxed-out credit cards, and twice picked her up from a police station. Aged nineteen or twenty, she'd roll up for family meals high on something, or drunk, or both, and she'd be truly obnoxious if anyone challenged her lifestyle.

'You're so dull and conservative and bourgeois,' she'd once said, and Fran had snapped back that luckily for her they were, or she'd be dead or a hooker by now. Duncan never said such things, but would give his daughter a gentle encouraging talking to and slip more money into her account.

Amazingly, Em had studied hard throughout it all, and got her A levels, a good degree and then, after two years on the dole, an MA, financed by Duncan to get her back on some sort of track. Thank goodness for the MA. If she hadn't done that, she wouldn't have met Alex and she wouldn't have become the sensible Em they knew now.

Fran checked the clock: almost half four. Another hour before the others arrived. How she'd love to have a nap herself; a really long one, right through till morning. She thought she might not celebrate any more birthdays. Not even the big ones, no matter how much pressure she was under. This was it, she decided, her last ever birthday gathering.

Ben woke up and reached for the remote. 'Can we put the news on? See how Obama's doing?'

'Of course. Can I get you anything? Cup of tea, coffee. Soft drink?'

'Got any Alka-Seltzer?' he asked, rubbing at his chest, then a bit further down. 'I've got the worst indigestion.'

Stomach cancer, pancreatic. She should quiz him, Fran thought, as she went upstairs to the medicine cabinet for a bottle of pink liquid. She'd ask him later, when there was more of a hubbub, and once they'd all had a drink. Or tomorrow. She couldn't bear terrible news on her birthday.

Passing their bedroom, Fran heard Duncan's yawning. She pushed at the door and found him lying on the bed, staring at his mobile. His slippers were off and his droopy eyelids looked ready for another nap.

'Who are you calling?' she asked.

'Just Alexa,' he said, half asleep.

'You mean Alex?'

His eyes popped open and he shifted himself upright. 'Alex. Yes, of course.'

'They're on their way now. Listen, why don't we make a start on the meal?'

'Good idea.' Duncan swivelled round and put his slippers back on. 'Spaghetti Bolognese, eh?' He shook his head. 'I wonder how I came up with that?'

'I've no idea,' said Fran, trying to smile, trying to buck him up. 'But I'm sure it'll be lovely.'

He burned the onions he'd meant to lightly sauté, and swore loudly and scraped them into the bin and threw the pan in the sink. Then he stood and rubbed at his eyes, but because he hadn't washed the onion off his fingers, he said, 'Yikes!' and had to dash back to the sink to throw water at his face.

'Not a good start,' he said, wiping at his wet shirt with a tea towel. 'Maybe I should let you cook, love.'

Fran stopped still and felt her blood pressure rise. 'What?' she asked, trying at first not to let the shakiness show, then suddenly not caring. '*What?*'

'I'm sorry . . . it's OK, I'll—'

'Just go, Duncan. Go and have another sodding sleep.'

'But—'

'Go!'

No more birthdays, she thought again, when he'd left and she was scouring the frying pan to fry more onions. They were too much like hard work.

FIFTEEN

Before his sister and her clan arrived, Ben had been enjoying himself, sitting in a companiable silence with his dad, watching the rolling news. There'd been some sort of altercation in the kitchen, and his father had come and plonked himself in a chair and not said a word. No, 'How's the job hunting going?' or, 'I hear you're staying for a while?'

His dad had always been someone who enquired; someone who'd come up with constructive advice, or at the very least an understanding and some sympathy. It spooked Ben, this silence, but at the same time he wasn't up to taxing chitchat, exhausted as he was from the packing and the stress of sharing a car journey with someone listing his shortcomings while averaging eighty. Still, he'd thought, as he watched his father's eyes slowly close, the corners of his mouth droop, it must be hard for his mum, suddenly having a moody bugger as a mate. Ben thought of Clementine Churchill, putting up with her husband's 'black dog' moods, and Iris Murdoch's poor husband, and it made him wonder if he'd given up too quickly on Julia. Although, thinking about it, she'd given up on him.

Everything had changed now, though. The news was gone and his father was actually talking, watching something with George called *Grandpa in my Pocket*. He'd come to life, which was great and reassuring, and Ben only wished he could do the same; have a bit of fun with his insistent niece.

Martha, now five and huge, was sitting on his foot asking for 'The Galloping Major'. What a memory she had. The last time he'd jigged her up and down to 'The Galloping Major' she been half the age and half the weight she was now. He took hold of her hands and tried, but his leg was incapable of hoisting her and he couldn't remember the words.

'Wow, you've really grown,' he said. Children were surely bigger these days. 'You're much too heavy for your poor old uncle.'

'Oh, *please*. Daddy can do it. Look, like this. Up, down, up, *down*.'

'Ow!'

'No, Martha,' came his mother's voice. 'Uncle Ben's tired. Aren't you, love?'

'Yeah, I am a bit tired.' Why hadn't he thought of that? 'Maybe later.' He looked over to the door at his mum's unhappy face. It must be miserable having to cook your own birthday dinner. He should offer to help, but Em and Alex were in the kitchen now, chatting and clattering away, and besides, there was still a weight on his foot. 'Off you get, Martha.'

His niece sighed loudly and rolled off in a dramatic Martha-like manner, knocking a small pile of DVDs from the coffee table. Ben waited for his father to explode or at least mutter some rebuke, but he and George were well into *Grandpa in my Pocket*, gawping together endearingly. That must be what happens, he thought, when you get older. You identify more with a two year old's world than with your own grown-up children's.

A familiar restlessness was creeping in, and that meant it was time for Brucofen. They were in his rucksack, which he'd left in the kitchen. He should do some unpacking while he was at it, and at least it would keep him away from the family. As much as he loved them – even Alex – he wouldn't have a thing to tell them about his sad and luckless life that they didn't know already. But maybe he'd watch the rest of the programme first. It had that bloke from *New Tricks* in and seemed pretty funny.

'Hi, Ben.' Em looked awful: stick thin, as usual, but her eyes were red and puffy, and her normally sleek hair was all over the place. She reminded him of those pencils they used to have, with a troll on top. 'I know, I know,' she said, reading his mind. 'I've got a bug, so don't come close.'

'Oh, OK.' He nodded at his brother-in-law. 'Alex.'

'Hey, Ben. How's it going?' Alex came over and gave him a man hug, because that was the kind of bloke he was.

'Good, yeah.'

'Well, that's . . . good.'

'Yeah. And you?'

'Alex has been offered a seriously well-paid job in Paris,' said his mum, but then her face screwed itself up in a 'Did I really say that?' way.

'Great,' Ben said.

Alex nodded. 'Yeah.'

'Well done.'

'Thanks.'

'Going to take it?'

Alex glanced at Em. 'I dunno.' She looked dazed.

No one seemed to know what to say, so Ben walked around his sister to get to the rucksack, but it wasn't there. A small tremor of panic hit him and his head raced through the things that might have happened to his stash. 'That old thing?' his mum would say. 'I took it to the tip/threw it on the bonfire while you napped.' There wasn't a pharmacy for miles and he had no transport.

'Your bag's in your room,' she said. 'Away from the little ones.' Her face told him she'd found the tablets. How stupid he'd been, how completely stupid, and you should never keep all your eggs in one basket.

'Which room is . . . ?'

'Where you slept last time.'

'Um . . .'

'At the end of the landing, at the back of the house. You'll find all your things there.' Again, she gave him a look, a really odd look. She knew. His mum knew his dirty little secret. He'd have to fabricate something, when his head was clearer. He'd lent his bag to a mate and found them there; something like that.

'Thanks. Listen, I think I'll go and unpack. See you guys in a while.'

Alex nodded. 'We thought we'd crack open the champagne at six.'

'Cool.' Ben said, while his sister made a face at him.

Ben frowned back at her.

'Champagne?' she said, well whispered – mimed, almost.

'What?' he tried to mime back, but everyone heard.

'Jesus, Ben.'

Alex reached out to Em. 'One bottle will be plenty,' he said. 'Don't worry.'

In his room, Ben locked the door against annoying kids, fired up the laptop and stuck the mobile wifi dongle in. It had been a techie friend who'd suggested getting one. 'Since you're always in cafés and libraries,' he'd said, rather cruelly. And it had been useful, because not everywhere had wifi, and then there was the hassle of asking some assistant for the password, which they invariably got wrong, so you'd have to ask again. He loved his dongle, even if it was a slow and expensive way of getting online. If it managed to find a signal and internet out here in the sticks, he'd be astounded.

Somehow it did. There were two emails telling him he hadn't been successful in job interviews, which was quite something. Normally, you didn't hear a thing. And there was one from a redundant former work colleague asking if he'd like to meet up for a 'drowning our sorrows' drink. Fuck that, Ben thought. He'd rather sit through *Titanic* again. He sent only one email himself. *Don't think you're keeping them,* he told Julia. *Ben.*

He plugged his headphones in and found an episode of *Friends,* one of the old ones, where they all looked fourteen and the script was razor sharp. He'd seen it before and was one step ahead but it still made him smile. He and a friend from uni had planned to write a sitcom once. They'd kept in touch over the years, he and Eddie, despite their very different career paths. Eddie was part of a touring theatre company, often performing in schools and other institutions, and because of poor funding having to play up to half a dozen parts. Eddie wrote for his little group but wanted to get something on TV, hence the sitcom set in the City idea. He and Ben met up in a pub in London once to discuss it, got completely plastered, then went back to their different lives and never mentioned it again.

Ben paused and sent Eddie an email reminding him of their planned joint venture, telling him he was well up for a bit of revenge on big business, and suggesting they got together to discuss. He went back to *Friends* then heard an email ping through. Again, he paused. *Sorry, mate. Believe it or not, I got a part in something at the Globe coming up. Another time, yeah? More later, learning lines. Eddie.*

Huh, thought Ben. He guessed he should email back and congratulate his old friend, but, as his mum was clearly aware, other people's good fortune grated a bit these days. It shouldn't, he knew, but what could he do? He'd reply some other time, like when he felt genuinely pleased for Eddie, as opposed to childishly bitter.

Ben shut down email and pressed 'play' again, and then someone was knocking on the door and waking him up. *Friends* had finished. He disconnected himself and went to unlock the bedroom door. It was his mum, looking like the house was on fire.

'Oh, *Ben*,' she said, and she put her arms around him and rubbed his back. 'I thought I'd never wake you.'

'I had my head—'

'Tell me what it is,' she said, standing back now, clutching both of his arms and staring hard, right into his eyes. She wasn't crying but she was close. 'What's wrong with you, love? Please tell me.'

SIXTEEN

London, 1985

After passing her driving test at the second attempt, Susie had shot out and ordered a little runaround, suitable for London traffic but robust enough to survive a full-frontal black cab. Now they could pop up to Grandma and Grandpa's, or down to the Kent farmhouse, without checking timetables and organising lifts at the other end. It felt terrific to be so mobile and independent, although at first she found it daunting to be driving her one precious child along motorways, or indeed any ways.

However, it wasn't long before she became steady and confident, and she so regretted not having learned to drive in her early twenties, when her father had offered her lessons. She'd been caught up in her resits then, and driving had felt like yet another thing to study, another test to take. What a difference a car would have made to all those years in Kent. Not that they'd been unhappy times, but going out for food, clothes or anything had been major operations.

Now the car had opened up their lives. Most weekends, when Duncan wasn't around and there were no birthday parties or prearranged sleepovers, she and ten-year-old Alexa would unfold a map and say, 'How about Brighton?' or, 'Let's go to Cambridge!' and off they'd set, with an overnight bag just in case. They'd listen to the radio or to some new band or singer Alexa and her friends were in love with, or they'd just talk.

The two of them had never had any trouble talking, and it had been Susie's policy from early on to be honest with Alexa about her father's situation. Daddy's erratic visits, and the fact that he kept very little in the flat, needed an explanation, and from the time she was old enough to understand, aged six or seven, Alexa knew she had a half-brother and -sister with a different mummy, and that Daddy lived mainly with them. She also knew her half-brother and -sister didn't know about her, because that would upset them.

At first, Brenda had called Susie 'daft as a brush' for sharing so much with her daughter, and Susie had wondered if she was a bad or immature parent for doing so. But she and Alexa were good friends, as well as mother and daughter, and somehow the truth, rather than a convoluted story, felt the only way to go.

Alexa also knew her half-siblings lived in Chelmsford, and barely a week went by without her begging her mother to drive them there, to see their house or catch glimpses of Ben and Emily. Neither she nor Susie had been allowed photos of Duncan's wife and children. He just couldn't, he'd said, and Susie had respected his wishes. But she too was curious. Ben would be fourteen and

Emily nine. She wondered, because Duncan had never said, if Emily was tall, blonde and well rounded like Alexa; if Ben resembled Duncan; what Fran looked like. She'd always wondered what Fran looked like.

In spite of telling Alexa it wouldn't be a good idea, Susie would often lie in bed and imagine driving up Duncan's street of thirties semis, finding his house number and then waiting in the car, with Alexa, until someone appeared. They'd need to do it when Duncan was away – genuinely away – on business. All that was needed was a little plucking up of courage.

In the end it was spur of the moment, which tended to be the way a lot of things happened with Susie. 'Shall we go to Chelmsford today?' she asked over breakfast, and Alexa dropped her spoon and ran from the room, crying, 'Hooray! Shall I wear my Puffa jacket? I want to look good, just in case. Which rucksack should I pack?'

'It's only a day trip!' Susie called out, but then she thought about it and ended up packing an overnight bag for herself. Anything could happen. Perhaps the family wouldn't be there that day, Saturday, but would be on Sunday. Duncan was in Prague, that she did know, because she'd called him at his hotel last night.

Once the decision was made there were no second thoughts; in fact it astonished Susie that they hadn't done it before. All she felt, as they drove north and eastward, was excitement and anxiety, and no guilt whatsoever. Alexa herself had gone terribly quiet, and when Susie asked if she was all right, she said, could they go to Chelmsford again, if they didn't see anyone this weekend?

'Yes,' she said, and then she promised they would, because a disappointing outcome this time would hang over them, and because she too was determined to see this family of Duncan's in the flesh.

It wasn't remotely as she'd imagined it. Not rows of grey and bleak pebble-dashed semis, but attractive houses and front gardens packed with lovely mature trees and shrubs, even on this grey winter's day. The trees and shrubs were useful too, for when they located number thirty-eight, she was able to park the car in a shady spot, hidden by foliage from the house they were in front of, and where they wouldn't be easily spotted from Duncan's house on the other side of the road and slightly ahead of them.

Duncan's house. How often he'd phoned home in front of her. All that time it had merely been a fuzzy unreal place, practically in another universe. And now here it was, all painted white with two large round bays and a red front door with a pretty oval stained-glass window in it, and yellow roses growing around and above it. There was a garage to the left, and because of the angle they were at, Susie could see the extension Duncan had moaned about during its construction.

Her daughter took a photo, then reached to the back seat for their lunch of sandwiches and crisps, and orange juice that would be horribly warm by now. Alexa didn't seem to be as fascinated by the house as Susie was. All she wanted to see were her brother and sister, and Susie could feel her daughter's tension. A tense Alexa was a quiet Alexa.

It felt rather wicked to be there, in Duncan's street, spying. But she justified it to herself. He knew where they lived, after all. He knew almost all there was to know about them. This was something Alexa needed to do, and that alone was a good enough reason. And it balanced things a little. Just seeing the house had already made Susie feel better, and she wondered how much resentment she'd been carrying around all these years; suppressing it and being relentlessly bubbly, because that was her nature.

'Mummy, I think a curtain moved!'

'Did it, darling?' Susie leaned towards the windscreen and squinted.

'Upstairs. The window above the door.'

'Perhaps they're home, then.'

Alexa took another photo with Susie's heavy and expensive camera. 'This is so exciting, isn't it, Mummy? It's like we're Cagney and Lacey doing a stakeout.'

Where was her daughter watching such things? At sleepovers, presumably. A few years back Susie had succumbed to a television. Although hooked on *Dallas* and other rubbish herself, she limited Alexa's viewing to the wholesome and educational. What her daughter did elsewhere was out of her hands, unfortunately. Letting go of control didn't come easily to Susie, who guessed it would only get worse in teenagehood, particularly as they were in London, with all its attractions and nightlife and streetwise youngsters. There was something to be said for boarding schools, she often thought, not that she'd ever entertain that idea.

The past ten years had been devoted to Alexa, and it had paid off. In spite of Susie's fears, she'd settled into school immediately, aged five, and she'd made lasting friends and shone in subjects her mother never had. Susie was openly proud of her daughter but secretly pleased with herself, too, for being a good mother.

And she'd continue to be the best mother she could, but perhaps it was time to find an extra interest; something to get passionate about. She'd spent five years of spare time – Alexa's school hours – getting to know London. From hushed Highgate to troubled Brixton, she'd soaked up the diversity and absolutely loved it. And with Primrose Hill a short walk away, she'd spent hours and hours at its highest point, enjoying the increasingly familiar view and working out where to visit next. She'd had tea at the Ritz and in the most basic of East End cafés, and once, when Duncan had Alexa for the day, she'd travelled by train and on foot to the mouth of the Thames. She'd never taken notes on her travels, or photos, but it was all there in her head – the feel of the city, if not the details.

But now she'd done London – not the museums and other duller-than-dull stuff, but the real London – and it was time for something else. She was in her early thirties with, hopefully, a long life ahead of her. The one thing she knew for certain was that she didn't want to move. They both loved the flat, and the area, and the fact that Alexa's school was so close, as was the next one she'd go to. They liked their neighbours in the block, and because of the communal gardens had got to know one or two in the adjacent block too. Some neighbours were nicer than others, of course, but the one Susie had really taken a shine to was Joel. Tragically widowed Joel, who'd lost his new bride in an accident eight years ago. Joel, with his dark eyes and his charm and wit, and his long, lingering stares at her, could so easily become her new passion, but she wasn't about to let that happen. The practicalities of juggling Duncan and Joel would be a nightmare, and things would become murky and confused for Alexa. Life was simpler with one man – one daddy – in the picture, even a very part-time one.

Alexa gasped and Susie looked up from *The Women's Room*. Someone was coming out of the front door. It was half open but no one could be seen yet, just a shadowy movement. It gave Alexa time to grab the camera from the floor but in her hurry she bashed it against the gearstick.

'Careful,' Susie said, worried more about the car than her Nikon.

'Who do you think it is?' Alexa asked, and then a very lanky boy stepped out and slammed the door behind him. Click went the camera. 'Do you think that's Ben, Mummy?'

'Oh, yes.' Susie was looking at a younger, shorter, skinnier version of the Duncan she'd met at London Star. She could almost smell the beery Anchor, the musty stationery room. 'It's Ben.'

Click, click went Alexa, as he walked down the short path and turned right, in their direction. 'What if he spots us, Mummy? We haven't really got a story, have we, you know, if they confront us?'

'No.' Susie wished now she'd gone for the tinted-windows option when ordering the car. She and Alexa slid down in their seats when he passed on the other side of the street, but they needn't have, since his eyes were fixed on the pavement.

He definitely had Duncan's cute nose, but Susie couldn't see his eyes on account of the thick curly fringe covering them. His hair was long at the back and long at the front, but cut short by his ears. He wore a pale denim jacket with a red-lined hood. His jeans were matching, and on his feet were a pair of clompy black boots. With the passenger windows open to avoid steaming up, they could hear the clomp. His shoulders were hunched and his thumbs were hooked into his jeans pockets. He came across as self-conscious and vulnerable, and every ten-year-old-girl's dream.

'Isn't he wonderful?' said Alexa, on cue.

'Shh. Yes, yes, he is.'

'My brother, I can't believe it.'

'Shh.'

Click went the camera again for a shot of his back, and after he'd turned the corner, Alexa slumped in her seat.

'Would you like the last sandwich?' Susie asked, and Alexa shook her head.

'But I would like the toilet.'

'OK, darling. We'll go to a café we passed a few streets away.'

'May I have a Coke there?'

'We'll see.' Since it was such a big day, she might just let her. They always drank Coke at Lucy's, apparently.

As she pulled out for a three-point turn, Susie wished for two things. One, that no one would take her space while they were gone, and two, that Ben wasn't on his way to the very same café.

Just before three, when they were thinking of heading back to the café, mother and daughter came out the front door together. Alexa fumbled with the camera, while Susie turned the corner of the page she was reading and closed the book.

The first thing that struck her was how alike they were: both dark-haired and slim. But what amazed Susie was how Fran was nothing at all like *her*, as though Duncan didn't have a particular type. Or perhaps it solved that longing-for-what-you-haven't-got thing that people suffer from. When he was with blonde and curvy Susie, did he crave dark and thin Fran, and vice versa?

She was surprised to see Fran light up on the path. Duncan wasn't a smoker but he sometimes arrived with the smell of cigarettes. From work, she'd always assumed, but now she saw it was from home too. Fran wore a longish floral wrap-round skirt, with a red shirt, black tights and brown pixie boots. Emily was in a ski-type jacket, pink and not unlike Alexa's, over pale jeans like her brother's. Her hair was held back with a slide and she was very pretty, but in a different way from Alexa.

There was a click, click of the camera, as the two of them walked through their front gate and turned, just as Ben had, towards them. They were chatting but not in a loud or animated way, and Susie wished she could catch what they were saying, or just hear them better. She prayed Alexa wouldn't speak loudly as they passed. So far she'd said nothing, just breathed heavily on the half-open window.

Fran put her hand on her daughter's quilted shoulder, as she peered past her for a good look at her rival. Click, went Alexa again, and then in less than a second, she'd slipped from Susie's hand, opened her door and jumped out.

'Emily!' she shouted across the road, and the little girl's head swivelled round for Alexa to take the perfect shot. She fell back into the car, slammed the door, and said, 'Let's go! Quick!' to her mother, as though they really were Cagney and Lacey.

SEVENTEEN

It was all hands on deck for a spaghetti Bolognese, and just before six they'd reached the final stage, with Em easing two handfuls of dried spaghetti into boiling water. They could open the champagne while it cooked, she'd suggested, and her mother had gone off to get Ben.

While Alex filled the dishwasher, Em prodded stubborn bits of pasta into the water. She'd liked to have had a shower but there was no time. She knew she looked a wreck, but in some ways she was more worried about her mum, who was drawn and pale and seemed very on edge. Living with her dad could have been causing it. She hoped that was what it was, rather than some underlying illness. What a nightmare that would be, having two sick parents. It didn't bear thinking about, even though Alex would be a total brick should it come to it. Unless he was in Paris.

She didn't want him to go to Paris, not now. She needed him. Here. It was weird, but he'd even begun to look better. Tall and attractive with a nice open face. Hadi was a bit on the slim side. Boyish, perhaps, where her husband was manly. And last night, after he'd led her to the bedroom, Alex had been so passionate and eager to please. And, strangely, considering how upset and stressed she been, he had pleased.

Maybe they could all go to Paris. It was a city she loved, and the kids would end up bilingual. Alex was fluent, of course, but Em's French was as bad as his was good. She'd do an intensive course, and then look for a job. Or she could offer tuition in English and art history, although it would be nice to get out of the home; work in another gallery, perhaps. If her French became good enough, she'd find something in admin. She was a natural organiser, according to her family. 'Bossy', was how Ben put it. She pictured them all in an elegant apartment, overlooking a pretty square. Martha all got up in French gear, with a velvet headband. George in culottes . . .

Em put the lid on the saucepan and turned the heat down. She'd tell him later to go for it, for the job. That she'd be prepared to leave London. It was what he'd been wanting to hear. Poor Alex, how foul she'd been to him, her kind and selfless husband.

When the birthday girl appeared holding the hand of a drowsy-looking Ben, her mum had something of a sparkle about her that hadn't been there ten minutes ago. She'd probably splashed her face and put makeup on. Whatever it was, she looked fresher and happier and pretty good for her age. Not that sixty was old these days. Em had tried telling her that recently and almost had her head bitten off. 'Look at Joanna Lumley,' she'd added, only to be told everyone said that.

The four of them trooped through to the sitting room with

the unopened bottle and five glasses, to find her father with his head back, eyes on the television, half closed. At his feet, his granddaughter was trying over and over to strike a match.

When it lit, Ben said, 'Fuck,' and Em screamed as the flame only just made the coffee mug on the floor. But it was Alex who put the tray down and calmly walked over and asked Martha and George if they'd like a fizzy drink to toast Grandma.

'Yes, yes!' they cried, while he eased a box of matches from his five year old and picked up the mug and one or two stray matches. 'Lemonade or fizzy water?'

'Lemonade!'

'Lemonade!'

'Ah, time for champers,' said her father, rousing himself. 'Lovely jubbly.'

'I'll get the lemonades,' Em said, and for the second time that day found herself shaking in a kitchen. If it hadn't been her mum's birthday, she'd have asked what she was thinking, leaving matches around for grandchildren to play with. And what was her dad doing, letting that happen? Obviously, she and Alex should have kept a closer eye on the kids, but honestly.

She went back to a scene, in Laura's garden on Bonfire Night. She and Laura, her best friend for years and a close neighbour, were trying to light a sparkler with a match, but they'd set fire to Laura instead. Em had been holding the sparkler, while Laura struck the match, wearing some sort of shiny ski-type gloves. On hearing the screams, her dad had rushed across, yanked the glove off and stamped on it. Luckily it was thick and Laura hadn't been burned. Then he'd told them off big time – Em in particular – about the danger of matches. Hadn't he told her never *ever* to play with them, or even pick up a box, or a lighter, etc, etc. The reprimand had stayed with her because her dad had been so unusually angry and loud, and because both she and Laura had cried a lot, mainly with the shock of the smouldering glove.

Em realised she'd overreacted just now, that she should have been composed like Alex. It must have been a flashback, but on top of that she was incredibly jumpy. Her bag hung on a kitchen chair and she delved in, fiddled around and withdrew her phone. She looked behind her, then quickly checked for messages. Nothing from Nigel. She was no longer expecting anything from Hadi. He could be in Iran, or on honeymoon, or dead for all she cared.

No, that wasn't true, but now she'd sort of collected herself, she just wanted an explanation. If Nigel didn't call, then she might go to his house one evening or at the weekend. She'd turn up and demand to be told why Hadi had gone, if not where. Whatever it was, she just needed to know . . . something.

After pouring lemonade in two plastic cups, Em took a deep breath and carried them through. Champagne, she thought, someone give me champagne. Perhaps she'd drink her brother-the-moron's share too, since he hadn't bought any. What was his problem? She used to tell people her brother was nice and super clever with it. These days he was nice but dim, and not even that nice. Calling her bossy. And who got their mother a wok for her sixtieth, but no champagne or flowers?

'Here you are, George,' she said. 'Martha.'

The champagne cork popped and Alex filled the trayful of glasses, then her father got up off the sofa and they all stood around listening to Em's semi-prepared speech about this wonderful, funny, caring mother and grandmother, and how she didn't look a day over forty.

'And may I say,' chipped in her father, 'that I couldn't have wished for a more perfect wife all these years. Happy Birthday, my love.'

Her mother beamed and said, 'Thank you.'

Kiss her, thought Em, but he didn't. Glasses were chinked and 'Happy Birthday's were said, while eyes wandered nervously to the spots of singed carpet at their feet.

They'd stopped on the way and picked up a cake with 'Happy Birthday' and little roses on it, and a box of candles and holders. In the kitchen she and Alex put six of the candles in a circle and lit them, then Alex carried it through to the rarely used dining room at the front of the house, while Em held each door for him. She and Alex had agreed that if this were their place they'd knock down walls to incorporate the smaller front rooms into one lovely modern and open space. 'But think of the heating bills!' her mum had said to the idea. At least with assorted rooms, it would be easy to escape from your partner, should you wish to. Em imagined there might be a bit of that going on these days.

It was Martha, climbing on to her chair, who led the singing. She'd be on the stage one day, or a politician. Alex had such a lovely voice, Em thought beside him. She was opposite her father, who sang loudly and enthusiastically, but when it got to the 'dear name' part, he stopped, looked in a bewildered way at his wife, sang nothing, and then joined in with the final 'Happy Birthday to you'. Em put it down to the multitude of names ringing out from different members of the family: 'Mum', 'Grandma', and a 'Fran' from Alex. It could have thrown anyone.

The kids were charging around, on a sugar high from the cake. Up the stairs and along the landing, then down the stairs and through the various rooms, slamming doors and shouting and screaming about the monster chasing them. The monster being their grandfather, lurking in corners or behind doors, then leaping out and growling. He was pretty nimble, Em thought, for someone in his late sixties who'd given up his golf, the only exercise he'd ever taken. Perhaps it was down to all the naps he took. She sat on the chair in the hall, pretending to read but keeping an ear open, just in case.

'Rrrarrgh!' she heard again, followed by the screams. It was eight fifteen, an hour after their bedtime, and they'd still have to have a bath, and stories, and then they'd take ages to go to sleep because they were at Grandma and Grandpa's, the most exciting place in the world.

Ben and Alex were watching the news and discussing the election, and her mother was talking to Uncle Pat in New Zealand. Em had had a quick word with him, trying her hardest to sound chipper. He'd got up early to watch the election too. The whole world was watching. She wondered what Hadi was doing, a sudden fondness hitting her. He had American friends in London, she knew, because he'd been with them the first time they met, and had even introduced them to her. Three guys, all music students; two of them black. He'd be cheering on Obama tonight, but where? In a pub, perhaps, or at a gig.

She got up and went into the kitchen and unwrapped her

phone. There'd been a missed call from a landline she didn't recognise but no message had been left. Nigel! It must have been Nigel. Hadi had always called from his mobile, so she'd never known his other number. She could go in the garden and phone him back, but thinking about it, what if it had been Hadi himself, calling from his new place? It was an 020 number, so somewhere in London. This needed some planning. There were the children to deal with, the game of Trivia her mother had requested.

'Everything OK?' asked Alex behind her. He went to the fridge and pulled out two beers, while Em pushed the phone up her sleeve. 'I'll just have this, then put the kids to bed. They can skip the bath tonight, yeah?'

'Yes,' she agreed with a quick smile. 'I'll get them away from Dad, if I can. And heat up some milk.'

Alex came over and kissed her forehead, then leaned back and cocked his face at her. 'You sure you're all right? Still poorly?'

'A bit.'

'Aahh.' He gave her a hug and she felt the icy bottles on her arm, inches from the phone. 'I'll be five minutes,' he said. 'Just catching up with Ben, poor guy.'

'OK.'

When he'd gone, she hid the phone again. She'd have to call back whoever it was, or she'd go nuts. But when, and how?

'I'm just popping to the garage for the kids' packed lunch stuff,' she told them. She'd declined recent offers of wine, having had a small glass with dinner on top of the champagne. She'd be fine to drive the three miles, absolutely fine. 'It didn't occur to us to bring it.'

'I'm sure we have things here you could give them,' said her mother.

'Oh, no, no. They're so fussy.' Alex was putting the children to bed and unable to contradict. 'Honestly, I won't be long, and the car's low on petrol too. We don't want to be queuing in the morning.'

Em slipped her coat on and was out the door before Alex could reappear and scupper her plan. He'd filled the tank on the M25. She drove away slowly and quietly, then pulled over by the village shop, switched off the engine and took out her phone. She pressed to return the call and, heart thumping, waited.

'Hello, you've reached Nigel Newsome. I'm sorry I can't get to the—'

Em hung up. She switched the engine on again, looked at the petrol gauge and sighed, then pulled out into the quietest High Street in the world and headed for a garage she didn't need. Since they'd already agreed the kids would take the next day off school, she'd have to come up with something for Alex.

In the garage's mini supermarket, she picked up a box of tampons. An unexpected period, she'd tell him.

EIGHTEEN

'"Who is the female writer of *The Liver Birds*?"' Ben asked, reading from a card that was yellowing with age. If *Antiques Roadshow* came to town he'd take their Trivia along.

'*Lyver*,' said his dad. 'Not liver, as in the bodily organ.'

His mum hooted with laughter.

'It was a sitcom in the late sixties,' his father explained. 'Early seventies. Set in Liverpool and about two dolly birds sharing a flat. Isn't that right, Fran?'

Now she really was in stitches. 'Dolly birds?' she managed to splutter, arms clutching at her middle. Why did people do that, wondered Ben. In case they literally explode with laughter?

'Carla Lane,' said Alex, whose question it had been.

'Correct!' said his dad.

'How do you know that?' Ben asked.

'We've had it before, dozens of times.'

'We have?' Ben was quietly worried. If it had come up that

often, how come he hadn't remembered? Unless they'd been playing without him. Yes, that must be it.

'If it was set in Liverpool,' he said, 'why were they called the *Lyver* Birds, not the Liver, as in liver and bacon, or even Liverpool, Birds?'

His dad shrugged, his mum calmed down and said she didn't know, and Alex, rather abruptly, stood up.

'Where's Em gone now?' he asked, picking up empty glasses. 'Can I get you all a refill? Fran, another vodka and tonic?'

She wiped tears from her eyes. 'Yes, please.'

'Same for me,' said Ben. It felt like time for a top-up of another kind too. 'Since we're having a break, I'll take a pee.'

'And I'll have a ciggie,' said his mum.

Ben nodded. 'Me too.'

'But you don't smoke? Tell me you haven't taken up smoking?' As well as drugs, she meant. Upstairs he'd owned up to Brucofen addiction, only to stop her thinking he was dying.

'Nah, don't fret. It's just, you know, Julia. And Obama. Big night, special occasion and all that.' He got up and said, 'I'll be out in a minute,' and then he ran up the stairs to his room, popped four painkillers, had a quick pee and ran back down.

The election coverage wouldn't start in earnest until elevenish. If he'd been at home, in the flat, with proper broadband and no birthday going on, he'd have linked up with some of the US cable channels and watched their manic outpourings. He'd read that they'd know for sure who'd won at around four o'clock British time, and decided he'd watch through the night while the others slept. There were some big plusses to being an out-of-work loser.

* * *

'May I?' he asked his mum.

'I suppose so,' she said, exhaling into the night and handing her fags over. 'If you must.'

Occasionally, just occasionally lately, he'd had a cigarette. Never in Julia's presence, because she'd have stubbed it out in his eye. He'd had one in Trafalgar Square, another outside the cookshop, while trying to decide about the wok. One in front of the Job Centre with the other investment bankers. A pack of ten, he'd bought himself, and there were two left. He could have smoked those instead of bumming off his mum, but then she'd think he was a real smoker. Plus he'd feel silly, because no one over twelve buys ten cigarettes.

Ben lit up and deliberately coughed a few times. 'Dear, dear,' he said. 'Ugh, horrible.' But then his mother looked suspiciously at him, and he grinned. 'OK, I admit I do have the odd one.'

'Maybe you and I have that addictive gene.'

'Hmm.' Ben inhaled. It made him feel light-headed and good, on top of the vodka. And the tabs would be kicking in soon – half an hour or so. He'd taken a few more than usual, slipping in a couple of dihydrocodeine, which came with paracetamol instead of ibuprofen. It was good to mix them up a bit. You wouldn't want to be taking too much of one thing.

'So, how long have you been on those Bru . . . whatever they're called?'

'Since I pulled that muscle in my back.' Julia had decided they should clean behind the washing machine. But she'd meant 'you' when she'd said 'we', and he'd wrecked his back heaving the thing in and out, all on his own.

'I remember,' said his mum. 'In the summer, just before you . . .'

145

'Got fired, yeah. It's OK, you can say it. Anyway, ordinary painkillers weren't doing it, and this guy I know said, here, try a couple of these, and suddenly the pain was gone, but on top of that I felt euphoric. The codeine's an opiate.'

'Maybe I should try them, or better still, give some to your father.'

'Don't even think about it. Honestly, Mum, they're evil. They say three days and you're hooked.'

His mother smiled and exhaled again. 'In that case, I'll definitely get some. It's not easy at the moment with your dad. Well, you'll find out, if you're not on planet zog along with him.'

'Planet what?' Ben laughed, then they both jumped as Em appeared on the path in the gloom, her coat wrapped tightly around her. 'Where have you been?' he asked.

'I felt a bit icky, so I took a walk around the garden. Sorry for deserting the Trivia.'

'Don't worry,' said Ben, 'we all have. It's really time you bought a new version, Mum. I mean, "What's the capital of Yugoslavia?" And who remembers anything about George Brown and Joe Grimmond, or who the fuck they even were?' Ben knew full well who they were, because politics had interested him since his student days and he'd even considered it as a career before big bucks were dangled temptingly.

His mum was creased up now. '*Poldark!*' she said, coughing on her fag. 'Even I barely remember that.'

Em wasn't laughing and she looked rough as hell. 'Ben!' she snapped, spotting the glow he'd been trying to hide. 'What are you doing smoking?' She looked seriously cross, which was a bit rich considering she'd have smoked her granny at one time, if she'd thought it would work.

'I, er . . .'

'Em, *please*,' said his mum. She shook her head at her daughter, barely perceptibly, in a 'not on my birthday' or 'think what he's been through' way.

Em made a disapproving grunt, coughed pointedly and went back in the house, where Ben watched her fiddle with her handbag, blow her nose into some tissue and dab at her eyes. Still Mummy's boy, she was probably thinking. If she hadn't lost it for all those years, Em might have remained the favourite, as she'd always seemed to Ben when they were kids. His pretty little sister, Emily, with her winning way with adults. He'd been the lanky, freckled, toothy, tongue-tied older brother only a blind mother could love.

Em was still pretty, but the way she looked tonight, she could even be back on the drugs. Unless she was ill. Thinking about it, hadn't she said she had a bug? God, his brain was crap these days. If they did one of those dementia memory tests at job interviews, he'd be unemployed for ever. Name the last four prime ministers, that kind of thing. Actually, he should be all right. Brown, Blair . . . Thatcher. Then in the seventies, it was . . .

'Who was the prime minister before Thatcher?' he asked his mum.

She dropped her cigarette in a pot. 'Are we still playing Trivia?'

'Winter of discontent and . . . oh, yeah, Callaghan.' Ben shook his fuzzy head. 'I'm so thick on these pills, but I can't stop taking them. In fact, I need more, I find, just to get the same kick, or just to feel OK.' It was a relief, he realised, to be talking about it.

'Perhaps we can work on it while you're here. I've had clients with drug dependency.'

'Yeah?'

'Are you sure you can't ease yourself off them, now you're not living with the girlfriend from hell?'

'Maybe.'

'We could go on walks and outings. To be honest, it'll be lovely for me, having you here.'

'Really?' It had been ages since someone said nice things to him.

'And I do like the wok. Thank you. How's your cooking these days?'

'Let's just say my style's been cramped.'

'Julia?'

'Mm.'

'You used to be pretty good. Remember that Christmas Dad and I had flu and you did it all?'

'Oh, yeah.' Em had been out of it on something, on the sofa.

'We'll do stir fries. It'll be great.' She stood up and said, 'Come here,' and for a while they hugged – slightly awkwardly, since his mum was five five and he was six two, and they were both in bulky coats.

It wouldn't be so bad, living at home for a while. He'd ease himself off the pills, like his mum suggested. Cook, take walks, watch *Loose Women* with no fear of Julia bursting in. Gradually, he'd get back to normal and be able to think straight. And he'd be company for his mother; be doing something useful for a change.

'Shall we go in?' she asked.

Ben opened the door and let her through first, then once inside, closed it, lifted the handle and turned the key to lock up. For a while he stared at his dumb reflection in the glass. Major, he thought. He'd forgotten John Major.

NINETEEN

London, 1985

What Susie didn't know, while she and her daughter were staking out Duncan's house, was that she was pregnant. It was around a fortnight later, as she poached two eggs for their breakfast, that a horrible and horribly familiar feeling welled up. It was a bug, she told herself, and she left Alexa in charge of the eggs and sat down until the nausea passed.

A home test confirmed what she'd been half fearing, half wanting. She phoned Duncan and told him, and after an initial shocked silence, during which she'd had to say, 'Duncan? Hello?' he told her how happy he was, but without sounding over the moon. She wondered, briefly, if he'd suspected her of spying on him; that Emily or Fran had said something. But knowing Duncan, he'd have confronted her – in a non-confrontational way – rather than let it fester. 'That's wonderful,' he added unconvincingly.

Well, he didn't have to be involved, if he didn't want to. She'd been looking for a new interest, something to get passionate about, and here it was, another child. The timing wasn't brilliant, since the baby would be due shortly before Alexa started secondary school. At least not for Alexa, who'd be going off to her semi-grown-up world just as she was being replaced – or so she might feel – by another little person. But nothing could be done about the situation, and with a bit of luck, Alexa would see herself as almost another mother, since she'd always been good in that role.

She definitely seemed excited by the news, phoning all her friends and asking Susie if they could shop for baby clothes. But the reality of someone needing lots of its mother's attention would be another matter. Still, if it came to it, she could always hire some help.

'Are you sure you're happy about the baby?' Susie asked her daughter one evening, when they were watching *EastEnders* because Susie didn't have the energy to forbid it.

Alexa gave her a firm nod. 'There are two of *them*,' she said, 'so it makes it more fair.'

'Two of . . . ? Oh, I see. Ben and Emily.'

This hadn't actually occurred to her, but yes, Alexa was right. It did make it more fair. And they'd be more solid, somehow. More of a family. A real family, instead of the waifs she'd felt they'd been, until Belsize Park had come along and given them substance.

'Daddy might spend more time with us,' said Alexa. 'If there's a baby. Especially if it's a boy. I expect Daddy likes boys better.'

Susie was horrified. 'That's absolutely not true, sweetie.

You know why Daddy can't spend all of his spare time with us. And he loves you, darling. He couldn't love anybody more than he loves you.'

Alexa went quiet and had her sulky face, and Susie suddenly regretted the Chelmsford trip. Seeing Duncan's family had made them more real to Alexa, who hadn't mentioned them since but kept the developed photos under her pillow.

'It's not fair,' she said, frowning at the cushion she picked at. 'Why do *we* have to be the secret?'

Susie tried to put an arm around her but was shrugged off. 'Well,' she said, 'it's because they came along first for Daddy. As you know, he was married to Ben and Emily's mother before he met me and she already had a baby in her tummy.'

'Oh, Mummy, *please*. A baby in her tummy? I'm not four years old.'

'Sorry, darling. I'm sorry.' Gosh, she was becoming difficult. Or was it just that until now she'd had it easy with Alexa? 'Anyway, Daddy and I talked about it at the time and decided he shouldn't leave his wife and baby-to-be.'

Alexa tapped her mouth in a mock yawn. 'Yeah, yeah.'

'Tell you what, darling. How would you like to phone Grandma and Grandpa and give them the news?'

Alexa caught her breath and clutched her chest with both hands. 'May I?' she asked, back to her old sweet self. Of course, it wouldn't last. Some of her friends were already going through puberty and could be jolly rude.

'Yes, you may.' Susie went to the hall and unplugged the phone and brought it into the drawing room, where there was another socket by the Chesterfield. 'Here you are.'

Alexa knew the number by heart, since she'd spent far more time talking to her grandparents down a line than face to face.

'Hello, Grandpa,' she said, and Susie slipped out of the room, pulled the door to and let out a sigh of relief. 'Oh, it's just *EastEnders*,' she heard through the gap. 'Yes, I *am* allowed to watch it . . . No it's not, it's good.'

Oh dear, thought Susie. Bad start. She hadn't exactly been dreading telling her parents about the baby, but had been putting it off. They may have shifted in some of their views, but not seismically. To the group captain and his wife, it would still be another illegitimate grandchild.

Sebastian arrived a week and a half early, looking exactly as Alexa had. It was an easier birth but Susie couldn't help worry about her daughter, down in the farmhouse with Brenda and all that entailed: germs and nearby cows, and all kinds of hazards. Sometimes it amazed Susie that they'd survived it, and that the twins continued to thrive there.

Her mother appeared too late for the birth, fortuitously perhaps. Since she and Susie weren't that close, the intimacy of the occasion could have been awkward.

'Isn't he super?' her mother exclaimed. 'Darling little Sebastian. Just think, a boy!'

Susie said, 'Yes, isn't it wonderful?' Suddenly it was confirmed for her. They'd always wanted a son, her mother in particular. She'd had a miscarriage after Susie, followed by years of no luck in the conception department, until they'd finally given up. Her father had revealed all this after a particularly fluid session in the mess.

Her mother, so prim in her Jaeger suit, gazed adoringly at her grandson, beaming and happier, perhaps, than Susie had ever seen her. And all things considered, this was rather good news. It could mean more grandparental input.

'Does he have a middle name?'

'Not yet,' Susie said, praying she wasn't about to suggest Bernard, her father's name. Sebastian Bernard would never do.

'I rather like James,' her mother said, looking wistfully at the baby, out of the window, at the baby again.

Susie didn't mind which James her mother still held a candle for, but it went perfectly with Sebastian. 'Spot on!' she said, hoping Duncan wouldn't mind. But considering he'd shown little interest in the event that was Sebastian, his opinion, even if he'd had one, would be irrelevant.

It took him three days to get round to visiting, but this was partly because he'd driven to Kent to pick up Alexa. By then, Susie was back in Number Ten and suffering post-natal blues. Her new best friend was the nanny, who'd been in her employ only half a day when Susie found herself crying on her twenty-year-old shoulder. 'Thur, thur,' Danielle had said, in her soft Lancashire accent.

Duncan picked up his son with a, 'Hey, big boy, look at you!'

'He has a name,' Susie snapped. Oh, do please stop, she told herself, but she simply couldn't. The oestrogen, or whatever, had taken over. 'But I doubt you'll remember it.'

'May I hold him, Daddy?' asked Alexa. There was a scratch on her face she'd got from a branch. Had Brenda let them climb trees?

'Would you wash your hands, sweetie?' Susie asked.

'Why? Daddy didn't wash his.'

'I know, but . . .' Why was she being so difficult? Jealous already?

'Come on,' Duncan said, putting the baby back in his basket. 'Let's both go and wash our hands. Mummy's right.'

'Mummy always *thinks* she's right.'

Susie sighed and closed her eyes. Motherhood was exhausting in one's thirties, and she hadn't even done a great deal, what with Danielle and her, 'Let me tek baby off now. You 'ave a lickle rest.' Susie enjoyed being spoken to like a two year old. And she enjoyed not having to do nappies, and dozing a lot, and the cups of teas that appeared half-hourly, as though Danielle had knocked up a conveyor belt.

'Clean enough?' asked Alexa, thrusting her palms in her mother's face.

'Thank you, darling. We had to do the same when you were newborn, didn't we, Daddy?'

'Mm?' said Duncan. The remote was in his hand, the TV went on and he searched for the news.

'Switch it off!' she told him. 'You have a new son, Duncan. Now show some bloody interest.'

'Mummy!'

'Sorry, darling. Sorry. I'm just . . .'

'Mummy's not herself,' said Duncan. He reached into the Moses basket for Sebastian, and he and Alexa did lots of cooing and, 'Ah, look at his little . . .' feet, fingers, etc.

And all was well for a while. Once again, and briefly – because Duncan had a meeting to get to – they played at being a family.

TWENTY

'I'm worried about Duncan,' said Fran. Alex had been checking the children and they were whispering on the landing. 'How have you found him?'

'A bit down, but then he was when he came for lunch, and the time before that. Well, for quite a while now. Depression can be quite common after retirement.'

'He's so drowsy all the time. That's often a symptom.'

'Is he on any medication?'

'Just something to help him sleep.'

Alex laughed. 'Seems to be working, then.'

'I deal with this all the time, but with Duncan I'm at a loss. The trouble is, he won't talk. He just dismisses any suggestion he might be depressed, and he's so tired that he's hard to have a conversation with anyway. Then there's the irritability.'

'Has he seen his GP lately?'

'Not for nine months. He picks up a repeat prescription when he runs low on sleepers.'

'Perhaps he should get checked out.'

'Yes, but I'd have to make the appointment because he never will.'

'It must be rough for you,' Alex said. He put a hand on her arm.

'A bit.' *Don't cry. Birthday.* An hour to go, then she could cry.

'Look, you know where we are, if you ever need a London mini-break.'

'Instead of the country one? Yes, please!' She laughed, but realised she'd been rude. 'It's a wonderful present, thank you.'

'Em's idea, actually. Sorry, if you don't fancy it . . . you know, at the moment.'

'Don't be silly. I'm looking forward to it.'

'And maybe it'll cheer Duncan up?'

'Here's hoping,' said Fran. How she'd love to go on her own, or with a fun-loving friend. A possibility, perhaps?

Alex said he'd check on Em, who'd gone to bed early and apologetically. 'See you downstairs.'

'OK.'

Fran adored her son-in-law. The first time he'd appeared with Em, she and Duncan both felt relief that their daughter had found someone so normal and nice, and nervousness that she wouldn't hang on to him. But she had hung on to him, or he to her, and it had all worked out so brilliantly. Lucky Em. Fran hoped she was appreciating Alex, while he was still a fantastic husband and father; before he retired and fell into despondency and apathy.

Her own parents had had a similar reaction to Duncan, who'd

come home for a weekend in 1967 and completely charmed 'Jean' and 'Les', as he was instantly calling them. She'd been a short-hand-typist for some stockbrokers when she and Duncan met one lunchtime in The Anchor. Fran had always thought that an odd name for a pub in the heart of the City, but then Duncan had taken her on a tour of the area and the river and given her a history lesson, and it began to make sense.

Having left school at sixteen and done a quick secretarial course, she'd gone straight to the City for her first job in a bank. While her best friends stayed on in the sixth form, Fran had been keen to get out there and live a bit, earn money. The last thing she'd wanted was to work locally, so she'd boarded the train, new certi-ficate in hand, and gone around the London agencies. The tests they put her through showed excellent copy- and audio-typing, but poor shorthand. This limited her job prospects, but once settled in a four-woman typing pool in the bank, she was fairly happy. The other typists were a laugh, and they'd all go somewhere nice at lunchtime, or in the summer they'd bring sandwiches from home and find a bench in the sun. After a year, Fran said goodbye to the bank and found a better paid job at a stockbrokers'.

Earning good money and working in the heart of the financial centre gave Fran a bit of status back at home, and almost made up for the fact that her friends would go on to be teachers and managers. She never regretted her decision to leave school at the first opportunity, then when Duncan came along, believed it had all somehow been fated. She was eighteen, he was twenty-four. She knew more or less nothing about anything; he knew so much.

Duncan had always been keen on history, and the books on

his side of the bed had tended to be about the English Civil War or the silk trade, or were biographies of Cromwell and others. As fascinated as he was, he'd still take months to get through a book, a few pages at night before fatigue took over. After years of complaining that he didn't have time to read, he now had all the time in the world but read nothing. Samuel Pepys had been beside the bed for months, covered in mug rings and with a bookmark in the prologue.

Fran thought a new interest would be good for Duncan, but how would he find a new interest, when nothing interested him? It was hopeless. He'd become hopeless. If her parents could see him now, she thought. She'd lost them both to illness a few years back; her father in 2002, and her mother fifteen months later. And today, on her big birthday, she'd been missing them. She tried to picture how they'd have looked, six years on and disease free. How they'd have related to their great-grandchildren. At least her mother had seen Martha a couple of times, and held her until she'd cried and been handed back to Em. Her parents would have been in their mid-eighties by now. Losing their minds, perhaps. Their deaths had been shocking and upsetting, but at least they'd both been with it to the end. As had Duncan's. More with it, in fact, than Duncan was now.

With that cheery thought, she went down to the kitchen and poured a vodka and tonic, and took it into the sitting room, where her husband was asleep – surprise – and Ben was stretched out, straight as an ironing board in the armchair, glued to David Dimbleby and his election panel. His eyes were glazed, his mouth was almost smiling. He looked like someone high on something, which, of course, he was.

Any idea that Ben might be welcome company and a big help with Duncan was going out the window. She couldn't feel cross with him, though, poor guy. His self-esteem had been battered; first the job, then the relationship.

As she stood there, alcohol in hand, staring at her son and her husband, the reality of her situation crept in. She had two projects on her hands now, on top of her clients. Of course, she could just leave them to it. Let them muddle along on their own, while she took a break. Now she was sixty she could head off with her bus pass.

'It's not looking good for Obama,' said Ben. Only his lips moved, nothing else.

'No?' she asked. She sat next to Duncan and put her feet on the coffee table. 'How many states has he lost?'

Ben had switched to Sky, where yet more people were trying to think of things to say for five hours.

'Oh, they haven't had any results yet. I just think it's best to be pessimistic in life, don't you? Then if things turn out well, it's a pleasant surprise.'

Fran nodded thoughtfully, with an inkling now of why her son was unemployed. Zonked out on codeine and expecting to fail. She put her head back and closed her eyes and pictured all the places she could go – Durham, St Ives, the Isle of Wight. All for free. Would her bus pass cover Scotland? Duncan hadn't bothered with his, saying real men didn't go on buses. Her husband had some quaintly old-fashioned ideas about certain things. Or, rather, had had. Now, she had no idea what, if anything, went on in his head.

TWENTY-ONE

Em had faked sleep when Alex checked her. Or perhaps she had been sleeping, so exhausted was she, she wasn't sure. As the light from the landing shrunk and disappeared and the door clicked shut, she opened her eyes fully and stared into the blackness. From beneath the duvet, she lifted her phone and dialled and listened again to the ring-ring, ring-ring . . .

'*Titanic* engine room.'

Em jumped. 'Oh, er . . . is that Nigel?'

'*Speeea*-king!' She heard background noises. People, the TV.

'Is Hadi there?'

'He's moved out. Sorry. You the one put the note through the door?' Either he had a speech impediment or he was drunk.

'Yes. Yes, I did. Thanks for trying to phone earlier.' Pushing the duvet off, she got up and crossed the room, opened the door and checked both ways on the landing.

'He owes me rent, if you see him. Hang on. Bottle opener's in the top drawer, Chris!'

She guessed they'd just got back from the pub. She saw the fridge stocked with beers for the long night ahead. Even teachers were staying up.

'Sorry, yeah,' he said. 'Anyway, Hadi's dossing at some mate's place. Can't tell you where. Said he'd bring the rent round, but I won't hold my breath. His old man gives him money, so I'm mightily pissed off.'

'I see.' She wondered if he should be telling her this.

'Do you want his mobile number?'

'I've got it, thanks. I'm actually a good friend of his.' Em kicked herself. Nigel could check her number and hound her for the money. 'Well, sort of,' she added quickly. 'He was due to give my son a lesson this week.'

'Right, right. When he brings the rent, ha-ha, I could ask him to give you a bell?'

'OK. Um, why did he suddenly go, do you know?'

'Thanks, mate!' There was the sound of a ring pull, then Nigel glugging something down. 'Well, between you me and BT,' he said, burping down the line, 'Hadi was banging some MLF and got warned off by her hubby. That's what he told me. He didn't say what the threat was, and for all I know he got paid off. Only he wouldn't have owned up to that, would he, on account of the rent. Oops, being a bit indiscreet, here.' He laughed, loudly, drunkenly.

Em said nothing. A thousand electric shocks had struck her, all at once.

'Hello?'

She cleared her throat. 'Gosh, what a thing to happen. I don't suppose you know the woman's name? Perhaps he's with her and I could contact him there.' Surely Hadi hadn't meant *her*? He must have had another married lover, one with a frightening husband. Em wasn't sure which scenario made her more sick, but she felt very sick.

'No, I don't. Only know she was an ex-junkie and her husband was a big bloke. Hadi said he drove a girly car, though.' He laughed again. 'Some little Citroën.'

Em dropped the phone and headed for the bathroom. She got to the loo just in time. And as she stood there, staring at spaghetti Bolognese in the bowl, head hung, sick in her hair, she was instantly back in the bad old days. Her junkie days. *Some little Citroën*, she kept hearing, over and over. Alex's courtesy car.

She showered, shaking and with her stomach all knotted. Wrapped in thick towels, she walked back to the bedroom, praying Alex wouldn't be there talking to the person she'd left dangling on her phone. Not that it would matter, not now. She took clean clothes from their case and continued to shake as she dressed. She was in shock and needed something for it. A drink would help, but that would involve going downstairs and seeing her creepy husband. Not only had he found out, he'd been to Hadi's house, threatened him or paid him off, and then acted perfectly normally at home.

Em sat on the bed, fully dressed but so jumbled emotionally that she couldn't think what to do. She got up and put some foundation on, and a little lipstick and mascara, and then she combed out her wet hair, rubbed it with a towel and combed again.

163

In the past, when she'd needed help, there'd always been one person there for her. Someone who wouldn't condemn; just listen and offer advice. But now she wasn't sure how helpful her dad would be. He clearly wasn't well himself. In spite of her mother being a psychotherapist, Em had always felt judged by her when she'd gone wrong. It was understandable, really, when it came to family. She could see herself being the same way with Martha and George. It was her dad who'd been the saint. The one she'd always called, often at work, and he was the one she wanted to talk to now.

Her father had had the same mobile number for ever. Em picked up her secret phone – or was it a secret any more? – and dialled.

It rang and rang, and then her father answered breathlessly, as though he'd run from a room. 'Alexa?' he said.

'Who?' Did he mean Alex? 'No, Dad, it's Em.'

'Ah, yes, yes. Is everything all right, you sound—'

'No, it's not all right. Could you come upstairs? I need to chat.'

'To me?'

'Yes, Dad. To you.'

Em met him on the landing and led him into Ben's room, as Ben was less likely to come and disturb them. She left the door ajar so she could keep a watch out, and sat on a chair with a view of the landing, while her father settled on the single bed. He looked tired and unusually podgy, his hands clasped on his round tummy.

'What's up, poppet?' he asked.

'I don't know where to begin.' She'd always been open with her dad in the past, but then it had been about drugs or debts, not about cheating on a beloved son-in-law.

'The beginning?' he asked, predictably.

'OK. Well, I just want to say I really love Alex. He's always been a wonderful husband and a brilliant father. But I don't know, it just didn't . . .'

Her dad sat up; seemed almost to wake up. 'It just didn't feel like enough?'

He always gets it, Em thought. Even now, when he's deep in some horrible place of his own. She shook her head. 'No.'

He nodded.

'And I, er, met someone. I didn't go out of my way to, it just happened. You know?'

He nodded again. 'I know.'

'Hadi, his name is. Or rather was, because he's done a runner.'

'Hadi? What nationality?'

'Iranian.'

'Really?' He suddenly looked shocked, and Em was thrown back to when she'd brought a Korean boyfriend home one Christmas. It had been a short-lived relationship, owing to lack of compatibility on all fronts, but Em had been surprised by her dad's coldness towards him. And over the years there'd been the odd racist joke at family meals, when she and Ben had been forced to berate him. Perhaps he wasn't the right person to be talking to at all.

'How on earth did you meet him?'

He meant how did you meet an Iranian. 'At a club. He's not a fundamentalist, or anything, Dad, don't worry. Just a musician, who was born here. And he's clever, got a doctorate. Anyway, it was a friend's birthday outing and we immediately clicked.' She took the scrunched-up tissue from her sleeve and blew into it.

'He was gorgeous-looking and great fun, and . . . Oh, I can't explain how these things happen, and end up taking over your life because you become kind of addicted.'

She tucked the tissue away and looked at her father, horrified to see tears trickling down his face. Maybe he'd become more racist in his old age, or he was even fonder of Alex than she knew. Or he was appalled by what she'd told him; disappointed in his daughter, yet again – this being the final straw.

'I'm such a cow, aren't I? It was a terrible thing to have done.'

Her father sniffed and dabbed at his face with his sleeve. 'No, no, it wasn't, Em. I completely understand.' He cleared his throat, then took a deep breath and puffed it out noisily. Then he did it again, like someone hyperventilating, or in labour.

'Are you all right, Dad?'

'Fine. Fine. No, I'm not. Oh God. Listen, sweetheart, if I tell you something . . . about something . . . something that happened a long time ago . . .'

Oh, no, she thought. No. He was about to say words she didn't want to hear. His secretary. Some horribly predictable affair. 'No, Dad. Please.' She got up, went to the dressing table and tugged four tissues from a man-size box. She handed him two. 'You don't have to tell me something you don't need to, or really shouldn't, just to make me feel less of a bitch.'

He wiped his face and quietly blew his nose. 'We're very much alike, you and I. People have always said Ben's like me, and he is, in looks. But . . . well, I haven't been good, Em. I haven't been a good person.'

'Yes, you *have*.' She sat beside him and put an arm around him. 'The best. Now let's go downstairs. Come on, yeah?' She patted his back in an up-you-get way, but he wasn't budging. 'I'll put the kettle on and make us a cuppa.'

'It isn't tea I need, Em. It's someone to confess to.'

Confess? She was becoming more and more uncomfortable with the situation, wondering exactly how it had turned itself around this way. Shut up, she wanted to say, pull yourself together, come for a walk around the garden. But now her father was sobbing noisily, so after giving the landing a final check, she shut the door, got the box of tissues for him and sat at the foot of the bed.

The clock said 11.43. Her day could end as badly as it had started. Or worse.

Her father quietened down and dabbed at his nose. With his head hung, he took a deep breath, then looked up at her with his puffy tired eyes. Christ, thought Em, realising just how depressed he was, and the impact her sordid little story must have had on him. How thoughtless she'd been, pushing him even further into the depths. He was about to ramble on masochistically, she guessed, about what a bad father he'd been, and how he'd been away so much of the time, and that was why she'd turned out the way she had, blah, blah. But she'd listen, because neither of them could go downstairs looking the way they did, and because there were only fifteen minutes of this crappy day to go, and tomorrow was bound to be better.

'It began,' he said, and then he stopped and sniffed, and his bottom lip quivered. He cleared his throat and puffed up his chest. 'It began when your mother was pregnant with Ben.'

'What did?'

'The affair. I had an affair, Em. It went on for decades, well, until I retired, essentially. But now I'm stuck here at home, I'm unable to see them.'

There was a silence while they stared at each other. His eyes welled up and Em felt her cheeks redden.

'Them?'

Now he looked sheepish, as well as upset. 'Susie,' he said. 'And . . . and the children.'

She couldn't ask; the words wouldn't come out. She just continued to stare, her face burning, her spine losing strength.

He nodded. 'My children.'

TWENTY-TWO

Once Alexa had gone through an early, and thankfully short, adolescent stage, she and Duncan grew closer than they'd ever been. Alexa was clever, articulate and interested in things. The two of them would go to a museum and still be discussing the exhibits over dinner; describing what they'd seen to Susie and, if he was still up, little Sebastian. Alexa always remembered to buy him something in the gift shop, even if his father didn't.

This hanging out with her father in museums didn't mean Alexa wasn't also a healthy fun-loving teenager. At almost fifteen, she was mad about clothes, loved going to parties, and casually dropped one boy – Ruben – into conversation.

'Is he Jewish?' Duncan asked one Saturday breakfast, after she'd partied at Poppy's. Duncan had picked her up at eleven p.m., bringing home to Susie, yet again, how much easier life was with two parents around.

'I think so.'

'You *think* so?' He laughed. 'Isn't it obvious?' He was coming across as prejudiced and Susie nudged his shin with her slipper. 'What?' he asked.

Joel was Jewish. Was that what this was about? Beautiful, sensitive, funny Joel. They'd had six months of wonderful clandestine lovemaking – kept secret, somehow, from Alexa, as well as her father. Susie had always gone to Joel's flat, on assorted pretexts. She'd resisted him for years, but after Sebastian left her with protracted postnatal depression, and Alexa was being so, so difficult, she'd fallen into his welcoming, compassionate embrace, and into his bed.

Once Duncan had become suspicious, following a note Joel had dropped through her door, she'd owned up – admittedly to a far more brief affair – and decided she and the children needed Duncan more than they needed Joel. The realisation that she could lose Duncan had hit her hard. They were soul mates, kindred spirits, and all that. Joel had helped Susie through a sticky patch, and if he felt used in any way, he didn't show it. He was still her best friend in the flats, something Duncan was uncomfortably aware of, she guessed.

'What's joosh?' Sebastian asked, and they all laughed.

'Honestly, Daddy,' said Alexa, 'what does it matter what Ruben is?'

'Of course it doesn't matter!' Duncan was sounding defensive. 'I was interested, that's all.'

'Daddy . . .' said Sebastian.

'Yes?'

'Can we go to the zoo today?'

Alexa pulled a face at her father.

'What's the matter?' asked Susie.

'It's just that Daddy and I planned to go to the Imperial War Museum. There was so much we didn't catch last time, wasn't there, Daddy?'

'War!' cried Sebastian. 'Do you mean guns and stuff? Can I come? Can I?'

Duncan gave Susie a help-me look. When they'd taken four-year-old Sebastian to the Natural History Museum, he'd used it as a running track. At one point they'd lost him for a full five minutes, although it had felt like an hour to Susie.

'Why don't we all go to the zoo?' she said.

Alexa groaned and Duncan smiled, almost painfully at Susie, then at his son. 'It's just that it's been sort of planned, Seb. And your sister and I like to stand and look at the exhibits and read about them, and if you came along, we'd be chasing you around.'

'I'll stand and read the zibits.'

Susie ruffled his hair. 'Tell you what, Sebastian. Let's you and I go to the zoo. How about that?'

Sebastian crossed his arms and pouted.

'Sounds like a great idea,' said Duncan. 'You can tell us all about it later.'

'It's not fair.' Sebastian went back to his cereal. Nothing kept him from his food for long. 'I *never* do things with you, Daddy. Like flying my kite or fishing or going to the zoo.'

He managed to keep the pout as he chomped through Sugar Puffs, and Susie's heart filled with pity for him. She'd have to have a quiet word with Duncan. His other daughter, Emily, was taking drugs and sleeping around, and that was drawing him more and more to Alexa. What was happening was obvious, and perhaps understandable, but Duncan wasn't getting the bigger picture, which was unlike him.

Susie and her son went to the zoo, while the other two took off for the day. Duncan and Alexa wouldn't only do the museum. They'd have lunch somewhere nice, walk around the park. If she were less sure of her place in Duncan's heart, Susie would be jealous of this father-daughter love affair. But, after years of Alexa believing her father preferred his other children, this could only be good for her. Still, poor Sebastian. Susie had been tempted to invite Joel along, but two things had stopped her. One, Duncan. And two, she thought Joel might have a secret girlfriend. Secret, because he still held out hope for Susie. It would have been fun, though. More fun. But she made a valiant effort, imitating the animals and making her adorable little boy chuckle; wishing Duncan would find him as adorable. One day, perhaps. Once Alexa was at university, or on a gap year. They all took a gap year these days. She wondered if young people knew how lucky they were, and other times she didn't envy the pressure they were under to do something terribly interesting that paid enough to live on. It embarrassed her, slightly, that she'd never really worked. Sometimes she felt as though her life had been one long gap year.

'Happy Birthday, Sebastian!' she heard Duncan yell at the other end of the line.

His son said a dutiful, 'Thank you,' into the phone, followed by, 'I know,' when Duncan said he couldn't be there, and, ''S OK,' and, 'I know.' He grew quieter with each of his father's excuses.

'Yeah,' he almost whispered at the end. 'OK . . . I will . . . Bye, Daddy.'

He handed the phone to Susie, who, knowing Duncan was still on the line, hung it up. There'd be words she'd come out with that Sebastian shouldn't hear. Their son had celebrated four birthdays, and his father had been at only one, two years ago.

Right! Susie thought. They'd continue with the day's events and not let anger fester. It was Thursday, Duncan's busiest day of the week; then he was flying to Madrid. She'd try to understand and she'd try to make the day so wonderful for Sebastian that he wouldn't notice his father's absence.

First was an afternoon trip to the zoo – now Sebastian's favourite place ever – with his best friends from playgroup, William, Abdul and Olivia. Susie and Olivia's mother collected all four at one o'clock, and managed to have a super three hours, and then it was all back to Number Ten for a birthday tea. Alexa organised games and Sebastian and his friends had a great sugar-fuelled time. Susie caught lots of funny moments on her camcorder, and hoped, some time soon, to shame Duncan with them.

On the whole, he was a good father to Sebastian. He played with cars and rockets and carried him on his shoulders, bobbing under low branches at the last moment and making his son giggle. He was patient with him and kind, but it all had a strained feel to it, and it was often limited. 'Right, better go and help Mummy in the kitchen,' she'd hear him say. Or, 'Gosh, is that the time? Daddy has to go.' There'd be an 'Awe' from Sebastian, then Duncan would come and talk to her, cuddle her, or watch TV for a while, then leave for his other life.

It was forced with Sebastian, that was the difference, in a way it hadn't been with Alexa. Fourth-time fatherhood was bound to be less exciting, but there was more to Duncan's distance. It was, perhaps, a child too far, in that it made his second family too substantial and real. Something Susie and Alexa had welcomed, without realising the psychological burden it would be for Duncan. Sebastian wasn't financially draining for him, since Susie supported her family single-handedly. But there was unspoken resentment, and it was terribly unfair, she felt.

They had it out over dinner in a Spanish restaurant. Alexa was baby-sitting – another plus of having a large gap between children.

'I know,' Duncan said, head hung. 'And I feel bad. I can't explain why, though.'

'Why what?'

'Why I don't have the same feelings for Sebastian as I do for Alexa.'

'Or Ben and Emily?'

'Or Ben and Emily.'

'Well,' Susie said. There it was, out in the open, at least.

'Obviously, I love him.'

'I'm pleased to hear it.'

'Of course I love him. It's just that . . . I suppose I've never felt as connected. And also . . .'

'Yes?'

He took a good swig at his Rioja and carefully placed the glass back in the ring it had formed in the cloth. He was calculating how to put something, she could tell.

'Yes?' she asked again.

'I've often wondered if you planned him. Without me.'

'Duncan!' Why had he never mentioned this before? They'd always been so open with each other.

'Didn't you have a thingy . . . a coil?'

Susie shook her head in despair. 'Yes. And don't you remember, he was born with it on his head.'

'So you said, but—'

'I don't tell lies, Duncan. You must know that about me? And if you'd actually been there, at the birth of your son . . . Which, incidentally, I know you could have been. Well, then you'd have seen the bloody thing on his head, like some huge joke.'

'So you don't tell lies, eh? What about Joel?'

'I didn't ever lie. And when you asked, I told you. And anyway, how have we gone from your indifference to your son to my one and only teeny-weeny, titchy-witchy affair?'

Duncan laughed and reached for her hand. 'God, I love you.'

'I know.'

'And I'll try harder, I promise.'

He wasn't quite getting it. She wanted it all to come naturally – the love. But perhaps trying harder was a beginning. 'Good,' she told him. 'Now, give me your squid. I don't know why you don't order paella without squid.'

'Because I know you'll eat it.'

'Ah.'

'Silly billy.'

'Nincompoop.'

'Come here.' They kissed across the table, just as they'd done a hundred times since the café in Cheapside. Then Duncan sat back. 'Poor kid,' he said, deep in thought, picking at his squid.

'Yes,' Susie agreed. Perhaps he was getting it.

TWENTY-THREE

Fran had left Ben and Alex cheering, as the election was looking better and better for Obama. What a momentous day, not just for her and her decade turn. How different anyone with dark skin would feel when they woke up the next day, knowing the most important person in the world was half African. There were a few hours to go, though, so she decided not to count Obama's chickens but to empty the dishwasher.

In spite of her reservations the meal had been good. And a joint effort, which was nice. And then there'd been the cake, which Em had thought to get, knowing it wouldn't occur to her father. Apart from a post-dinner doze – before the Trivia but after haring around with the little ones – Duncan had been on good form. 'Good form' being relative, of course.

Yes, it had been a lovely get-together. Em was under the weather and quiet, and Ben was high or numb, or both, but that was all OK, because where else should a person feel free to be themselves, other than at home; the family home. And at least it was all over now – the birthday. It was twenty to one. They were predicting a win for Obama, but she'd see a few more state results before going to bed.

Fran was about to throw tea towels into the washing machine, when she saw Ben's things still there, all spun and ready to go in the dryer. Or, better for the environment, on the airer. Tugging out the assorted unfamiliar items, she smiled to herself, pleased, on balance, that her son had moved in. He would add another dimension to the household, and to their lives.

As she and Duncan got older, their circle of friends, including those made in and around the village, had somehow diminished. People had stopped throwing the parties they used to, and these days the two of them rarely went out for dinner, whether in a restaurant or someone's house. Everyone had slowed down, run out of energy, it seemed, and she couldn't remember the last time they'd had more than their oldest friends, the Goodwins, over for food. Fran recalled suggesting to Duncan that they threw a party, last summer sometime; catch up with people they hadn't seen for ages. It was during a good run of weather, when they could have lit up the garden and eaten al fresco. 'What on earth for?' he'd said. 'All that effort for people we barely see.'

She fetched the airer and extended it to full height. Perhaps with Ben here, Duncan would finally cheer up, and they'd get back into the social whirl. She imagined what that might be like, having to look good and be bubbly after a day at the centre listening to anger, resentment, suicidal thoughts. Exhausting, that was what it would be like. On the other hand, she used to do it. *They* used to. For her fiftieth birthday, they'd hired a hall, invited

177

a hundred people, organised the food and booked a band Em knew. How her life had wound down in just ten years.

Fran hung her son's black jeans on the top rail and wondered if winding down was a good or bad thing. Her parents had been pretty active in their sixties. Always holidaying, having bridge evenings, going to the theatre on a coach with 'the gang'. In fact, they'd become more active with age. Their world had expanded, whereas hers and Duncan's had shrunk. The current bout of depression wasn't helping, but it had started before that. The 'Do we really have to go?'-type comments from Duncan had begun . . . when? In his early sixties, she guessed. Fran knew he'd been dreading retirement. He'd said so often, and she'd tried not to take it personally, since she worked only Tuesday to Friday and was always home by four to avoid traffic. She'd pictured them doing much more together, but now life at home was so dull, she'd thought of adding hours. Working Mondays too. Monday could be such a long day, tacked on as it often was to a very long weekend.

Ben had some nice clothes. Young clothes. Things Duncan wouldn't consider, but which might actually suit him. She and Ben could take him shopping. Give him a new image – arty and urban. New look, new man? Who knew, maybe it would work.

Moving the airer to one side, Fran put on the old waxed jacket that more or less lived by the French doors. She went out and lit up, and sat thinking about how it would be from now on. The big birthday was over. Her son had moved in. Change was definitely in the air.

When the back door creaked opened, she looked around, expecting it to be Ben on the scrounge for another ciggie. But it was Em, resembling a ghost, so pale was she.

'Dad's in Ben's room,' she said shakily, and then she started crying. Em had never been a crier, but now she was sobbing in a horrible, heart-wrenching way, like someone overacting on stage. But this was for real, Fran could tell.

She put out her cigarette and stood up. 'What is it, love?' she asked, and now she was hugging her skinny coatless daughter rather than her big son.

'There's something he wants to tell you. I'm so sorry, Mum, but he's in a terrible state and he's insisting you go up and listen. I don't know if it's true. God, I hope not.' She let out a wail, then breathed in jerkily. 'I'll come if you want, but I don't know if . . .'

'Has he told you?'

'Yes,' she said, and another long wail came out. This was serious. Had Duncan been to the doc without her knowing? Been given some news? He was dying of something horrible. Now it all made sense.

Fran led them both into the warm, sat her daughter on a chair and wrapped her jacket around her. When Alex walked in and saw them he stopped dead.

'I thought you were asleep?'

Em turned her swollen face and glared at him. 'How did you find out, Alex?'

'About what?' He crossed his arms defensively, Fran noticed.

'*You* know.'

Alex took a deep breath. 'Your texts. On that phone. The one you kept hidden, or tried to.'

'Oh. Oh my God. Alex, I'm so sorry. Let me explain.'

'The texts said it all, no need to explain. And, then, well . . . I followed you.'

'What!'

'I'm sorry?' Fran said. Suddenly, she was in a very bad play and *everyone* was overacting. Was this some sort of preplanned murder mystery? Was Duncan on the bed, playing dead and covered in ketchup? 'Have I missed something here?'

Em shook her head. 'Go and see Dad. Please. I'll come up in a minute.'

'OK. Well . . .' Fran nodded at them both and left the kitchen. She passed the sitting room and a 'Yay!' from Ben, and went up the stairs and along the landing, stopping at the bathroom to close the cabinet door and switch the light off. Turning back, she tugged the light on again and went over to the basin and mirror. Her face looked tired and dry, so she unscrewed a jar, lifted her specs and slapped on moisturiser. It was a delaying tactic, because she was visibly shaking now, like her daughter. She could hear the raised voices of Em and Alex. This was no play.

She was terrified of what she was about to hear, while at the same time not sure she should take it seriously. Duncan could have some imaginary illness. In her experience, depression and hypochondria often went together. She just hoped he hadn't scared his daughter too much, particularly as she had some crisis of her own going on.

Fran dabbed away excess cream with tissue, and when she lifted the loo seat to throw it in, saw that someone had been sick. Duncan with his terminal illness? Em with her flu? Ben, because he'd taken too many bloody pills?

She got the loo brush out and scrubbed and flushed, then washed her hands, stood up straight and, looking in the mirror at a shiny face, said, 'Here goes.'

*   *   *

She couldn't wake him up. Duncan tended to sleep deeply once he'd taken a tablet, but she'd have to wake him because he was flat out on Ben's bed, and there'd be nowhere else for Ben to crash.

'Duncan!' she said firmly, rocking him from side to side until his eyes finally opened. Again, it went through her mind that he was acting, but he did look quite dreadful. 'Come on, love. Come to our bed.'

'Yeah, yeah. Sorry.'

'Here, give me your hand.'

He lifted an arm, only what he gave her wasn't his hand but a small brown bottle. It had no lid on and was empty. She read the label, then watched his eyelids droop again. He'd picked up a prescription recently. Last Friday?

'Duncan!' she shouted, slapping his face. 'How many? How many have you taken? *Duncan!*'

'All of them,' he told her, his eyes two slits. And for the first time in months, he laughed.

Fran stared at the bottle. The date said 31 October, and there'd been twenty-eight tablets. After checking the floor, around and under the bed, she stood up and took in her great lump of a stupid, selfish, comatose husband.

'Oh, Duncan,' she said, turning and leaving the room in search of a phone. She was crying. She was allowed to cry now.

PART TWO

TWENTY-FOUR

October 2009

For a while Ben had suffered from empty-nest syndrome. The departures had been sudden and emotional, and there he'd been, left all alone in a rambling house full of reminders. He'd worried so much about them. How they were, whether they were safe, whether they were eating. And had they thought to call or email? Not often enough. Well, that's parents for you, he'd tell himself, while he'd got on with his recovery.

With no tax or insurance on his mum's car, and the nearest chemist miles away, he'd eased himself off codeine, mainly by drinking himself into a stupor each long and lonely night. He ordered food and drink on the internet, and it was delivered to the door, but couldn't resort to buying drugs that way. He'd got aspirin and ibuprofen from the village shop, but they'd done nothing for him, and after a while he couldn't see the point and gave up on painkillers.

What he'd needed after that was to get off the booze, so he'd looked around for something to do in the dangerous evening hours. The choice seemed to be a book group or, ironically, a part-time position in the village pub. Since the book group meant ploughing through prize winners set in the Indian subcontinent, and since they only met once a month, he went for the job at The Fox. Five evenings a week, from six p.m. until the last customer left. Jim and Sylvia gave him a trial, which he duly cocked up, but they took him on anyway, because two barpersons had left and they were desperate, and unlike their son Joey, Ben could talk to the customers.

With a much clearer daytime head, he got to work on writing his story. 'Crunch Time' he'd called it. A sort of half-true, half-made-up account of his experiences in the Square Mile. Faction, he believed the word was. There'd be a hero, based on himself, and the untrue bit would be that 'Jake' would somehow save his company from going under. But one day, two weeks in and still on page seven, Ben realised he'd lost enthusiasm. He not only found it hard to make hedge funds gripping, but he couldn't quite see how Jake would achieve his objective without it all sounding fake.

Jake, fake, he'd thought, as he sat there on the verge of giving up. *Jake the Fake . . .* good title for a book. A children's book? And then, somehow, in some sort of unconscious-channelling-type way, he'd bashed at the laptop all day and produced the story of a little boy, who, if he pressed the mysterious button on his keyboard, got transported via the World Wide Web to the past.

Over the weeks, one story followed another, with Jake the Fake pretending to be someone he wasn't, in order to sort out some problem with his twenty-first-century knowledge, but ending up learning a useful lesson. Mostly, he learned to appreciate the life he had. It was *Doctor Who* meets *Mr Benn*, but with a child protagonist and no real heroics. Maybe it had already been done, but that didn't bother Ben and he decided not to check. He enjoyed writing *Jake the Fake*, mostly because it made him laugh, and not many things had over the past year.

In fact, he'd often find himself giggling on his way to work, or at work, thinking of something he'd written that day. There were bound to be other Web-travel stories, but his would be better. He'd sell millions and Hollywood would snap it up, and get big names to do the cartoon voices. Scarlett Johansson for Jake, definitely. Then he'd get to meet her.

The best thing about writing *Jake the Fake* was that he no longer missed having people around. He hoped his parents were happy and doing well, but he also hoped they wouldn't come back. An author needs space, he'd tell himself. Although not too much, and that was where the pub came in.

He poured Mandy her vodka and orange and placed it on the bar. She was late fifties, buxom, extremely blonde and liked to engage in suggestive banter. She should really have been standing where he was, but Mandy had three flower shops – Fleurtations – and didn't need to work for minimum wage.

'Oh, go on,' she said, sliding the glass back. 'Give me a big one. You know you want to.' She had a deep throaty chuckle, and when she laughed her chest joined in.

'Sure you can take it?' Ben asked.

After three months, he was finally relaxing into his new role.

It no longer felt demeaning to serve drinks to people with real jobs, because now he was an artist, and artists were supposed to struggle.

'It wouldn't be the first time I've managed a double,' Mandy said, and off went the wibbly-wobbly chest.

She often brought her son in. He was Ben's age, and she'd thought they might be company for each other, since both were newly single again. 'Gary and you could go clubbing,' was her thoughtful but scary suggestion.

Everyone in the village knew what had happened last year. That Ben had been chucked by Julia and deserted by his parents. That his father had taken an overdose, and that Ben had discovered he had another sister, and a brother too, and that his philandering real sister had been put on a short leash by her husband and dragged off to Paris, city of adulterers. They knew all this because Ben had told them. It was one of the drawbacks of working behind a bar, the way people got you to open up.

Mandy was being kind, he knew, but her son's entire neck was tattooed, and because he pumped too much iron his arms were like parentheses. Without question, Gary would pick up jail bait, dance like a dick and get into a fight. And besides, they were too old for clubbing.

'How's that going down?' Ben asked Mandy.

'Very nicely, thanks.'

While he waited for something indecent to follow, he wiped the bar and washed out glasses. He was on his own tonight, but business was slow, so he didn't mind. It was preferable to a quiet shift with Joey, who was nineteen and only talked computers.

'It's the swallowing I like best,' said Mandy, and he clattered around and pretended not to hear.

Since Mandy was his mother's age, he found their banter pretty gross, and hoped it wouldn't put him off sex for ever. It was only the appearances of Lizzie from the stables – a semi regular – that reassured him it wouldn't. These days he thought about jodhpurs a lot. That had never happened before.

The Fox was a likeable pub, clean and light and friendly. He remembered being brought here for Sunday lunches ages ago, when his parents first moved to the village. But later his mum had talked about it going downhill. Some new landlord and an unfortunate episode. A parish councillor and her husband had got food poisoning. Environmental health were called in and the local paper ran a story. The latest tenants, Jim and Sylvia, were trying to rebuild the reputation with figs and chorizo and all that. The restaurant was usually much busier than the bar, which suited Ben nicely, and if he was lucky he got to take food home with him; heating it up the next day in his red wok. The Fox wasn't a bad place to work, and a thousand times nicer than the bank.

Now, of course, his parents wouldn't come here at all. Even if they wanted to, he'd have to bar them because everyone knew absolutely all their business. Ben realised he'd been indiscreet, but what could he do? He'd seen it as much-needed therapy, but without the laughable fees.

'So how's your dad getting on?' Mandy asked. She'd never met him or his mother, but probably felt she knew them intimately.

'Last I heard he wanted to come and pick up stuff.'

'With Camilla?'

Em had christened her that, after it all came out and she'd stormed over to Belsize Park, guns blazing.

'Christ, I hope not. And what if she brought the brats?'

His sister had come up with that too, despite Alexa and Sebastian being fully-fledged adults, and according to their father, very nice. Although he would say that. It was still hard to take in at times, this double life his dad had been leading. But really, there had been an awful lot of absences. You'd think his mum would have cottoned on. His father would almost never be at his parents' evenings or some school play he'd had three lines in. He and Em had got used to it, though, and it didn't feel that odd to have only your mum turn up for things, because loads of friends only had a mum, anyway.

Ben had always wanted a brother, but now he had one, he didn't particularly want to meet him, and he felt an uncomfortable jealousy. It was the same for Em, he knew, and although she was hundreds of miles away, this big nightmare of a thing had made them closer. They spoke on the phone once or twice a month now and tended to do a lot of speculating, or they shared new-found information. Things like, 'Hey, Sebastian just lost a big case!' Alexa's partner was a well-known comedian, and Google images came up with pages of photos of them – sometimes all glammed up for an awards ceremony, sometimes out shopping, wearing hats with ear flaps and looking like *Big Issue* sellers. Sebastian's one internet photo was on his law firm's website. Like his sister, he was very blond. Yes, they talked a lot about Alexa and Sebastian. 'Dad would never have chosen those names,' Em had said. A small comfort for them both.

'They might be really nice,' Mandy was saying. 'You never know. And it was hardly their fault their dad was a bigamist.'

'Hey, steady on. Dad didn't marry Camilla. Although, thinking about it, someone should check.'

'There are three people in this marriage,' Mandy said, doing a Diana.

Ben laughed. 'Nothing like a threesome, I always say. Eh, Mandy?'

Damn, he thought, seeing her expression. He'd heard rumours of Mandy swinging and had always managed to stay the right side of a proposition.

She drilled into him with her blobby-mascara eyes. 'Is that an offer?'

A familiar face appeared over her shoulder, and Ben had never been more pleased to see her son and his purple neck.

'Hiya, Mum.' Gary kissed the blonde head. 'Hiya, Ben.'

'What can I get you?' Ben asked, as if he didn't know by now.

'Pint of best, if you please.' He sat on the barstool and unzipped his jacket. 'Heard from your mum?'

'Yep.'

'Left Oz yet?'

'I'm not sure.' Ben worked out the date. 'Yeah, yeah. She must be on her way to Japan.'

'And what about that verruca she picked up in Sydney?'

To his credit, Ben blushed. 'Oh, all zapped.' That was it, no more disclosures between the beer taps.

There was an email from his mum with 'Konichiwa' in the subject box. Previous emails had said 'Howdie' and 'G'day'. She gave him a phone number and said she'd put more money in his account to cover 'any odds and sods'. That was a relief. The washing machine had banged worryingly for a while and the Hoover had packed up. Ben was aware he'd let the place go, as was the way with creative folk.

His mother went on a lot about cherry blossom, said it was getting much warmer, and listed the temples and shrines she'd been to, with links so he could see them.

He'd check them out later. He was tired and needed to rest his brain. Tomorrow he'd finish *Jake the Fake and the Air-Raid Shelter*, in which Jake learns how to get on with people in a small space, and never again moans about sharing a bedroom with his brother. It wasn't *Ulysses* – not that he'd know – but it was pretty damned good.

TWENTY-FIVE

London, December 1966

Fran squirted Youth Dew on her wrists and behind her ears. It was her favourite smell in the world, and as she breathed in the gorgeous mix of spices Estée Lauder had come up with, she hoped it might be a smell Carl Wintersson liked too.

Vicky was beside her in the ladies, squeezing her ampleness into 'her little black number', as she'd been referring to it all day. It matched her dyed hair exactly and was a bit *too* little, but Vicky had a big personality to match her body and would get away with it. A white feather boa finished off the outfit, making her look like a liquorice allsort. From a pile of bags and clothes, Vicky fished out false eyelashes and glue.

In place of falsies, Fran had painted a row of lower lashes beneath each eye, the kind she'd seen Jean Shrimpton and Twiggy and other models with. But unlike theirs, Fran's lines weren't perfectly straight and they crinkled when she squinted. Being short-sighted, she squinted a lot, but she could hardly wear her glasses to the office Christmas party, not if Carl Wintersson from Overdrafts was going to be there. And he'd said he would be. In fact, he'd made a point of mentioning it in the typing pool, giving her one of those looks.

'I think he fancies you,' Vicky had said, like she was Miss Marple and Carl hadn't made it obvious every time he brought Fran something to type; some threatening overdraft letter that she always felt bad doing because she'd want to die if she got one like it.

From where she sat at her desk, beside the big window partition, Fran could see along the corridor, and when Carl Wintersson came out of his office with paper in his hand, she'd casually slip her glasses off and pretend to read whatever she'd been typing. She sometimes wondered if she knew what Carl really looked like, so often had she seen him through a haze.

No, she knew all right. He was fair-haired and olive-skinned – his name sounded Scandinavian, maybe that was why – and he wasn't exactly handsome, but he had mischievous brown eyes and a sweet little nose. He was skinny and about five inches taller than her. His blond hair was straight and a bit layered, and when he walked along, even indoors, it was blown back by a non-existent breeze. It looked as though it would feel baby soft if you touched it.

Carl seemed like a nice person. He'd caught Fran a hundred times with her glasses on and he still showed an interest, so perhaps she was being daft about them. The girls had said what about contact lenses, but they'd be too expensive, and the idea of putting plastic in her eyes made her go faint. She was doomed to a life of myopia, so would just have to find a husband who'd love her, glasses and all.

No, she decided. And she wiped the wonky lines off with a tissue. It was too risky. Just the tiniest thing, like pretend eyelashes, could put a person off another person.

The three of them – Fran, Vicky and Sandra, but not Eileen, who was married and 'couldn't face any more gropey office dos' – trooped up to the third-floor executive room, carrying the coats and bags that would have got locked in if they'd left them in the typing pool. One corner was a dumping area, and so they piled on their things, while hanging on to their handbags, then smoothed down their clothes and made their way over to a long table covered in drinks and a buffet.

Some of the girls had gone to town, a bit like Vicky, and were covered in festive silver and sequins, and wore sparkly tights. But Fran decided she was quite happy in her red, orange and white geometric minidress and white slingbacks. She'd put a smidgen of white lipstick on, to balance things. Not too much because her dad had said she looked like the living dead in it.

She wanted to ask Vicky or Sandra if Carl was there, because as she'd walked across the room she'd deliberately kept her eyes down. The last thing she wanted was for him to think she'd snubbed him, just because she couldn't see.

But then he said, 'Hello,' right beside her.

'Oh!' She acted surprised to see him, stupidly, but Carl Wintersson made her nervous. 'Hello.' She picked up the one glass of champagne they were each allowed and smiled at him. He was in a suit, like all the men were. It was dead easy being a man: they washed, shaved and put clothes on. No having to decide about eyelashes.

He reached for a glass. 'Don't tell anyone, but this is my second. Hey, don't look so shocked. Bill doesn't like champagne and I bet there are quite a few blokes who won't have theirs. Look down there at the beer section. That's what they're here for.'

'I see.' Fran quickly knocked back all her drink, because she didn't feel she'd enthralled Carl with her powers of conversation so far. The bubbles made her cough and she patted at her chest.

Carl laughed and picked up another glass. 'Here. Drink Dave's as well.'

'Um . . . oh, OK.' She'd never stood that close to him for that long and it felt a bit odd after the formality of the office.

'Come on, let's go and find a seat. I want to know everything about you.'

'That'll take all of a minute,' she said, and he took her free hand and led her to a corner on the opposite side of the room from the man who was setting up a tape recorder.

As it turned out, Carl was the chatty one and Fran learned everything about him. He was a Scorpio, like her, and their birthdays were just two days apart, his the second, and hers the fourth of November. Only he was two years older. He had ten O levels, she had five. Like Fran he hadn't stayed on at school, and after joining the bank at sixteen, he'd quickly worked his way up to second in charge of his section.

'I really wanted to be an artist,' he told her, going deadly serious while he explained about the family troubles that had stopped him doing his A levels and applying to art school. 'I loved drawing and painting so much, and the teachers said I had a special talent and could go far, but my mum and kid brother came first.'

This impressed Fran and made her wonder whether she'd have given up on a burning ambition, if her dad had walked out and left them penniless and her mum seriously ill with cancer. It was hard to know, she decided, when you didn't have a passion like that.

Her family was the opposite of Carl's. Dead ordinary, she wanted to say, but stopped herself in time. It wasn't his fault, the things that had happened. 'My dad's a carpenter,' she told Carl, 'and Mum's a housewife. Her family's Irish and she tries to be a good Catholic but Dad's an atheist, so it's hard for her. And I never want to go to church with her any more, and Patrick's stopped too.'

'Patrick?'

'My brother. He's at university but he comes home a lot.'

'I've got one too. Sixteen and out with his friends all the time.' Carl went back to talking about his father, and how he'd struggled with the commitment of a family, and how he'd hit the bottle and finally gone to Sweden, where his father had originally come from, and where an ancient uncle had taken him in. While Carl poured it all out, almost as though he'd been dying to for ages, Fran nodded and made sympathetic noises. But then he stopped and said, 'Do you fancy a dance?'

The tape recorder had got going and Len Barry was singing '1–2–3'.

'Yes.' She hid her bag in a corner under a chair. 'Let's.'

The room was strewn with decorations and bunches of balloons, and Fran couldn't believe she was still in the stuffy bank. It all felt so magical as she danced the evening away with Carl and barely talked to anyone else, unless she was on her way to the ladies and got waylaid.

Carl was borrowing a friend's place for the night, in case he missed the last train. 'Just a bedsit,' he told her, 'in Streatham. But you're welcome to come back for a cup of coffee, if you'd like to. I mean, I'd like you to.'

Did he mean just coffee? If she went she'd miss her last train too, and that would mean sleeping there. Fran liked him a lot, and when they'd been dancing close to the slow songs, she'd felt things stir in her where maybe they shouldn't have. But the thought of doing it for the first time scared her. Partly because there was so much she didn't know, since no one had fully explained how sex worked. Not her parents, nor school. The girls in the office talked about it, but never in a detailed way. Sometimes, she wished they would.

'Yes,' she said to the coffee. He took care of his mum and brother, he wouldn't try anything on, not the first time. One of them would sleep on the floor, then she'd take tomorrow off because she'd have to go home and change. 'That would be nice.'

It *was* nice. They did it five times, and in the end Fran had never been so sore, but somehow she didn't mind. It was all part of being a woman, she supposed. It could have been the condoms making her sore, like a reaction. Several times in the night she'd thought about the pill and how she might have to go on it, but that it would involve asking Dr Bostock, who'd known her her whole life. Unless there were other places you could go . . .

When they woke up properly at eight o'clock and Carl got all amorous again, Fran decided to grin and bear it, but then he told her he might have to stop because he was a bit sore, and she laughed and said me too, and he washed and dressed in fresh clothes and gave her one last kiss and went off to work.

She could leave any time, he'd said, since his friend wouldn't be back until the evening. So she slept on in the tiny room with its bed, a wardrobe, bookshelves, and a mini kitchen with lots of pans and utensils hanging on the wall. It was cramped but neat. You'd have to be neat, she guessed, in a room the size of a cupboard. It wasn't proper sleep, though, because she was all churned up and dreamy, and all the lovely things they'd done filled her half-asleep head. And the bedsit was right above a shop of some kind and the dingaling of the bell when people came and went kept jolting her awake. But that was OK, because for the first time ever, she really felt part of the adult world, where you spent the night with someone you hardly knew in a stranger's bedsit over a shop in Streatham. It would be a while before her schoolfriends in Essex would experience this kind of thing. If ever. She smiled to herself in her semi-asleep state, listening to the dingaling, dingaling. How fabulously floaty she felt. She had a boyfriend, at last. A proper relationship that involved going to bed. It was a relief and it was lovely.

The following Monday, on her first day back after Thursday's party, Carl didn't come to the typing pool at all. Instead, Sharon from Overdrafts appeared three times with Carl's letters. Sharon had never brought her typing before and as the day wore on and Fran caught glimpses of Carl going in and out of his office but not once coming in her direction, she got the most horrible sinking feeling in her stomach. The worst thing, almost, was catching the others giving each other looks when they thought she wasn't looking.

On the train home she felt devastated and foolish, and like a slut or a scrubber. How could Carl do all that intimate stuff and say those romantic things and then completely ignore her? She knew from her magazines that boys could be difficult and hard to fathom, and that their sex drives made them behave in a way they later regretted. And that was why a girl shouldn't go all the way too soon, because she might lose the boy's respect. Was that what had happened? All weekend she'd been dreaming about Carl and hardly able to eat, while he'd felt the exact opposite. She was ashamed and embarrassed, and wished she could give up the bank job immediately and find something in Essex, where people were nice and behaved properly.

By the time she got home, she hated Carl Wintersson; herself too. She went upstairs for a bath, ignoring her mum's questions about whether she was all right. London was horrible, the bank was boring. She didn't like Vicky and the others, not really. They were so catty about people. Her now, most likely. She'd never felt so miserable in her life, and she wished she'd stayed on at school, instead of trying to be all grown up before her time.

The next morning was the same but somehow worse. She could understand Carl feeling embarrassed at first about going with someone in the office, but after five days, he ought to have been brave enough to come and talk to her. Get things back to as normal as possible. A couple of times, Fran saw him in the distance, and again he sent Sharon in with his handwritten letters. Last week she'd adored his writing with its loops and flourishes, but today she found it silly and pretentious. Each time Sharon dropped things on her desk, Fran would sift through for a message from him, just some friendly and encouraging words on a compliment slip. But there was never anything. She'd been thoroughly dumped after one night. Used, then chucked, just like that. How bad she must have been at the sex bit, for him to treat her this way. Or, she thought again, he'd lost all respect for her. But he couldn't ignore her for ever. It was a big bank, but not that big. And he was just down the corridor. They'd bump into each other at some point, sooner or later.

It turned out to be sooner. When Fran was leaving with the others for lunch in a restaurant – a preplanned pre-Christmas treat – Carl was coming into the building through the revolving door. He stopped and looked at her in a startled way, and then said a sheepish 'Hello', and carried on walking towards the lift.

The others had gone through the door but Fran was stuck to the spot, watching Carl Wintersson's back, his hair flying in his hurry to get away. He didn't look round, and when the lift came and he stepped in and finally turned, he stared back at Fran with no expression at all on his face. No smile, no nod, no look-I'm-sorry shrug. His arm reached for the buttons and the lift doors closed.

Fran felt her legs shake and hoped she wouldn't collapse and make an idiot of herself. The others were calling her, but instead of joining them for the lunch they'd been planning for weeks, she made her way to the stairs and climbed heavily and methodically to the second floor and the personnel department. There, she gave a week's notice in writing, and was told by the personnel officer that she was owed ten days' holiday.

Down on the first floor, Fran gathered her bits from her drawers – a bar of Dairy Milk, the family photos she'd brought in for the others, a Georgette Heyer, a spare cardie and three old magazines. She left the chocolate for Vicky and the others, with a note saying goodbye. She put her address in capitals and asked them to keep in touch. After saying they should all meet up once she found a new job, she signed it and added three kisses, one each. Fran didn't want to see them, but it felt polite to suggest it.

She picked up the cardigan and her folder of photos and left, walking right past Carl Wintersson's office with the same feeling she'd had when her granny had died.

TWENTY-SIX

Duncan was on a chair on the narrow balcony, beside the smallest fold-up table in the world. On the table was a coffee, on Duncan's lap and in his hands was the *Telegraph*.

'Michael Jackson's still dead, then,' he said. Nobody heard him. Susie was at life drawing and Rasine was hoovering.

He turned the page and there was a picture of Japan's new first lady, who looked like a perfectly sane and lovely woman, but who'd claimed she'd ridden a UFO to Venus. What's more, her husband – about to become leader of a fairly powerful country – believed her. The one tiny flaw in Miyuki's story was that she described Venus as beautiful and very green. A parallel Venus, perhaps. At one time, Duncan had been through a quantum mechanics spell. Multiverses, and all that. It had been fascinating, if incomprehensible, and even now still brought him comfort; the idea that out there, in the cosmos, could be at least one other version of himself, who'd done everything right in life.

Wasn't Fran going to Japan? He'd tried to keep up, via the kids, but they were pretty vague themselves. Wherever his wife was, he hoped she was all right, and not melancholic and full of bitterness. According to Em, who tended to communicate more than Ben, her mother was having a great time. All alone on a round-the-world trip? Duncan couldn't think of anything more dispiriting, but then Fran had always been strong. A little too strong at times. Self-sufficient, anyway. Reserved . . . guarded.

It was odious to make comparisons, but he couldn't help appreciate the visceral nature of his relationship with Susie. Even now, after ten months of twenty-four-seven living together, they'd hold hands in the street, cuddle on the sofa, have long lingering kisses at the drop of a hat. And after ten months they were still 'rampant in the boudoir', as Susie put it. At their age, too. They'd always been tactile, but he'd attributed that – wrongly, it turned out – to the brevity of their periods together.

Duncan folded the *Telegraph*, put it on the table, drank some of his coffee and bent down for another paper. It was very warm for October, and almost better than the predominantly bleak summer had been. Not that they'd hung around for all of it, jetting off in July to oversee work on Susie's place in Pau. It had been warm there, at the foot of the Pyrenees on the French side. The plan, once the work was finished, was to spend half the year there, the other in the UK. With Alexa and Seb based in London, Susie would never move in entirety to another country.

He, inevitably, and perhaps like a lot of men, had a less intense relationship with his children. Em and Ben kept in touch, and that warmed him, although the disappointment and hurt was still evident in their calls and emails. Duncan was both thankful and amazed that they had, initially at least, been so understanding. But apparently, the attempt to take his life had played a part in their forgiveness. It had showed his desperation and remorse, Em told him over a lunch, when he'd finally recovered his appetite.

Desperation, yes. He'd been desperate to spend time with Susie, and to see Alexa and Seb. He'd felt completely cut off, that had been the problem, ever since retirement. There'd been the odd snatched meeting, the occasional visit to the flat, plus a great deal of talking on the phone when Fran was at work. Although that had dwindled after a while, owing to his depression and the fact that he'd run out of interesting things to say. But perhaps he wouldn't have felt so low if she hadn't mentioned bloody Joel quite so often. Joel was the one other man Susie had been physical with in all those years.

As far as he *knew*, Joel was the only one, but then Susie was generally quite open. She'd owned up – not that she'd had anything to feel guilty about – when their short fling ended. It was just three months out of a thirty-year relationship but it tore Duncan's heart to shreds whenever he dwelled on it, or when they came across Joel washing his old Porsche or sitting in a deck chair on the communal lawn. Or when Susie went off to the residents' reading group that Joel, damn him, had to belong to. Why the heck couldn't the man move somewhere else?

It was ridiculous, Duncan knew, to continue to feel jealous, and the issue was riddled with double standards. But it had hurt, and it still hurt. After retiring, when he'd become trapped and powerless, the idea of Susie taking up with Joel full time had become an obsession. When he hadn't been able to get hold of her, he'd tried Alexa and Seb, asking them over and over what their mother was up to, whether she was seeing 'that man'. Looking back, he could see how completely nutty his behaviour had been. Overbearing and, yes, desperate. It was a wonder he hadn't driven them away; he must have come close.

But remorse? No, Em hadn't been right about that. He'd never regretted meeting Susie and creating a half-life with her. And he loved Alexa and Seb, and couldn't ever wish they hadn't happened. He had occasionally felt remorse for staying with Fran once he'd met Susie, and for having a second child with her – sweet Emily. But no amount of waterboarding or matchsticks under the nails would make him tell his daughter that.

Duncan was always so happy to see her, however long she'd been gone – half an hour, a weekend. Today, she crashed through the door, along the hall and into the kitchen with arms full of shopping, and a, 'Darling, fire up the coffee, would you? I'm literally gasping.'

'Shall I make lunch?'

Susie pulled a face and said she wasn't hungry. 'Honestly, if you'd seen the scrotum on today's model, you'd be off food too.' She dumped carriers and delved into her large shoulder bag. 'Here,' she said, and he took a drawing from her.

'Oh dear.' Duncan turned his head away. 'And I thought I was sagging. He must be, what, seventy-five?'

'Older. I was actually rather kind. Sort of air-brushed the poor fellow.'

Susie had discovered her gift for drawing late in life, but how nice that was, Duncan often thought. Just when you believe you've exhausted your natural talents, up pops another. He, himself, was still waiting for an exciting skill to reveal itself, but there was no hurry. Life was relaxed and easy, but at the same time it felt full. This evening, for instance, they were off to the Comedy Club to see Alexa's partner, Matt, perform. Dinner first with Seb and his 'latest squeeze', as Susie called her.

In the bath, Duncan recalled some of his close shaves. He didn't want to, particularly, but his mind often went where he didn't want it to. Life had definitely been simpler for a man with two families before mobiles and emails arrived. That was when the capacity to cock up increased many-fold. And Duncan almost had, so often.

Like the time he'd accidentally sent Fran an email from work saying he couldn't wait to park his car in her garage again. He and Susie had begun to use euphemisms, many of which involved snakes and sausages – luckily for Duncan, the one Fran received hadn't. It was all terribly childish, but Susie seemed to enjoy it. Her sense of humour was surprisingly unsophisticated, and he'd put it down to boarding-school pranks and giggles in the dorm after lights out. She'd titter at her future son-in-law's stage act, but not in the hearty way she'd laugh at a knock-knock joke. And she adored puns. It was endearing, really.

Fran's reply to the mis-sent email had been along the lines of, when had the garage last had space for a car, and was he sure he was over his flu? The horror of his error had made Duncan blush to his roots, and following that nasty moment, he'd always replied to an incoming email, rather than create a new one.

Both of Susie's children strongly resembled her: blond and bonnie-faced; tall and strong. Sebastian had a bit of the Boris Johnson about him, with his floppy locks and quick lawyerly way with words, only he was more athletic-looking. He'd definitely got his mother's eyes, nose, mouth, everything. As had Alexa, who was so much like Susie, it almost freaked him out. It was as though the Great Director in the sky had decided Duncan's limited involvement should be reflected in Alexa and Seb's genetic makeup. Their exterior makeup, anyway. Sometimes he minded and, by way of consolation, imagined their kidneys and aortas to be the spitting image of his.

'Cheers!' said Seb.

They were in a Lithuanian restaurant. Well, that was what Seb called it because it sounded cool and different, and there seemed to be a competition on to come up with obscure London eateries. Seb was in the lead so far, with his 'excellent Burundian place in Wandsworth'. They were in fact in an Eastern European restaurant, with Hungarian, Polish and you name it on the menu. The proprietor just happened to be Lithuanian – which, in Duncan's book amounted to cheating.

'Cheers!' the two of them said back; Seb's girlfriend having mysteriously gone down with something. Duncan guessed she was on her way out.

He still hadn't quite got used to being able to drink on an evening out. Village life had its attractions, but that tedious drive from the station after a night on the town was never going to be one of them. He and Susie had downed a G and T at home, and since they were bound to go for a drink after the show, there'd be a price to pay tomorrow. Why was that? Why did the body take less alcohol as it aged? Surely it should be the reverse, a gradual building up of tolerance, as was the case with coffee.

If the ten-year-old Duncan had drunk six coffees in a day, he'd have never seen eleven.

He'd pace the alcohol, Duncan decided, and there was his bladder to consider too. He wouldn't want to draw attention to himself later, not with a sharp-eyed comedian on stage with a ready prostate gag.

Alexa arrived late, all bouncy and wild-haired, having escaped from the hospital for a few precious hours. My daughter the consultant paediatrician, thought Duncan smugly. He was proud of all his children – even Ben – but Alexa's career was the one he'd followed the closest. Having always felt responsible for train-wrecking her mother's medical aspirations, Duncan had been a constant source of support for Alexa, both financial and moral.

'How was your day?' he asked, and he caught a scowl thrown his way by Seb. Had he asked his son how his day had been? No, thinking about it, he hadn't.

'Frenetic,' said Alexa. 'Heartbreaking. The usual. I tell you, I'm never going to have kids.'

Susie patted her daughter's arm. 'You have the most difficult job in the world, darling.'

Alexa put a hand on her mother's. 'But the most rewarding too.'

Seb sighed a sigh they all heard, before beckoning the waiter over. Susie quickly decided on a goulash, and after orders were taken and menus the size of broadsheets handed back, Duncan said, 'And how was your day, Seb?' For a while, he wondered if his son would answer.

'Fine,' he said with a sharp smile.

*　　*　　*

Matt was his usual funny self, if you liked that kind of thing. There were the same old themes – driving, supermarkets, call centres, restaurants, girlfriend. Matt put his own fresh twist on them, though, and managed not to say anything remotely accurate about his and Alexa's relationship. As a couple, they were in the public eye a lot, and anyone interested enough in celebs would have known that Matt's real-life girlfriend was a serious person with a serious career, and not the premenstrual airhead of Matt's act.

As he sat there, listening to Seb's guffawing and Susie's limp chuckles, Duncan asked himself how necessary all the sexism was in this post-Les Dawson age. Matt was probably what Fran used to call an unreconstructed male. In fact, it was usually himself she was calling that. It was something one could get away with at sixty, but Matt was just thirty-four. Younger than Alexa, in more ways than one, and to Duncan's mind, nowhere near good enough for her. But she seemed happy. And, so long as Alexa was happy, he'd pretend to like the vain and arrogant person his daughter aimed to marry.

'Hey, great act,' he told Matt outside the club. They'd go somewhere more staid for a drink, in order to avoid autographs. Meanwhile, they were all in a circle. Susie and himself, Seb, Matt and Alexa.

'Thanks, Duncan.'

'Hilarious.'

'Glad you liked it.'

'Mm, especially the relationship stuff, ha-ha.' He hoped Matt would get the sarcasm.

Alexa grimaced and shook her head at Matt. It was a disapproving head shake, and it was the first tiny crack Duncan had
ever seen in their relationship. Tiny, yes, but it filled him with a
mean-spirited optimism.

TWENTY-SEVEN

January, 1967

The letter arrived on a Saturday, just as she was going out to meet her friends for a milkshake and some clothes shopping.

Dear Fran,

I didn't know you'd handed in your notice until today when Vicky told me. She gave me your address and from the looks I got, I guessed you were upset with me and that's why you left, and if that is the case I am so sorry. It was rude of me to ignore you and not explain, so here's my explanation. My little brother Stefan was supposed to stay with our mother while I was in London overnight, but he went out with his mates, who are trouble, and Mum had a fall when she tried to get to the bathroom and couldn't get up, and when Stefan got home in the early hours she was almost unconscious with the cold and pain.

My brother phoned for an ambulance and Mum was admitted to hospital, where she still is. They say she broke two ribs. I think the doctors think it's not safe for her to be at home, even though that is where she wants to be. Anyway, I was feeling very responsible and was worried about her psychological state and if I ignored you I suppose I didn't want to be reminded of what I was doing while Mum was lying in agony. Anyway, I think she'll be home soon, so at the moment there's no chance of me having a girlfriend I can spend plenty of time with. You are in Essex and I'm in Hampshire and it would be impossible. Someone pops in during the day to see Mum but I have to be there at night. I should have told you all this before Christmas but I didn't know how and as you can imagine my mother was on my mind. I think you're lovely and I enjoyed our night together more than you'll ever know, and if I'm ever free I'd like to see you, but I expect now that you wouldn't want anything to do with me. The whole business has made me sad and I feel guilty that I left my mum and that I treated you badly.

He signed it 'Love Carl', and when Fran had finished reading it the third time, she folded it, said, 'No one,' to her mum, who'd asked who it was from, and then she put the letter in her handbag and hurried to meet the others.

She found a card in Smith's. It had an abstract painting on the front, which seemed better than flowers or a country cottage. Then back at home, after she'd done a fashion show for her mum, modelling the stuff she'd bought, Fran shut herself in her bedroom and wrote inside. She thanked Carl for his letter and said she understood. She added that she'd grown tired of the bank and had been thinking of leaving anyway. It wasn't true but she thought it would make him feel better and her appear less emotional. She was sorry to hear about his mother, she wrote, and she hoped she'd get better soon. That was a silly thing to say, Fran realised, because she wasn't going to get better. But she left it because he might think she was talking about the broken ribs. She put her phone number and told him to ring her if he ever needed to talk. 'Love Fran', she put at the bottom, before writing his name and the bank's address on the envelope. 'Private and Confidential', she added diagonally, so that Malcolm in the mailroom wouldn't open it.

The next morning, she posted the card on her way to an interview with some stockbrokers in Fenchurch Street. Fran didn't feel half as bad as she had before Carl's letter arrived, only she did feel a bit silly that she'd given in her notice in temper, or whatever it had been. She should have acted more like an adult and gone to talk to him in his office, or sent him a note. But it was too late now and she'd just have to put it all behind her and not think about how much she liked him, because, as he said, the situation was impossible.

Someone called Mr Turner offered her the job, to start the next day. He was even happy with her shorthand and said she might work her way up to secretary, if she proved herself efficient and reliable. They were offering more money than she'd earned at the bank and an extra week's holiday a year. It all sounded too good to be true.

Fran was introduced to two other typists she'd be working

with and they looked like they might be just as much fun as Vicky and the others, but better still, they were closer to her age. One was called Marie and the other Liz, and they were both smoking, so the small office was quite cloudy. Fran wondered if that would bother her, as she wasn't used to being in smoke-filled rooms. Her parents had given up years ago, and the girls at the bank had been addicted to chocolate, not nicotine.

The offices were quite modern, compared to the outside of the building. Although the three typists were in a separate room, it led out to one enormous area full of people on phones, mainly men. Nice big plants were dotted around and there were modern paintings on the pale green walls. Venetian blinds made the sun come through the huge windows in stripes. It was nice, Fran thought. It felt nice. And on her way home again, via a bit more clothes shopping in Oxford Street, she felt grateful to Carl in a way. He'd got the losing-her-virginity thing out the way, and he'd been responsible for her finding a better job. If she'd put off writing the card a while, she could have told him about the stock-brokers and where to find her. Never mind. If it was meant to be, they'd bump into each other one lunchtime or something.

Liz and Marie laughed at Fran's Tupperware box. 'Come on,' said Liz. 'We always grab something at the Coffee Bean and then go to the pub.'

'Oh. Well . . . all right.' She put the lid on her mum's beef-paste sandwiches and joined the others taking their coats off the stand. Marie pulled a beret on, almost down to her eyes, while Liz covered her hair with a small scarf and tied it under her hair at the back. Fran didn't have a hat or scarf, and outside she tugged the hood of her coat up against the cold and felt very unchic as she followed the others.

After buying a ham roll she couldn't really afford because she'd spent so much on clothes, the three of them hurried to a nearby pub, where Liz had a dry sherry, Marie a Babycham and Fran a bitter lemon. It didn't take long to see why her colleagues liked coming to the pub. Within minutes, four young men were chatting up Liz and Marie. The two of them got very giggly and as she wriggled around, Liz's skirt rode higher and higher up her thighs. Fran sat on a stool with her glass, wanting to join in, but not wanting to. Watching the flirting reminded her of Carl and the party, and their night together. She missed him, she realised.

He stayed in her head all afternoon. Poor Carl. She almost felt as though she'd treated him badly, which was barmy, she knew, and she thought about taking a detour past the bank on her way home in the hope he might be leaving. But since the story of their one-night stand had probably got around, she really didn't have the courage.

At Liverpool Street station, Fran bought her first ever packet of cigarettes. Ten No. 6. She'd had a few puffs over the years, usually from boys wanting her to try, but it was Liz making her have one with her coffee that morning – 'Go on, be a devil,' – and then another in the pub, that had given her a bit of a craving.

She lit one up and smoked it as she walked up the hill to her house, but it tasted foul and she gave up after three drags. It was horrible. She probably didn't have what it took to become a smoker.

The next day they all went to a different pub, one Liz and Marie hadn't tried before. It was really busy and popular, and because

Liz was wearing the shortest skirt ever made, she was like a magnet to the men. At one time she had five blokes chatting her up, and her blonde head swivelled back and forth, while she talked and giggled and sipped at her sherry and accepted lights. Marie was talking to a slightly older man, and Fran sat on a stool not that far away but on the edge of the circle. She drank her bitter lemon, and watched them all and wondered whether she really wanted to do this every lunchtime.

After a while, one of Liz's entourage moved over to Fran and asked if she'd like another drink. She didn't really want one because you could only drink so much bitter lemon, but she said yes she would, thanks.

While he turned his back and ordered more drinks, Liz shot her the evil eye, as though he'd been the one she'd been most interested in. Fran could understand why. He was quite gorgeous, and maybe he was deliberately playing hard to get. It was a good ploy and it seemed to be working, and Fran didn't mind because at last someone was paying her attention.

'Lovely,' she said, when he handed her the gassy bitter lemon she didn't want.

'She's quite a girl,' the handsome boy said, with a nod in Liz's direction.

'Very.'

He was staring at her legs, while his pint mug went up to his mouth, then down and up again.

'I'm Fran, by the way.'

'Sorry?' It was getting noisier and noisier, and Liz had obviously said something hilarious.

'I said my name's Fran!'

'Ah!' He held out his free hand to her. 'Duncan!'

She shook it and said, 'Hello, Duncan!' and smiled, and wondered if he, or any of them, would have been so formal with Liz.

'So you work with those two lovely girls?' he asked.

Fran hesitated because it sounded slightly insulting. In the end she nodded and took a sip of her drink. Carl thought she was lovely, or so he'd said.

Duncan was giving her an odd look. 'I mean, do you three lovely girls work together?' He smiled beautifully at her, and she told him yes, at a stockbrokers', but she'd only been there two days. She didn't know what to say after that, when his eyes drifted back to Liz.

'Why's this pub called The Anchor?' she asked in desperation. It was the dullest thing she could have come up with, but Duncan turned to her, his face all lit up, and he went into an explanation, all about the river and commerce in the past.

'Are you interested in history?' he asked afterwards.

Fran was sure she would be. 'Yes. Yes, I am.'

He told her he was too, and that next time he'd bring her a book to read, all about the Thames and the City.

'I'd like that. Thanks.' Next time?

'What's the name of your—'

'Are you coming, or what?' Liz was asking her, and Fran jumped off her stool and followed her friends, because she'd never find their office all by herself. She and Duncan waved at each other. She should have quickly told him where she worked, even if it was only Liz he was after. But they were outside now and it was too late.

218

'You want to watch that one,' Liz said. 'Looks like he could be trouble.'

'OK. Thanks for the advice.' Fran smiled to herself as they walked back. She'd never see Duncan again, or she'd see him and he'd have forgotten all about her, and about the book. But it didn't matter. She'd managed to make sexpot Liz jealous, and that felt good.

TWENTY-EIGHT

Em wondered if she should have been French all along. They knew how to live and they knew how to love. They venerated passion and understood where it could lead you. She felt French and was beginning to look French, with her little classic cardigans and carefully arranged scarves. And here, naked on top of her student, in an apartment that was small even by Parisian standards, she was behaving very French.

During lessons, Em insisted they speak English, but when they made love they used mainly French. She was picking up a lot. He taught her obscenities in his own soft and romantic language; words that if you said them in English, in the heat of the moment, would make you feel you were in a porn film. Florian was far too young and far too pretty, but it didn't seem to matter to him. One thing she'd learned early on was that a French man could find an older woman sexually appealing, in a way that would baffle an Englishman. She loved Paris, absolutely loved it.

Afterwards, they flopped back on pillows that smelled of stale sweat and cologne, out of breath, fingers entwined. *Mon Dieu*, she thought, keeping up the French. Florian turned on his side and kissed her cheek.

'Ow you say in English, I want making sex wiz you all days and nights too?'

Em laughed. 'We don't. That's the problem.'

'Please. You must tell.'

She turned on her side too, so that their noses were almost touching. 'I want to fuck you senseless, twenty-four seven?'

'Eugh. Is so agly, your language.'

Ugly.'

'Aagly.'

'Nearly.' She kissed his nose. 'Did you do your homework?'

'*Ah, non. Je suis désolé.* I ave been buzzy in ze restaurant.'

It was an uphill struggle, trying to teach this young chef English. If she were lucky, it could go on for years. 'You know I'm going to have to punish you.' She ran her fingers down to his groin and found him hardening again. God, young men were the best. 'You'll have to be given extra work to make up for it.'

'*Tu es très stricte.*'

'I know.' She gently rubbed him to life and pushed her tongue in his lovely young mouth. Cigarettes and garlic – *délicieux*.

They went to the café for their lesson, sitting outside in the autumn chill because Florian more or less chain-smoked. She made him nervous he said, as did learning English.

He could never concentrate, that was the problem. While his left leg jigged away, he was eyeing up pretty girls, ordering more coffee, doodling, stroking her arm. He wanted to work in London, he claimed, where even French chefs in French restaurants were expected to have passable English. Florian was twenty-three and that disqualified him from becoming a love interest for Em. Sex, yes. Love, no. And that, in a way, made it all easy.

There'd been a strong emotional attachment to Hadi, she realised. Alex had put an end to that, of course, and he'd had every right to. Her husband had not only stayed with her, he'd fought for her; frightened her lover off. How that had made her feel about Alex, she couldn't tell. There'd been gratitude that he'd stayed and held the family together, but deep down she'd raged with resentment for both Alex and Hadi. Cowardly Hadi, who'd met so many of her physical and emotional needs. Talking it through with her mum had helped, strangely. And it had been very much a two-way thing; her mother gaining from Em some idea of why her husband had seen another woman all those years. In the two or three weeks she'd stayed with them, her mum had gone from a wreck to a go-getter; constantly on the computer in the final few days, planning her trip. When they'd dropped her at Heathrow she looked better than she had for years, and she'd been so excited. Em had wished at the time that she'd recover from lost love as quickly as her mother had. But it had taken time, and she still thought of her Iranian lover; that connection they'd had.

In fact, she badly wanted another Hadi, but in the meantime Florian would do. And, yes, it was easy. They could text each other openly – strangely jumbled Franglais texts – because he was her student. One of four she was teaching English to, mainly in cafés. Which was fun. And, at present, it felt like just enough work, what with the children and the apartment, and the extra-curricular with Florian.

They were working on the second conditional. 'Repeat,' she told him. 'If there were more potatoes, I would make a Cornish pasty.' She tried to gear things to his area of professional interest.

'*Mais, non!*'

'English, Florian.'

'Ze Cornish pasty he has no taste! Eef ah ad more potatoes, ah would make *dauphinoise.*'

'OK. Repeat. If there were more potatoes, I would make *dauphinoise.*'

'No, no, baby. Not doh-fin-was. *Dauphinoise.*'

'*Dauphinoise?*'

'*Non, non. Dauphinoise.*'

Em sneaked a look at the time. Five minutes to go. 'Shall we call it a day, Florian?' She'd been with him two hours and he was getting on her nerves.

'OK. I ave to go in ze restaurant now.'

'*To* the restaurant. Remember?' They'd spent so much time on prepositions, she wanted to weep. If she hadn't made great progress with Celine the banker, she'd think she was a crap teacher. Em closed her books and stood up. 'See you Thursday, then.'

Florian took a drag on his cigarette, looked her up and down and winked. 'Wear ze red, OK, baby?'

He was referring to underwear. 'OK,' she said, wishing he'd show his teacher more respect, but pleased he'd got a sentence right.

* * *

223

Back home there was another email from her dad, saying he'd like her to meet Susie. Properly. Not like the time she'd flashed in and out of the flat in Belsize Park, hurling abuse and barely listening to either her father or his mistress. A gathering, he was suggesting, in Long Bellingham. *Ben seems pretty tied to his pub job and has no transport. I have a few things I'd like to pick up, so it makes sense to meet there.* The end of the month, he suggested. *There are wounds that need to begin to heal, for all of us.*

He was right, but the idea of some strained 'family' gathering appalled her. Would the brats be there? Em noticed he'd carefully not mentioned them, but 'a gathering' implied more than four. At least her poor mum wouldn't be subjected to it. In Japan now, and doing Europe after. How she was affording this trip of a life-time was a mystery, but she and Ben had assumed she'd cashed something in – savings or an insurance policy. Unless mega-rich Susie had coughed up to get her rival out of the picture.

It had to be got over with, Em supposed, this proper meeting with the love of her father's life. Funny how she'd once thought *she* was that. Thank God she hadn't known, as a child, what was going on. Early enough for it to have scarred her for ever. But perhaps she'd had an inkling that things weren't right. Her dad was so often away; more than anyone else's father. It hadn't felt like neglect at the time, but now she knew the facts, it certainly did. Was that why she'd got into drink, drugs and boys – to fill the gap left by her father?

Em didn't believe in dwelling on past wrongs, or revenge, or bearing grudges. And a year was long enough to digest the horrible events and behave in an adult and rational manner. She replied to his email with a yes. It would be good to see Ben again. He'd been promising to come to Paris, but from his emails and calls it seemed the pub would collapse without him. Why he cared was hard to fathom, but then Ben himself was hard to fathom.

She clicked on 'send', committing herself to something she both feared and relished. There was nothing like a bit of drama to make a person feel alive.

She bought pretty pastries for the children, then collected them from the international school that Alex had decided to push the boat out for. It was expensive, but Martha and George were happy in their respective class and kindergarten, and because they were there all day, Em was free to work. And play. She might still yearn for Hadi, but she was happy, and she knew Alex loved his job and his new polite colleagues. There was one in particular he spoke a lot of. Maxine. Maxine this, Maxine that. Would she mind if he had an affair? Maybe. But this was Paris and adultery was mandatory. What could she do?

After school, they went to the park, where well-turned-out children played on roundabouts and with balls, never too noisily, too boisterously. The equally well-turned-out mothers sat chatting on benches, calmly seeing to grazed knees, popping healthy snacks in their children's mouths. This was an affluent part of Paris, and Em knew that a few metro stops away was another world of tower blocks and poverty, drugs and violence. It was a world she didn't intend to think about, let alone visit. This was Paris to her, the city everyone knew and loved.

Martha was talking to a little girl, in French, quite fluently to Em's ear. Alex had been teaching her, as well as the school, and Em was slightly concerned that if she didn't do something soon, Mum would be left behind. She imagined the day her children began saying things about her in French, sniggering behind their hands. Since Florian had taught her only unusable words, she mostly got by with her schoolgirl French. She'd have to learn, go to classes and learn. Or find a private tutor? Em felt her stomach tighten at the prospect of that. What it might lead to, should the right one come along.

There was no doubt about it, Paris made her feel heady. Perhaps the trip back home would be good for her, though. She'd see her dad and brother and, more than likely, Camilla and the brats. A little taste of reality, then back to Paris with an even greater appreciation of its charms.

Martha ran up and spouted something Em couldn't follow.

'English, please?' she said, and Martha turned to her new friend and said something that made them both giggle. It was happening already. As proud as she felt, Em wanted to tell Martha she was being rude.

A French tutor, she told herself again, slowly conjuring up a picture of him.

TWENTY-NINE

They were climbing Primrose Hill. Kites flew, leaves swirled and Duncan was out of breath.

Susie slipped her arm through his to help him along. 'Darling, you must drink less and join a gym.'

'You know I'd rather die fat and unhealthy.'

'Walk more, then. We don't need to taxi all over the place. Let's make a pledge to go everywhere on foot in the next week!'

She had a way of making things sound a jolly wheeze. Even walking. 'Well . . .'

'We could get those thingamabobs, that count one's steps.'

'Yes, yes. But first, could we sit for a while? It'll make a change to see the view from here, don't you think?'

'Very well. But, darling, it's terribly unfair that I get to have you full time just when you've become an old crock.'

Susie had never been one to mince words. 'I'm sorry, dear,' he puffed, and they sat down on damp grass, both of them resting crossed arms on their raised knees. 'Echoing' it was called. He'd learned that from Fran. When one person copies the other's stance. She'd taught him quite a lot about body language, not realising, perhaps, that he was then bound to interpret her body language towards him. The folded arms when they'd chatted in the kitchen or elsewhere; the legs crossed away from him on the sofa. The back confronting him in bed – although not always. Fran may not have had Susie's libido, but she hadn't been frigid; just less enthusiastic. And who knew, maybe she'd even enjoyed the act occasionally. Everyone's different, he'd had to tell himself.

Sometimes, when out somewhere, he'd forgotten he wasn't with Susie, reaching for Fran's hand, only for her to slip it away at the first opportunity. His arm around her shoulder wouldn't automatically be followed by her arm around his waist. That was how it went with Susie – a natural, tactile, affectionate two-way thing.

But still, he'd loved Fran. She was clever and informed in a way Susie wasn't. They'd discussed current affairs over dinner, or over Sunday breakfast with the newspapers. There'd been an intellectual connection that was lacking with Susie. Did he miss it? Occasionally, yes. But he and Susie goofed around so much, even at their advanced age, that there was no time for human rights or the environment. He'd read somewhere that people become less interested in issues as they age; that it was partly due to brain-cell loss, but there was also an element of, 'What's the point of caring, when I won't be here much longer?'

He could feel it happening to himself, that was for sure. Giving up on an article after two paragraphs, reading Lee Child instead of biographies of historical figures. He remembered, not that many years ago, regularly staying awake through *Newsnight*. Now the

Radio Two on-the-hour headlines were plenty. Susie liked Radio Two.

They'd listened to Radio Four all the time, he and Fran; once she'd discovered it when Ben was a baby and she'd felt her brain atrophying. It was her mind he was first drawn to, in the pub that day. He'd felt sorry for her, sitting on the sidelines, while her two tarty workmates lapped up male attention. Fran was just as pretty, but she wasn't flaunting it. She was young and shy and unsure of herself, but once they'd got chatting she'd shown an interest in history. Talking to her had begun as an act of kindness, but there'd been something about her he'd found attractive. The witty remark, the twinkle in her eye. And she'd shown an enquiring mind, which she'd kept, even after her husband's had completely seized up. Fran would actually read a newspaper, slowly, thoroughly; whereas all he could manage was to flick through the stack Susie had delivered, picking out the quirkier stories, and rarely getting to the end of those. Politics bored him and there was nothing he could do about poverty in Zimbabwe, so why torture himself reading about it? He'd become shallow, but did it matter? Would the world change overnight if he got het up about things? No. In fact, the world might improve if he simply chilled; had a little fun in his dotage. Worry led to stress, and stress made you ill and a burden on the NHS. And he should know. He looked at his partner and felt thankful. If he was going to regress to a happy-go-lucky, childlike state, what better person than Susie to accompany him.

'I spy?' she asked, but didn't wait for an answer. 'I spy with my little eye, something beginning with . . . "s".'

'Um . . .' This wasn't fair. With the limitless view of London,

229

it could be anything. 'Sky?' he asked. 'St Paul's? Spaniel?' She shook her head at each guess. 'Springer Spaniel?'

'That would be "s, s", you clot!'

'Of course.' Duncan sighed. How he hated 'I spy'. Suddenly, he wanted to discuss stem-cell research. Following Susie's eyes, he found them on his feet. 'Shoes?' he asked.

'Correct!' She unfolded her arms to applaud. 'And I do believe they're not helping.'

'What?'

'Your shoes, darling. Totally unsuitable and possibly the reason you're struggling. We should buy you some trainers if we're going to walk more.'

Duncan thought only oiks and rappers wore trainers. 'I'm not sure I—'

'Let's do it now.' She was on her feet and helping him up. 'Come along. Upsy-daisy! Race you to the bottom?'

Or even the economy. A nice quiet discussion about greedy banks and businesses . . . He wondered where in the world Fran was right now. How she was. If she was meeting interesting people. Interesting men. Discussing interesting things. As he slowly descended in elegant but slippery shoes, he waved at Susie, already at the bottom. Voluptuous, bubbly Susie.

Presumably, Fran would be even trimmer now, after all the dashing around, sightseeing, running for planes and trains. She must have seen some things too. Places he'd have liked to explore when abroad, but business had taken up his time. All those countries and he'd barely left the hotels. Working on something half the night. For the first time ever, he envied Fran.

Pau was lovely, and Susie's place was going to be fabulous, but he knew from past holidays, and from their weeks in France in the summer, that Susie was a stay-at-home holiday-maker. She liked to sun herself, reading, and she liked to wander around a market, gathering items for dinner. But churches and museums and, basically, all the things Duncan enjoyed, did nothing for her. 'Honestly, darling, you've seen one dingy, draughty church, you've seen them all.'

This was a shame, Duncan felt. There was nothing worse than having someone impatiently waiting in a pew for you to finish.

The plan to spend half the year in a small town in France was beginning to unsettle him. Maybe he'd suggest three months, or that she'd spend longer there than he would. Then perhaps he could hang out with Fran a bit. No. No, she wouldn't want that. What was he thinking? She must hate him so much. Dear, sweet Fran. She may not have been demonstrative, but he'd always enjoyed her slim figure. And all that unruly dark hair. Now sleek and blonde, of course, in response to the grey – and who could blame her. He felt a little tug, deep inside. It was all so confusing, this love business.

The email from Em wasn't what he'd expected. She was coming. How wonderful! He'd begun by asking Em because it would be essential to have her there, and now all he had to do was ask the others. Or perhaps he'd be more authoritative and issue a summons. He could use his daughter, since she was on side. 'Emily and I would like us all to congregate at Tudor House in Long Bellingham, on Saturday 31 October.' It sounded a bit Agatha Christie and sinister, so he added, 'for a sort of get-to-know-you lunch.'

Duncan stopped typing and frowned at the monitor. Would

Sunday be easier than Saturday for everyone? Alexa might have to swap shifts, whichever day. But Seb may well prefer to rest on Saturday, after a busy week in court. And it would be Hallowe'en on the thirty-first, which could mean more customers for Ben. He deleted the date and put 'Sunday 1 November.' All Saints' Day, it said in his diary. Not exactly appropriate, but who would know?

He finished penning the email, popped it off to all concerned, then wondered what work this gathering might involve. He and Susie ought really to go the day before, in case Ben had been slobbing out for the past year. They could stay at The Fox, if they still did rooms. He quickly googled and found they did. Emotionally, it wouldn't be possible to stay in the house. Most of the time he managed to block out the blurry images of his last few months there – depressed as hell and brain dead with it – but memories could flood his head at any moment. Like that final, truly ghastly day, when he was home from hospital and Fran was silently packing, refusing to say where she was going. He found out later, after she'd left without a goodbye, that it was Em and Alex's place. They were having a similar crisis themselves, and apparently Fran's presence, along with her therapy skills, were a big help. Within a few weeks, she'd flown to America. Just like that.

He was organising this event for purely selfish reasons. It would be a kind of exorcism, going back to Tudor House. And with Susie and Alexa and Seb in tow, and others' feelings and comfort to consider, he'd be less likely to get emotional. It was a big ask, he knew, but he wanted them all to get along. He'd suggest that Em brought the children; that would help. And Alex too. Alex was always an asset socially.

Duncan fired off an email to Em, saying it was great that she could come, and please bring the family because he missed seeing Martha and George. He told her the new date, realising, too late, that the children would have school the next day. Or did they have half-term holidays in France? Were his grandchildren even *at* school? Better not to ask, he decided.

He got up from the desk and half bounced, half floated across the room. The trainers Susie had picked out were the ugliest things he'd ever owned and made him feel like a retard. But they were bloody comfortable. He just prayed stylish Joel never caught him in them.

He found Susie lying knees-up on the Chesterfield, a book wedged between her bosom and her thighs. He'd stopped asking what she was reading because she sped through books at a rate of knots, and was unable to remember them once finished.

'Darling?' he said.

She placed a finger on the page. 'Yes?'

'I was thinking of a gathering, sort of all of us. At Ben's place. Alexa, Seb, Ben and Em.'

Susie turned the page corner and closed the book. She sat up and twisted herself around, her feet guiding themselves into moccasins. She clasped her book and smiled at him. 'By Ben's place you mean your old family home?'

'Er, well. Yes.'

'I see.'

'What do you mean?' This wasn't going as smoothly as predicted. Of course Susie would refuse to go to the home he'd shared with Fran. How thoughtlessly male of him. He'd been impulsive too, sending off the emails before consulting her.

'What do I mean by "I see"?' She smiled quizzically at him, head cocked, as though he were one of her children, aged five. 'One says, "I see," to give oneself time to think.'

'I see,' Duncan said, and they laughed.

'Are you sure it's a good idea, darling? All those frightful memories being dredged up?'

'Ah.' The penny was dropping. Susie was concerned for him, rather than herself. He ought to have known she would be. 'A good egg' was how Alexa had once described her mother.

'I suppose we could, if you think it might help lay a ghost?'

'Fran? Well, she won't be there. She's in the Far East, I believe. I do have to go and pick up papers and other bits I left. Things I'd rather weren't chucked out or sold once Fran returns. My father's coins and so on.'

'I see.'

They laughed again.

'What were you thinking?' he asked after a while.

'Hm? Oh, that we ought really to hire a van. My little car won't hold much.'

'No, no, it won't.' Ever the practical one, she made him feel safe, and he loved that. Loved her. The good egg that was Susie. 'A van it is, then.'

THIRTY

London, 1967

Carl phoned Fran out of the blue one evening, to say his mother had died.

'Oh, I'm so sorry,' she told him, because people always said that, as though it was their fault.

'Thanks.' He sounded very upset and talked about the funeral the following Monday and how there was so much to do. Fran would have offered to help if it had felt right to do so, but she hadn't been part of his life and had never met his mum. What surprised her was that, with all the things he had to do, Carl had found time to phone her, of all people. Was it that now his mother was out the way, so to speak, he suddenly felt free and his thoughts had gone back to having a girlfriend?

'Can we meet up?' he asked. 'When this is all over?'

Fran felt cross but she also felt sorry for him, and on top of that she remembered how much she'd liked him and what a lovely romantic night they'd had. 'I'm going out with someone,' she had to tell him. 'I'm sorry.'

'Oh.'

He sounded miserable, and again she was torn between liking him and not. What had he expected? There'd been no contact apart from that letter. 'But I suppose we could meet for lunch. I work in Fenchurch Street.'

Carl said he was surprised she'd been so close and they'd never bumped into each other. 'You should have said.'

'Well, there was Duncan.'

'Your boyfriend?'

'Yes.'

'Maybe we could have lunch together?'

'OK.'

They arranged it for the following Friday, which meant keeping quiet about it for over a week, and hoping Duncan wouldn't catch her in some café. They were to meet by St Paul's at one. Duncan wouldn't be anywhere near there. More often than not he was in a pub with people from the insurance company. Every now and then she'd join him, but it was all a bit raucous and she could feel in the way. The reason she went was to keep an eye on him, and to make sure there were no Liz-types there, turning his head.

On the whole, she thought she could trust Duncan, and he was already talking about them getting engaged, so he must love her. Although it crossed her mind more than once that he might have talked about engagement just so she'd go all the way with him. After the Carl episode, Fran couldn't help but be cautious.

She'd lost confidence in herself sexually. Either that or she asso-
ciated sex with loss and heartache. She and Duncan kissed and
petted, but she was keeping him at arm's length, and although
she knew it was driving him nuts, it appeared to be working
because he was still around.

'I hope the funeral goes well,' she told Carl.

'Thanks. See you next Friday, then?'

'Yeah.'

Fran put down the phone and grinned. How she'd love to go
and tell Vicky and the others at the bank what had just happened.
That Carl still fancied her. Maybe she'd get in touch and see if
they wanted to meet up. She had said she would, after all. And
she'd tell them about Duncan and how she was practically engaged.
Show them a photo to prove how handsome he was. Tomorrow,
perhaps.

She went back to *The Man from U.N.C.L.E.* and said, 'Just a
friend,' to her inquisitive mum. 'From the bank I used to work
in. His mother died and he's a bit upset.'

'How awful.'

'Yes.'

Her mother's eyes darted between the telly and Fran. 'Did I
hear you say you're going to meet for lunch?'

Fran sighed. Her mum and her trumpet ears. 'Maybe.'

'Do you think that's wise, love? Wouldn't Duncan mind?'

Her parents had taken an instant shine to him the first time
she'd brought him home, and he'd grown on them with each visit.

'I'll tell Duncan. I expect he'll come too.'

She watched her mum relax back into the settee with an 'Oh,
good' and then she tried to follow *The Man from U.N.C.L.E.*,

237

while her insides got more and more churned up at the prospect of seeing Carl.

A most unexpected thing happened outside St Paul's. She and Carl had a hug and a quick kiss, but then they had another kiss, a longer one, and they seemed not to be able to stop. And then she was touching his hair, and he hers, and their tongues were going frantic. Right there, in the street.

'I've missed you,' he said, and she put her mouth back on his and ran her hand down his back, over the jacket he was wearing; then her hand was inside his jacket and on his waist and his back, stroking him through his shirt. This was so wrong. So very wrong. She had a horror of someone seeing her and reporting back to Duncan.

Finally they stopped, and Carl buried his face in her neck and said, 'I've got the key to the Streatham flat. Mick's away on a long weekend. What do you say we go there?'

'Now?' Had he planned this, she wondered, but she didn't care. 'I'll phone the office and say I'm poorly.'

'Me too.'

They made their phone calls, then somehow got to Streatham without molesting each other any more, and back in the bed again, made lovely love.

'It's the chemistry between us,' Carl said, when they were starting up the second time.

'Yes,' agreed Fran. It had to be. She'd never felt like this with Duncan, although he was nicer-looking than Carl and a better shape. Chemistry! It was a relief to have a word for it because she'd worried on the train to Streatham that she might be a nymphomaniac. But if she was one of those, she'd want to do it with every man she met, not just Carl.

Stopping for a rest, they lay in each other's arms, looking up at the cracked ceiling and talking about what had happened since they'd seen each other. Things they would have discussed if they'd made it to a café. She told him a bit about Duncan, feeling disloyal, but he *was* the biggest thing in her life. Well, he had been. Now she was confused. Should she chuck Duncan and make a go of it with Carl and his chemistry?

'My kid brother's moved into a flat,' he was telling her, 'with his friends. He's doing an apprenticeship at a garage.'

'So you're on your own in the house?'

'Yep. I might sell it once the will's all sorted out. The money will help finance my, er, studies.'

Fran sat up and looked at him. 'Your studies?'

'Been offered a place at art school.'

'No!'

She could see he was trying not to show how thrilled and proud he was. 'They liked my work and said I could start in September.'

'That's not far off, at all. Hey, clever you!' She kissed him on the lips and sat up again. 'You'll have to show me your art some time.' She wondered if she should be saying that, if this was just another one-night stand. Could you have a daytime one-night stand?

'Yeah, I'd like to. In spite of Duncan, you'll come and up and see me, won't you? It's a bit of a trek, I know.'

'What do you mean?'

'Oh.' He coloured up through his olive skin. 'I didn't say, did I? It's in Liverpool. The art school.'

'Liverpool?' Fran whispered.

He kissed the top of her arm. 'Sorry.'

'Couldn't you get into one down here?' She flopped back and stared at the crack again. It was always going to be like this with Carl, she could tell. They'd be intimate, then he'd go off.

'I did try. Kind of. Also, I thought life would be cheaper up there, rent and so forth.'

'That's true.' She wanted to cry but had no idea why, not really. She had Duncan, and as she was always telling her friends at home, she was almost engaged. Duncan had a good solid job and future, whereas Carl was going to be a poor artist for the rest of his life, living on coffee and cigarettes once his mum's money ran out. Not that he smoked. She could see him with a pipe, though, and a beard in some big attic full of canvases. Thinking about it, it sounded quite romantic. If he asked her to go with him, to live, she just might. But it didn't sound as though he would. And he hadn't suggested she finish with Duncan and go out with him. If he was so keen on her, he ought to put pressure on her. Why wasn't he? She didn't really know Carl, she realised, or understand him. Had he even meant it about visiting him? At least she knew where she was with Duncan, and she suddenly missed him.

He and Fran had arranged to meet after work, to go to the flicks. How she was going to face him, she didn't know. But there wasn't time now to go and find a phone and cancel, because Duncan would be setting off for the pub soon, where they were to meet at six.

'I'm really pleased for you,' Fran said as she and Carl dressed. She meant it and she didn't. He was always doing things that made her cross, or at least disappointed her.

* * *

They parted before they needed to, just to be on the safe side.

'Bye, then,' Fran said with a quick peck, as though he was an acquaintance, not someone she'd just done it with twice. But Carl grabbed her and held her tightly and said, 'I really like you, you know?' and when she looked up, his eyes were all watery.

'And I like you,' she said. And then she added, 'A lot,' because just 'I like you' didn't really sum up how she felt. If he asked her to leave Duncan, she would. But he didn't. He just held her and cried, and she couldn't help thinking it was more to do with his mother than with her.

'Phone me at home or at work?' she said, finally pulling away, aware of how late it was.

'I will.'

'Promise?'

'Promise.'

They had one last kiss and Fran walked off, dizzy from lack of food, or from love. She tried to remember what film she and Duncan were going to see, which pub she was meeting him in. Pull yourself together, she told herself, and gradually it came back. *Bonnie and Clyde*. The Anchor.

'What happened?' asked Duncan, when she went up to him. He was sitting on a small stool, around a table with work colleagues she recognised. He pointed at her hair and laughed, and she realised it was still wet on the ends from when she'd had a spray-over with the shower hose.

'Oh . . .' she said, thinking quickly, 'I, er, got some chewing gum stuck in it and had to wash it out.'

Duncan made a face at the others, embarrassed at having a

241

girlfriend who got gum in her hair. Fran sympathised, but if he knew what she'd really been doing . . .

'Shall we go?' she asked. The film started at seven and she needed to get sweets and popcorn because she was weak with hunger.

When she'd finished the tub of popcorn and wiped salt off everything, Duncan took hold of her hand and held it for the rest of the film. Every now and then he'd whisper a comment, like, 'People say I look like him.' He did look like Warren Beatty, she realised. Every girl's dream. Why then was she dreaming of Carl, who looked more like that one in The Monkees with the tambourine? Each time Duncan turned to her he did a double take and asked if she was all right. Fran would nod and try not to look at him. She had no idea what was going on in the film, or in her life. All she could think about was Carl and his body and his kisses, and she felt terrible, and at the same time, just wonderful.

THIRTY-ONE

'Shit!' Ben read the email again. No. No, no, no, no. 'All of them? Here?' He'd been doing this a lot lately, talking to himself.

He got up and ran along the landing, slid down the banisters and climbed over the newel post and stood for a while in the sitting room. 'Shit,' he said, as though seeing it for the first time in a year. He was viewing it through others' eyes, and it wasn't pretty. The only recognisable thing was the TV. Everything else was hidden under . . . under what? What the hell was it all? Where had it come from? In the kitchen, the floor was barely visible for papers and leaflets and bags of this and that, and dirty clothes and sheets. Or maybe they were clean. There was a stack of used plates, bowls, cups, saucepans, all next to the encrusted wok. 'Shit!' They couldn't all come here. No way.

He meandered his way upstairs, past piles of this and that on each and every step, then back at the laptop he tried to compose a firm but polite refusal, along the lines of how ridiculously busy he was with the pub and his writing, and what with the severe plumbing problem – a lie – which had put the toilets out of action, and the fact that you couldn't get a plumber in Long Bellingham for love nor money . . .

He was wondering if 'severe' was egging the pudding, when an email pinged through from his father. It was one he'd forwarded from Alexa, saying she'd love to come and had rearranged her shifts in order to be able to do so. It was followed by one from Em: *Hi Ben, great idea, don't you think? It's half term for Martha and George, who are so excited about seeing Grandpa, and staying at Tudor House again. Haven't yet broken it to them that Grandma won't be there! She's in Japan now, did you know? Hope all's good. Em x.*

He was fucked; no two ways about it. But maybe . . . He picked up the phone and called the pub. 'Hi, it's Ben,' he told Joey. 'Is your mother there?'

'Uh.' It was his most-used word. 'Uh . . . dunno.'

'Your dad, then?'

'Dad! It's uh . . .'

'The Fox at Long Bellingham,' came Jim's welcome voice. 'How can I help you?'

'It's me. Ben. Listen, I need a cleaner and wondered if I could borrow yours. It's a pretty big job but I'll pay well.'

'How well?'

'Um. Say, fifteen an hour?'

'Christ, I'll do it for that.' Jim chortled, which Ben took to mean he wasn't serious. He said he'd have a word with Moira, who 'did' for him and Sylvia every morning.

'Cheers,' Ben said, and Jim wished him a nice day off, and asked what he was planning on doing with it.

'Oh, this and that.' He'd become more circumspect recently.

'And a bit of the other?'

'With luck, ha-ha. Bye, Jim. And thanks!'

Well, that might be one problem solved, but there were others to consider. Ben hadn't been hospitable for a year; in fact, longer, because of the way things had been between him and Julia. How would he go about entertaining people? He did it at The Fox but that was different. And would he have to feed them all? The brats and little Martha and George, and Camilla? *Susie*. He must start thinking of her as Susie.

His mind was racing, when it should have been creating; *Jake the Fake and the Cotton Mill* – a particularly moving tale of life for ten year olds in late eighteenth-century Lancashire. Never again would Jake moan about having to do housework for pocket money. Ben deleted the email he'd begun to his father and thought he'd wait before replying. There were questions to be asked and plans to be made. The idea of being 'on holiday' appealed, but then again he'd quite like to meet this family who'd lived in the shadows. It occurred to him that he could be coming back from holiday on 1 November, then there'd be no way he could organise anything. Someone else would have to do it; like his dad and Camilla. *Susie*.

Ben felt too stressed to write and, now that he'd seen the conditions he lived in, had a strong urge to be elsewhere. London? He called Will, who'd been made redundant the same time he had, and they arranged to meet for lunch. Will had got himself another job in another bank and Ben almost felt sorry for him.

'And what are you up to?' Will asked.

'Er, well, actually I'm writing a series of novels.'

'Hey, cool. Tell me more later. Money beckons, better go.'

It was his first trip back to London since moving to Tulip House. In fact, it was his first trip anywhere. What a recluse he'd become, he realised, as he sped towards the metropolis. Had trains always gone this fast? There was a tension in his stomach, but he couldn't tell if it was the prospect of a joint family party causing it, or just going back to the Smoke.

How had almost a year gone by without his actually doing anything, seeing anyone or going anywhere? Outside of the village, that was. Somehow, the little shop, The Fox, the super-market deliveries and his writing had sustained him. He hadn't felt a lack; not at all. He'd been content to stay home and write nonsense and stroll down to the pub for a shift and fantasise about a young stable girl. Ben hadn't realised just how contented he'd been with his simple life until now, with his insides all knotted and acidic. He rubbed at his middle as the bullet train flew through fields and small towns, then miserable-looking suburbs. The first thing he'd do was find a Boots and get some indigestion tablets.

'Hey, how're you doing, Ben?' Will looked him up and down with ill-disguised horror.

It was true, he could have made more of an effort. 'Good,' he said. 'And you?'

'Never better.'

Ben sat down at the small round table. 'Sorry I'm late.'

'No problemo. Shall we order a bottle? Red or white?'

The Birthday

'Oh, ah . . .' It was so long since he'd drunk anything but beer, he couldn't remember his preference. 'I'm easy.'

'White, then. I find I sleep better in the afternoons.' He cackled annoyingly, and it came back to Ben, the way Will laughed at his own jokes. 'Soooo,' he went on, 'you're a published novelist now?'

'Well . . .' Ben did the wavering-hand thing. 'Let's just say there's a possible deal in the pipeline.' One day there would be. What sane publisher would turn Jake down?

'Cool. Who with? Bloomsbury have just won an auction for my cousin's book.'

'Hey, that's fantastic. Listen, I think I'll hang my coat over there.'

'Sure.'

At the coat rack, Ben dug into the pocket of his old grey mac, and fiddled with the box of Brucofen he'd picked up with the antacids. He popped two tablets out of their strip, then another, and shoved all three in his mouth while pretending to yawn. What a dickhead Will was, and what a truly bad idea this had been. He'd already got lost, hence his lateness, and almost been killed by a Lycra lout on a bike. London was terrifying. How did his dad cope with it?

They were at the coffee stage of their never-ending lunch, and Ben's head was woozy with alcohol and codeine.

'Things have worked out well for you, then,' Will was saying. 'About to be a published novelist, co-owner of a gastro-pub, and shagging a pretty Olympian horsewoman. I'm pleased, I really am.'

'Cheers.'

'Listen, I'm going to have to split. Shall we get the bill?'

'Sure.' Ben gesticulated to the waitress and when the bill arrived, it was placed in front of him. 'This is on me.'

'Very kind. Thanks, mate.'

After tapping his pin in the machine, Ben's card was rejected. Not the pin, but the card. Frowning and saying, 'That's ridiculous!' he tried again and it was rejected again. This was total humiliation, and if he hadn't been high, he'd have wanted to die. But, despite half a bottle and three pills, he remembered his old trick and examined the card, then thumped his forehead. 'Shit, I brought the wrong one out! I'm so sorry, Will.'

'No worries,' said his friend, a hand delving into his jacket. There was no telling if he believed him. 'I'll see to it.'

'Cheers.'

'We should do this again,' Ben said outside.

'Absolutely.'

'On me next time, obviously.'

'Well . . . good to see you, Ben.'

'You too.'

They shook hands and did a bit of awkward patting, then went in different directions.

It had been a disaster, yes. But as he floated back over London Bridge, he had nothing but warm feelings for Will, and the way he'd been so pleased about Ben's successes. That had been nice.

He stopped at every pharmacy *en route* for a large box of Brucofen. With all this family business coming up, it was best to be on the safe side.

'OK,' he'd said at least five times, when told he shouldn't take them for more than three days. And, 'Really?' when informed codeine can be addictive, and, 'No,' when asked if he was any other medication. Did antacids count?

THIRTY-TWO

May 1979

A letter came from Carl saying he was getting divorced. Fran had heard nothing since his last letter, two years earlier, which had been redirected by her parents, and which had announced he was getting married to someone called Delia. Quite bizarrely, since there'd been no contact for ten years, he'd invited her to the wedding, along with Duncan, '. . . if you're still together.'

She'd replied immediately, with congratulations and an apology that she wouldn't make the wedding. She described her family, her house and Duncan's work, and gave him their address and phone number, in case he and Delia were ever in the area.

And now this letter had arrived, out of the blue. Again. It was all very Carl, she thought. No consistency. He wrote that he and Delia hadn't been compatible after all, but went into no detail. 'I'd love to see you,' he finished with, 'if you're free to visit any time. You wouldn't believe how often I've thought of you.' There was a Devon address, a village near Tavistock.

She wondered if it was serendipity. In a fortnight it would be spring half term and the kids were going to her parents from Sunday to Thursday. Duncan would be in Saudi Arabia on business. Anywhere else on the planet and she'd have begged to be taken along. In fact, she'd been miffed since hearing of this business trip because she so rarely had a break from motherhood and a chance to join him. 'Never mind,' he'd said, seemingly unbothered. 'There'll be other opportunities.'

Fran mulled it over for a few days. In the end, she decided she could always visit Carl but stay in Tavistock. She wrote back with the dates she was free and asked him to recommend nearby accommodation. She heard from him by return post, with a, 'Great, see you then!' He enclosed directions to his house, but no B&B or hotel.

She'd expected an ancient and remote cottage, but Carl's house was in a row of terraced redbricks on a fairly busy road. He'd said to park around the back and come through the garden, and so she turned down the lane he'd mentioned and found a high wooden fence and gate with a huge number five on it.

Fran had planned to stay three nights but her feet were growing cold, so she left her suitcase in the boot, hooked her handbag over her shoulder, and took a deep breath at the gate before clicking the latch open on to an unexpectedly stunning garden. There were vine-covered arched walkways and strange pieces of artwork and Greek goddess statues. The slate and brick path led her past a beautiful pond, covered in a net and surrounded by rushes and grasses and tall daisies. It was all so lush and colourful, and if it was like this now, she thought, how would it look in a month, in the middle of summer? The garden wasn't wide but it went on and on, until she came out into a patio area, and there was Carl, reading a book at a table, feet up on a chair.

'Fran!' He leaped up and came and hugged her, so tightly she almost left the ground. He leaned back and took her in. 'You haven't changed. I'm so glad.'

'Neither have you!' It wasn't true. His hair was thinner, and more fair than blond, and he'd put on weight. There were bags under his eyes that hadn't been there twelve years ago and a bit of a second chin. But he was still Carl, and he felt good.

'What, no luggage?' he asked, letting go of her.

'Um . . .' He might have been saggy and baggy but the attraction was still there, still strong. She had no idea why, and she had no idea what to do. What had she come for, if it wasn't to see if the old spark was there? The chemistry. But she hadn't thought it through; deliberately, no doubt. Could she really break her marriage vows, she wondered, now she was here, seeing him in the flesh, touching him? She'd always be a Catholic girl, despite the registry office wedding, and adultery was a sin. But who was to say Duncan hadn't broken his vows? Got lonely in some sterile hotel room . . . not that it would make this any more right.

Fran had asked him once, outright, if he'd ever picked up someone on a business trip. She must have had a couple of drinks to have been that bold. On the whole, she and Duncan didn't touch on tricky emotive subjects. 'A one-night stand?' he said, all indignant. 'That's something I would *never* do. Never.' But he was good-looking; there must have been temptations. She'd most likely never know for sure.

'My case is in the car,' she told Carl, and with those words, and with the warm look he gave her when he heard them, Fran knew she was doomed.

He carried the suitcase, while she followed him back down the narrow path, admiring the garden. 'Was it you or your wife, who—'

'Me. Everything in the house too. Delia was what you might call . . . sedentary.'

'What does she do? For a living.'

'Hm, let me think. Oh, yeah, fuck all. Well, she tries to be an artist with integrity. We all try that and we all end up producing commercial tack and teaching. Not Delia, though. Wouldn't sell out. Wouldn't lower herself. Anyway, she's gone to sponge off Mummy and Daddy.' They'd reached the back door and he turned round. 'Sorry. Didn't mean to sound bitter, only she ran up a lot of debts I've only just found out about.'

'Oh dear.'

He hoisted the case through the back door, then himself, and Fran followed. The kitchen was as fascinating as the garden.

'Wow,' she said, slowly spinning around. How dull and conventional her own was. When she got home, she'd weave hops around the units, and hang interesting photos of garlic bulbs and naked people, and have plants on every surface beside jars of pulses and preserved fruit. She'd paint the walls bright yellow and hang assorted old mirrors, and find two cats – real ones – to adorn the windowsill.

'Tea?' Carl asked.

'Please.' She wandered around, looking at things, stroking them. 'I love this room. And it's airy but cosy at the same time.'

He smiled at her and she noticed the teeth she'd forgotten about; white against his tanned skin and perfectly straight. He wasn't conventionally handsome but his smile was quite lovely.

'This end bit's an extension, to let more light in.' He pointed at four Velux windows in the sloping ceiling. 'I hung on to the features in the original kitchen, and the old range keeps the place warm. A bit too warm in summer.' He smiled again and she saw laughter lines fanning from around his eyes. She liked the little signs of ageing. She liked Carl.

Age must have slowed them because it was a full hour and two cups of tea before they fell on the double bed in 'her room' and began peeling clothes off one another.

Fran said, 'Why does this always happen?'

'I don't know.' He kissed her again, then stopped. 'Two passionate Scorpios?'

'You remembered!'

'I always remember your birthday. Two days after mine.'

'That's right.' How sweet of him. She'd actually forgotten.

They were fumbling and embarrassingly clumsy, but all Fran wanted was skin on skin, more and more kissing, and sex. She couldn't believe it but she absolutely had to have sex.

'It was never like this with Delia.'

'Nor with Duncan,' she said, when Carl finally pulled a fresh-smelling white sheet over them and pressed his soft podgy skin against hers.

*   *   *

Later they walked on Dartmoor, and the next day, with fingers hooked through hers, Carl showed her around Tavistock. They went to the abbey, where they managed to kiss unseen among the ruins, then into town and the covered market and specialist book-shops. He showed her some of his own paintings in the affordable art shops, and collected money from one or two sales.

'I can't believe people buy this stuff,' he said, slipping twenties into his wallet.

The day before she was due to leave, Fran phoned her mother and asked if they'd hang on to the children one more day. She was visiting an old work colleague, she explained, and the car was playing up. The mechanic said he'd have it ready late the following day.

'I'll set off early Friday and see you all around three.'

Her mum didn't mind at all, and Fran spoke to Ben and Emily, who sounded happy enough. There were new children the same age next door, she was told, with a swing and a sandpit, and they'd all gone to the swimming pool twice, and Grandpa had taught them to dive, only Em kept belly-flopping.

'With armbands, I hope!' Emily couldn't even swim. 'What a shame I can't join you for the last day,' she told Ben. 'My stupid old car!' How she hated lying, but since they were having a lovely time without her, there was no harm done.

Carl taught art A level, so he too was on half term. 'Normally, I'd be working upstairs during the holidays. But that can get lonely. This is much nicer, being with you.'

He'd resisted showing her his work, because he was departing from the commercial landscape stuff he loathed doing, and experimenting

255

with more abstract ideas. 'I'm doing more photography and designing an installation at the moment.'

He showed her his diagrams and drawings in the attic bedroom, and had to explain to her what an installation was. 'I was into Marcel Duchamp and the Dadaists and Surrealists at college.' He laughed at her blank expression and took a book from a shelf. 'Here.'

'Thanks.' It was big and heavy and full of glossy photos. She sat on a paint-splattered chair and opened it.

'Anyway, it's all pie in the sky. In twenty years, I'll still be selling crap and teaching kids as deluded as I was.'

'No,' she said. 'I don't think you will.'

He laughed. 'Thanks for believing in me. Anyway, I'm renting some space so I can get constructing. We'll see.'

Fran slowly worked through the book of weird and wonderful objects, not quite getting it, but guessing they'd be more im-pressive in the flesh. She stopped, feeling Carl's eyes on her and looked up.

'I've really enjoyed this,' he said.

Fran felt a rush of emotion; feelings she'd pushed down so she could concentrate on having fun. 'Me too. But . . .'

'But what?'

She closed the big book and put in on the floor, then got up and went over to him. 'I can't do it again,' she said, wrapping her arms around him. 'You know that, don't you?'

He sighed and stroked the back of her head. 'Why not?'

'Because next time it would be premeditated, in a way this wasn't.'

'It wasn't?'

'OK. Well, I sort of convinced myself I was just visiting an old pal. Platonically. I asked you to find me accommodation, remember?'

'Oops, sorry.'

Fran laughed, and they kissed for the millionth time. 'Yep,' she said, pulling back and looking into his eyes. 'It's all your fault.'

'I love you,' Carl said.

'Do you?' She tried to recall the last time Duncan had said that, and couldn't. They'd never come out with it that often, what with work and babies and exhaustion.

'You're supposed to say, "I love you too."'

'But I'm a married woman!'

'Leave him.'

'No.'

'Why not? Do you still love him?'

'I don't know. Yes, I suppose I do. But not in the same . . . it's different, that's all. There are the children and we're a unit. I couldn't do anything to jeopardise that.'

Carl sighed again. 'I should have asked you back then, shouldn't I? Twelve years ago.'

Fran nodded, but wondered what kind of a mess she'd be in now if she'd stuck with Carl. He was lovely but she'd discovered he could be controlling; deciding what they'd do, where they'd eat and so on. She was used to Duncan's easy-going ways, she supposed, and she had to remember Carl was the host; they were on his home territory. But when she took a fancy to an Italian restaurant they passed, he'd said there was a Thai one she'd like more. Oh, yes? Fran had thought, fancying a good pizza. They'd eaten Thai and it had been delicious, and Carl had looked very proud. She guessed he'd drawn up a list of things to impress her with, and that he'd be better once he relaxed.

And Carl didn't want children, he'd said. Never had, never would. It went back to his own childhood, with his father deserting and his mother falling ill. 'I'd be terrified of letting them down.'

No, luck had made her stick with reliable, solid, child-loving Duncan. There may not have been the highs she'd had with Carl, but highs weren't everything. Did she love Carl? Yes, but she wasn't about to tell him, because that might lead to all sorts of trouble.

The children returned on Friday, and Duncan on Saturday. On Sunday, Fran cooked a roast and the children told their father all about their time away, and how good it was that Mum's car broke and they had to stay an extra day.

'What was it?' Duncan asked her.

'Oh, it was making a noise. Whining. Well, more of a whistle. So it went to a garage Liz uses.' She'd nominated Liz as the 'old friend' from the stockbrokers' she was going to see. She was real, or had been, and Duncan remembered her.

'And what did they say it was?'

'Mm? Oh, I don't remember.'

'Well, where's the invoice?'

'I'm not sure. I might have left it at Liz's.'

'Daddy, tell us about Saudirabia,' Ben was saying.

'Yes, do,' said Fran.

'Not much to tell, really. Except it was hot. Very, *very* hot!'

'As hot as an oven?' asked little Em.

'Hotter!'

'That must have been wicked,' Ben said.

'Wicked's the word!'

Funny, Fran thought, when Duncan reached for the potatoes and his sleeve rode up one very pale arm. He didn't look as though he'd been in the sun. But then people in hot countries tended not to go out.

'It wasn't the fan belt?' he asked.

'Uh, maybe.'

Duncan looked at her quizzically. He'd done that a lot since returning. Could he tell? Did she look different – sort of wanton or sexually sated and still flushed? She *felt* different. Very different.

THIRTY-THREE

22 October 2009

Em was packing. The next day, the children would be on half term – or *Toussaint*, as Martha kept correcting her – right through to 4 November. The plan was to go home by rail, visit friends in London, then hire a car and tramp over to Alex's parents for a few days before heading to Long Bellingham on Sunday the first for the 'Big Chill', as Alex referred to it. 'You know, that film in which old friends meet up for a funeral and it all goes wrong.'

He was staying in Paris for four days to continue working on something with Maxine. Red flags were waving themselves frantically in Em's face, but she kept averting her eyes. A little balancing of the books might be just the thing their marriage needed. And, besides, any fling Alex had would help validate Florian, and any who'd follow.

She folded Martha's little cardigans and her French dresses and skirts, and not for the first time wished her mother could see and listen to her new cosmopolitan grandchildren. They'd Skyped once or twice, but it wasn't the same. Still, there'd always be Christmas. She'd said she'd be home by then and had hinted that she might come via Paris. Em hoped she would because she'd heard Paris was magical, then, with its pretty white lights and fabulous window displays.

In her emails and Skype calls, her mother wasn't giving anything away about her emotional state, and Em worried that she was in denial; something she'd certainly get her clients working on. Hopefully, she wouldn't crash and burn once back in Tudor House, with all its memories; not to mention Ben driving her nuts with his messiness. Em had popped up once just before leaving for Paris, shortly after everyone's godawful Christmas, and although her brother had only had the freedom of the place for a month, it looked like a student house, times ten. Perhaps she'd arrange for someone to go and clean up, a day or two before her mother's return.

If she were in her mum's shoes, she'd sell the house and start a new life somewhere else. Her parents had moved there, all excited about their new project, after she and Ben left home. They'd done quite a bit of cosmetic work – painting and repairs, nothing major – and they'd filled the garden with shrubs and trees and colour, and generally created a great place for the family to visit, and a place they'd both loved. At least they'd appeared to love it. And that was going to make it hard to live in again, surely?

Em decided to have a word with her father about giving the house to their mum. He had no money problems, unless Camilla was tight. And he had his pension. With what she'd get for the house, her mother could buy a little apartment in Paris and be near them, and maybe meet a charming silver-haired French divorcé or widower.

Yes, Em liked that idea, but in the meantime, she had bags to pack and lists to write for her husband. And she had presents to buy for everyone; Camilla and the brats. Em was aware the presents would be a kind of showing off. Look! We can bring you food that looks like a work of art! Chic scarves! Heavenly perfumes! Aren't we interesting and sophisticated, living where we do! It was totally pathetic and transparent of her, Em knew. Sebastian was a top lawyer, and Alexa a successful consultant going out with a famous comedian. But she'd always had a competitive streak, and those two were a lot to compete with, for someone who knew she'd let her father down badly. Did Ben feel the same guilt? Years of financial support while he studied, only to end up a barman living rent-free at home?

She tried for a while to get into her brother's head, but gave up and went to look for George's one-flippered Pingu, which always caused a meltdown if left behind.

THIRTY-FOUR

24 October 2009

Ben was packing, only he was having trouble because Moira had been in three days in a row and turned the place into a show-house. Where the fuck were his clothes?

He finally found his tops on shelves in the master-bedroom wardrobe, and there also were his jeans, on hangers and looking decidedly ironed. He pulled open a drawer and discovered his socks. Identical, in pairs. Tops rolled together like Siamese twins. He couldn't remember when he'd last worn matching socks, but it was some time in 2008.

After scooping up half a dozen pairs, then a couple more, he found the drawer below full of pressed boxers. The woman was seriously addicted to ironing. Still, everyone to their own, he thought, suddenly aware it was Brucofen time. Well, almost. Twenty minutes. It was the stress of the family gathering, he told himself every time he popped them. And having to leave home for a week. Not that he *had* to leave. He'd just prefer to roll up mid-occasion, making him a guest rather than a host. All that having to greet everyone and make sure they had drinks. No thanks. His dad said they'd be up either Saturday or Sunday, and since Ben wouldn't be there, they'd arranged for caterers to come in. So, his cunning plan had worked. His father and Susie had taken control. The down part was that Ben was compelled to leave, and promptly, before he trashed the place again.

Ben whipped jeans and trousers off hangers and threw them over his shoulder. The other wardrobe door revealed shirts, lined up like soldiers on parade and with the sharpest sleeve creases. How many for a week, what with the tops and T-shirts? He slipped three of his favourite shirts over one arm and marvelled at the joy of packing when you were organised. Not even Julia had lived this anally, but from now on he would. If he wasn't hunting for things, he'd have more time to be creative.

He felt bad now about being short with Moira, who'd somehow always wanted to be exactly where he'd been over those three days, making him jump over the Hoover, the floor polisher, the mop, the black bags she was filling with God knew what. The house had smelled of chemicals and the bathrooms of bleach; floors had been wet and lethal but without one of those signs you're supposed to put up. Bedspreads and sheets and rugs had hung over doors. How was a person supposed to write *Jake the Fake and the Potato Famine* in such chaos? If he recalled rightly, he'd asked Moira that several times and with some ferocity.

Now, here were all his clothes, clean and proud-looking and ready to dip into. His shoes too, paired up on the rack at the bottom. That someone had gone to such trouble to make his life easier was strangely touching. He'd get her a present in London to make up for his rudeness. Or should he do it now, before she had time to bad-mouth him at The Fox? Thinking about it, it would be too late for that.

With property coming out of the doldrums, they'd had an offer on the flat that Julia had accepted without thinking to consult him. Since he'd had no idea of its current worth, and since Julia must have realised that, he'd held fire. The truth was he'd come out of the sale £15,000 better off, when not that long ago they were staring a loss in the face. And he was grateful that Julia had taken over the selling of the place, despite being shacked up with another lawyer in Camberwell. Simeon. Ha! Simeon probably knew Sebastian. Perhaps Simeon, Julia and Sebastian went to one another's dinner parties. How *Brideshead* would that be? Christ, he hated poncy London . . . although he had been invited to an interview at an investment bank in two days' time and for some bizarre reason had accepted.

A suit!

He worked his way past the regiment of shirts and found his lucky one. It was his oldest suit, bought in Marks and Spencer and twice saved from Julia's charity clear outs. It came out only for interviews and other nerve-racking meetings. Knowing it brought luck had a calming effect whenever he wore it – a talisman with a St Michael label. He unhooked it and its hanger and staggered back to his rucksack under half his wardrobe.

Ben tried to imagine how it would feel going back to the flat for a while. Would Julia have left essentials, such as a bottle opener?

Duvet and sheets? A TV? He should have asked, but bothering her with minor details could feel demeaning, so he'd sleep in his coat if necessary, open beers with his teeth and watch telly on his laptop. He'd need his dongle to do the latter, but that would involve finding the thing. After failing to pack his rucksack in any decent and respectful manner, he went off in search of a suit-case for his ironed clothes.

'There,' he said, half an hour later. He was tempted to call Moira and have her come and see how neat the case looked, but went instead to his parents' study, where, heaven be praised, the wifi dongle sat in a small tray, lined up with other computer acces-sories. Ben picked it up and kissed it. If Moira hadn't been sixty and married and didn't smell of Cif, he'd have made a move.

THIRTY-FIVE

4 November 2008

There were one or two cards she hadn't got round to opening, so while Duncan had his post-breakfast doze, Fran went back to the messy pile on the end of the kitchen table, and picked out three that were still sealed. Although they'd kept in touch, fairly loosely, over the years, she was surprised to find one from Carl. Then again, she had sent him one for his sixtieth.

He'd dropped her a line following that, thanking her for the card and saying, in a matter-of-fact tone, that his decree absolute had just come through for his failed second marriage to Polly, a potter. 'Sixty and alone, hey ho,' he'd written. Fran had responded with a 'sorry to hear that', but that she was pleased his career was going well, and that she'd been following his world tour online. 'Your teaching days are well behind you now!' she'd said, in an attempt to bolster him. 'Didn't I tell you?'

She deliberated about putting his card out, for although Duncan would take no notice of it, Em almost certainly would, and there'd be a mini interrogation about who Carl was and why she'd never heard of him. So Fran tucked it back in its envelope and went up and hid it under her fancier, rarely used lingerie in a wardrobe drawer. She wondered if Polly the Potter had worn skimpy black lace underwear for Carl; whether he was seeing anyone now. He hadn't said, but there was a new address, in Tavistock itself, and a new phone number, plus mobile and an email address. She'd send him an email, thanking him.

All day it warmed her to know that Carl had gone to the trouble of hand painting a pretty abstract garden scene. His new garden, or the old one? Her head went back to that half term all those years ago. The passion, the sun . . . the passion. She took a deep wobbly breath – remembering then, comparing it with now – before closing the drawer and going down to wake Duncan. There was food to be bought, a small party to organise. Balloons for the little ones? That might be nice.

THIRTY-SIX

Alex couldn't come to Gare du Nord as something urgent had come up. So he saw them off in the taxi outside the apartment block, with two kisses each because that was what *les enfants* expected now, and a 'See you in a few days!'

It would have been nice to have had him around at the station, but taking Eurostar was easier than catching a plane, and it was still early in the day and no one had reached the grumpy stage. The kids had a backpack each, full of games and magazines and little treats for the journey, so they'd be fine on the train. And once they reached London, they'd take a cab to Cat's place. Thanks to their grandparents, Cat's children owned every toy in the Argos catalogue, and had rabbits and a giant trampoline. Martha and George couldn't wait.

Em sat back in the taxi and looked forward to it too. It was nice to have a break from the teaching. Most of her one-to-oners were bright and demanding, and although Florian was making no headway, his appetite for full-on erotic *amour* was wearing her out. She ought to find someone less libidinous. A man in his thirties, at least. Someone clever and educated, like Hadi had been. Was. He was still somewhere in the world, presumably. Making beautiful, thoughtful love to a lucky woman. His wife, perhaps. Pillow-talking sleepily and intelligently. *The blind man is laughing at the bald head.* Where was he? Following Alex's admission, there'd been no need, in the end, to go back to Hadi's house and grill Nigel, although she'd often wished she had. To have an address or an inkling of where Hadi had gone would have been something, and better than the feeling he'd just evaporated. Too late now. The trail would have gone cold, as they say in cop shows.

Young Florian's one other passion was food, and he tended to give lecturettes on the subject, even in bed. Especially in bed. How you must never over-whip your omelette eggs, or use cooking apples in a *tarte tatin*. Hadi, on the other hand, would talk about Iranian philosophy; Zarathustra and others. Most of it had gone over her head but it was a turn-on in a way an omelette would never be.

'Mummy, have you got Pingu?'

The words shook her out of her reverie and she saw George had emptied his things all over the seat and floor. 'I put him in your bag this morning.' Em unstrapped herself and picked up the books and crayons and biscuits. 'He must be here . . . You didn't take him out again, did you? At the apartment?'

George nodded.

'Why?' She ran a hand over the floor of the taxi and sat up again.

'Pingu always cleans my teeth with me.'

'And you forgot to put him back?' She tried not to sound as though she was scolding him, although she was. How was she supposed to think of everything?

He shrugged. 'I want Pingu, Mummy.'

'Well, you can't have him,' said Martha. She was cuddling her black doll, Sylvie. Provocatively, Em felt, and it wasn't helping. 'Ha-ha, you've left him at home and he can't come on holiday.'

Em scowled at her daughter and said, 'Listen, George. I don't expect Pingu likes travelling much because of having only one flipper. I bet he's really happy to be staying home.'

George started crying. 'He wants to come!'

Martha laughed. 'How do you *know* that?'

'He *told* me.'

'No, he didn't.'

'Yes, he did.'

'No, he didn't. Penguins can't talk.'

George was sobbing now, and Em realised nothing she could bribe him with would make up for Pingu.

'Instead of having Pingu,' she tried, regardless, 'how about a ride on the London Eye? We could go to the Aquarium too? That would be fun!'

'I want Pingu . . .'

'I'll buy you another one, sweetie.' She tried to hug him but he wasn't having it.

'*Myyy Piiinguu,*' he wailed. He was close to the gasping-for-breath stage, tears streaming, all snotty. Then there'd be those mini convulsions. Em found a tissue and checked her watch. They'd left in plenty of time in case the traffic was bad, which it

271

hadn't been. '*Pardon, Monsieur . . .*' she said, leaning towards the driver.

'We go back for Pingu?' he asked, already indicating.

The driver seemed like a perfectly nice person, but Em wasn't about to leave either her children or luggage with him. While they all trooped back into the apartment block with their bags and cases, she hoped the North African-looking man waiting in the idling car wasn't taking offence. The lift took them to the second floor, and when they got to the door of the flat, Em was surprised to find it wasn't double locked. Alex was still home? So much for having urgent work to do.

She unlocked and pushed it open with a casualness she'd later regret. Because there, at the end of the corridor, in the kitchen, was her husband's bare bottom, encircled by the bare legs of the woman lying on the table in front of him. He looked up and saw them, his face red from exertion. For a while, everyone seemed to freeze. Then, when what she was seeing registered – it was only seconds but felt longer – Em spun the children round and ushered them back out.

Martha looked up wide eyed. 'What's Daddy—'

'Shh!'

'Can I get Pingu?' George asked, oblivious, hopefully.

'I'll get him,' said Em, and before George had a chance to rush back in, she stood her children firmly by the wall and told them not to move an inch.

'What's an inch?' Martha asked, and Em showed her with two fingers.

'OK?'

'OK,' they said.

She went back in. Alex and his woman – Maxine, presumably – had disappeared. Em closed the door behind her and walked as noisily as she could along the wooden floor. On reaching the family bathroom, she found it locked, but knocked on it with a shaky hand.

'*Oui?*' came a female voice.

Em closed her eyes and breathed in deeply 'Is there a Pingu in there?'

'*Ah . . . oui.* Yes.'

'May I have him?'

She heard a few creaks then the unclicking of the lock. Pingu was handed to her through a five-inch gap by a woman whose face was hidden. Em saw only a thick gold bangle and a thin cream-coloured strap on a pretty bare shoulder.

'Thank you,' she said, then back outside, the door to the flat firmly closed, she handed Pingu to George and was asked again by Martha what Daddy had been doing.

'Gymnastics,' she said, her voice shaky with anger. What was Alex thinking? 'With his gymnastics teacher.'

Martha said, 'Oh,' and picked up her bag. 'Come on, or we'll miss the train.'

When they headed towards the lift, Em prayed Alex wouldn't come out and try to explain, apologise, create a scene. She pressed the button for the doors to open and looked back to check. Alex didn't emerge, but there on the floor by the flat was Pingu.

Em pointed and said a weary, 'Pingu?' to George, who ran back, picked up his beloved penguin, and dragged him by his flipper to the lift.

* * *

What she'd witnessed didn't register properly until they were under the sea: the bit of the journey that always unnerved her and made her thoughts turn to darker matters, like their family breaking up. She may have had affairs but she'd never truly considered leaving her husband. This Maxine business was worrying, since, as far as she knew, Alex had always been faithful; loyal to her, to his little family. Em hadn't been able to tell if Maxine was pretty, but she'd seen lots of long dark hair, and the legs wrapped around her husband had been slim. Judging from the shoulder she'd glimpsed, Maxine – if it had been Maxine – was petite. And she wore expensive perfume, Em knew, because it lingered on Pingu from the five seconds she'd held him. Would Alex be the type to fall head over heels and decide to be with the woman he loved? Or would he be very French and keep his marriage and love life going at the same time?

George was asleep with his head on her lap, and Martha was leaning over the table, drawing and colouring. She had two parents who drew well, so it wasn't surprising she was good. Already, their daughter leaned towards the arts and struggled slightly with *les mathématiques*. Or rather, got bored with them and made silly mistakes. Martha had joined a drama group, and several of her English compositions had been praised. Perhaps she'd be an actress or playwright. Em had had no idea, at that age, what direction she'd go in. She still didn't really have a clue.

In his sleep, George rolled around on her lap, clutching Pingu. Once more, Maxine's perfume wafted Em's way. It was nice, actually, and not one she recognised.

'What are you drawing?' she asked her daughter.

Martha lifted her arm and pushed the pad Em's way. 'It's Daddy. He's doing gymnastics with his teacher.'

Em's eyes widened at the amount of detail her daughter had absorbed in those few seconds, but she had her daddy sort of somersaulting the bare-legged woman, in the way Alex would sometimes do with Martha when she held his hands and climbed up his front. Nobody seeing it would think it was porn, but Em nevertheless tilted it away from the couple opposite. What relief she felt, seeing how her daughter had viewed the scene.

'That's really good, Martha.' She slowly turned the page to a blank one. '*Now*, why don't you draw . . . your school? Then you can show everyone.'

'Like Grandma and Grandpa?'

'Er, yes.' She should tell Martha her grandmother wouldn't be there. Nearer the time, maybe.

'OK,' Martha said with a yawn, dragging the pad back her way. 'Are we nearly out of the water, Mummy?'

What with the gymnastics, Em had forgotten for a moment where they were. 'I do hope so,' she said, putting her head back and closing her eyes. To block out thoughts of the surrounding sea, her head filled with Martha's drawing, then the scene itself. She wasn't jealous, that was the strange thing. Just cross that he'd been shagging instead of helping get the children home. And on the kitchen table. How unhygienic. The children ate their cereal there in the mornings, did their homework – *les devoirs* – there after school. Even George, poor thing, had a bit of *devoirs* each week.

How could Alex do that? Em thought.

But then she remembered the time, soon after they'd met, when they'd offered to make lunch and had managed an upright quickie in his parents' walk-in larder. It had been risky and exciting; Em half perched on a shelf of marrowfat peas and Maggi seasoning.

She sighed. 'Alex,' she mouthed, not quite saying it. She laid her head against the shaky window and stared at blackness. 'Don't go.'

THIRTY-SEVEN

31 October 2009

Duncan had forgotten what a big thing Hallowe'en had become in Long Bellingham. Considering the village had no school and only a rusty slide and set of swings, it housed an astonishing number of kids. And here they all were, dressed up and weighed down with bags of sweets they really shouldn't touch before bed.

'Aren't they splendid!' Susie said.

Duncan drove the van slowly, in case a tiny Dracula got bumped from the pavement. 'Yes,' he agreed. He used the distraction to turn off Radio Two. The phone-ins, the middle-of-the-road hits and Susie's poor singing voice had added to his edginess. He'd been nervous, truth be told, about coming to Long Bellingham again. Wondering if he'd be repulsed by it all, by the memories it would drag up; that he'd have to turn back and ruin everyone's weekend. But almost the opposite was happening.

As they drove through its heart, past the pub they'd be coming back to, he felt an unwelcome rush of homesickness. Pull yourself together, he told himself. It's not your home. And when it was your home you were miserable.

'What pretty little houses.'

'Yes.' He'd forgotten the place was so picturesque, and with pumpkin lanterns in windows, all the more so.

They were heading for Tudor House, where they'd give it the once-over before booking into The Fox. Ben was holidaying somewhere and due back tomorrow, and although he'd promised everything was in good order, Em had insisted they check it out because 'good order' was a subjective concept. The caterers would arrive at eleven in the morning, and although everyone would be too tense to notice a little chaos, he and Susie would make sure there was space for the food, and no underwear or dead mice around.

He needed to focus on the positives. How wonderful it was going to be, seeing the main family – not a description he'd ever use with Susie – again. Martha and George, especially. Once or twice, he'd considered popping over to Paris, but taking Susie wouldn't have felt right somehow. Too soon. And he hadn't wanted to go alone because that would have left her with Joel. Ridiculous, really. Susie had sworn she and Joel hadn't been physical since their brief affair, and he believed her, but perhaps the insecurity would never go. He'd led a life of deceit, so was bound to suspect others of it too.

He indicated left, checked no children were around and went over the path and on to gravel.

'Oh!' Susie pointed back at the house sign. 'We're here?'

'Yes.'

She put a hand on his thigh; an action that had more than once led to car sex, even in recent years. Unseemly, some might call that; he just saw them as young at heart. 'Darling, are you all right?' she asked. 'You're terribly quiet.'

'Oh, I'm fine.' Of course he wasn't fine. He looked up at the dark house before them. Fran was silently packing . . . he was asking her not to go. Had he actually asked her not to? It was all very hazy. They'd pumped his stomach and he'd been feeling wretched while she filled her cases. Earlier in the day, Ben had said, 'Here, Dad,' and given him pills for the headache, with a warning they'd space him out. They had. Something had. Shock, perhaps. Or just life. Before that day ended, unable to cope with Fran's departure, he'd moved in with Susie.

'Duncan?'

'Mm?'

'Come along,' she said, getting out with an armful of lilies. 'You'll simply have to bite the bullet.'

'I know.'

His tactic, in the end, was to walk purposefully into each room, quickly scan and leave. Standing before the master bedroom, he paused, then turned the handle.

'Oh God,' he said, his eyes doing a tour. There on a hook, on the door to the expensive but rarely used en suite, was Fran's chunky robe; the one she thought made her look fat. Even a fat suit wouldn't have made Fran look fat, but there'd been no telling her. She hadn't taken it with her, then. Too bulky, perhaps. He'd bought her that nice silky one in Tokyo. Maybe she'd taken that.

The bed – the one they'd tested in the shop and pretended to fall asleep on – was exquisitely made. No way had he left it in that neat condition last November. In fact, from the moment they'd entered the house it was clear it had been professionally cleaned. Either that, or Ben had gone gay in his near-middle age. Duncan smiled. Just the sort of thing Fran would tell him off for saying. He pictured her in her pretty blue and white kimono. She could have bought another one, of course. In Japan.

The floorboards creaked behind him. 'Darling, are you OK?' Susie stopped dead and looked in the room. 'Oh. I see.' She rubbed his back. 'Why don't you go downstairs, and I'll check the rest of the bedrooms?'

Good old Susie. 'OK. Thanks.'

Having booked in with the young girl at a makeshift reception, then taken their bags to their room, he and Susie went down to the bar for a drink. They'd be dining at eight, which gave them an hour to chill out by the fire after the stresses of the day.

The pub had changed for the better. The clutter, from when the brewery had given it a farm theme, had all gone, and the décor was bright, clean and simple. The lighting was soft and cheerful, rather than garish, and the air was filled with attractive cooking smells, not the old deep-fat fryer. Duncan and Susie sat side by side on a modern cream sofa that must have been a bind to keep clean in a pub. They held hands as they drank a very decent Sauvignon Blanc and chatted about Alexa and Matt, and the concerns they had with their relationship. Or rather, the concerns Duncan had.

'He undermines her,' he said.

'I haven't noticed.'

'It's subtle.'

'Well, it could be her success is intimidating, despite the fact that he's successful too.'

'Mm. Her success is more solid, more intellectual. And more worthwhile, of course.'

'Whereas his celebrity could go "puff" and be gone? Yes, I see what you mean.'

'Mm.'

They both sat nodding. It wasn't often they disagreed, and when they did it was about trivial things, such as TV programmes. Susie followed every soap going, which Duncan had found delightfully incongruous at first. But not now. Recently, they'd bought another TV for the bedroom, so that he could blissfully indulge in the history channels, while Susie watched mayhem in the Queen Vic. It was a how-the-other-half-lives thing, Duncan could only conclude. He couldn't recall any TV disputes with Fran; they'd more or less liked the same things. *Waking the Dead, Morse, The West Wing* – programmes that tested their plot-following skills.

'. . . Parker Bowles is coming,' said a woman on a bar stool. 'That's what I heard.'

Susie turned to Duncan and pulled a 'Fancy that?' face. She was quite keen on the royals, and had a photo in the hall of Prince Philip chatting with her father on an airfield. When Seb said he'd met William, she'd wanted to know every little detail of the encounter. It was endearing, if incomprehensible, to Duncan.

'Camilla?' asked a man on another bar stool.

'That's what Ben calls her. Bit of a toff, apparently.'

A panicky feeling hit Duncan. His Ben?

'Bloke's got a nerve,' said the barman, who looked as though he might be the manager or publican. 'They both have.' Working alongside him was a youth with identical features but more hair, all swept forward like a strong wind had hit him.

'It's the wife I feel for, poor thing.' The woman speaking was late fifties, Duncan guessed, and attractive, if overly buxom. 'All those years of deceit.'

The man they were telling shook his head. 'The bloke's a glutton for punishment, if you ask me. As if one family weren't enough. All that stropping and never cleaning up and demanding the latest toys.'

Duncan sensed Susie shifting uncomfortably, and he did the same.

'And that's only the wives!' said the woman.

The barman laughed. 'I bet you keep up with all the latest toys, Mandy.'

'Oooh, you,' she said, giggling along in her low-cut top. '*Anyway*, seems they're all meeting up here tomorrow. At the house, that is. Can you imagine it, Jim? Both families? My bet's on a bloodbath.'

Duncan quietly cleared his throat and whispered to Susie. 'Do you think we should . . .' His eyes darted to the dining-room door.

'Absolutely.'

'What, the brats as well?' said Jim.

'The brats?'

'Camilla's two. One's like a lawyer and the other a doctor. Poor Ben's gonna feel a real thicko.'

Duncan and Susie were on their feet now, having got up in slow motion to avoid detection. Duncan began taking small careful steps, like Tom sneaking up on Jerry.

Jim said, 'Hang on!' and Duncan's heart stopped. 'Wasn't he a City boy before? Working in one of those banks that went tits up?'

'Oh, yeah. I forgot about that. I've only got to know him since he came to his dad's rescue. His father tried to top himself, you see. Ben moved home to help, but his dad buggered off to Camilla's, and his mum, bless her, went round the world to recover from the shock of it all. Well, you would, wouldn't you? When your husband's owned up to bigamy and taken an overdose.'

'Cowardly,' said Jim. 'That's what I call it. And on his wife's birthday too.'

'No!'

'Shocking, eh?'

'Shocking.'

'Ready for another, Mandy? On the house?'

'I wouldn't say no.'

'So we've heard, Mand. So we've heard.'

When they reached the door to the dining room, Duncan began breathing again. His face was flushed, his palms were sweaty on the glass stem. What Susie made of it all, he had no idea. She looked as embarrassed for him as he felt for her. Camilla? He'd seen the similarity himself, but still. And the suicide attempt? It seemed the whole village knew his business. He'd kill Ben when he saw him.

THIRTY-EIGHT

He stood on what they laughingly called the balcony and looked out over the river. What a great view it was. And a neat little flat too. The buyer had dropped out, having not got the finance together. But neither he nor Julia would be particularly worried. The market was on the move again and any future offer was bound to be higher. It might even be worth waiting. A touch of redecoration, some new kitchen counters and maybe they'd be laughing in a year or two.

Eight fifteen. Tomorrow he'd have to get up early and make his way by public transport to Long Bellingham. It was funny that this had been his old life, and now that – Tulip House, The Fox – felt like his old life. How things can turn around in the space of a few days. He breathed in river air and listened to passers-by on the river walk below. It was busy tonight because of Hallowe'en, although why grown people got carried away he'd never know. Any excuse to throw a party, or for pubs and restaurants to rake in the cash.

There'd been a few fireworks too, from idiots who'd got Hallowe'en and Guy Fawkes confused. He blamed America for exporting the trick-or-treat business. He liked blaming Americans for things, although not so much these days, now Obama was marginalising the Republican backwoodsmen.

He could really do with not going tomorrow. Nobody knew where he was. He could claim a cancelled flight, or some other travel delay. They'd hardly miss him. But then there was the big part of him that really, really wanted to go and meet the brats. Then, when they asked, 'And what do you do, Ben?' – as they inevitably would, unless primed by their father not to – he'd say, *très* casual, 'Actually, I've just been head-hunted for a position in the prime brokerage division of a leading investment bank.' Only the 'head-hunted' would be a fib but it was too good not to throw in.

How he'd swung that, Ben had no idea, but he'd given most of the credit to M&S. Apart from when sleeping, he'd kept the lucky suit on for the entire three days he'd waited for the bank's decision. Christ, a job again. He still couldn't quite take it in. He should call the pub and tell them he wouldn't be in on Monday. Or maybe he'd do a few shifts before moving back. He wouldn't start at the bank for another two weeks. Yeah, a couple of shifts might be nice. He'd miss the old crowd: Mandy and Gary, Jim and Sylvia.

He stubbed out the cigarette and dropped it in the dog-end dish. He ought to stop the smoking, and something told him he would once he was busy again. He shivered and went back in, sliding the window shut and heading to the kitchen to stir the carrot and butternut squash soup. He blew on a spoonful and sipped some. Delish. Spicy and delicious. He bunged olive ciabatta in the top oven and opened a Rioja. It was a good one. He'd splashed out. Well, why not? He was on a decent salary now, or soon would be. And how welcome it would be after a year below the income tax threshold. Not that there'd been many outgoings in Long Bellingham, what with his mum's regular injections and the fact that he'd had no life.

Had it really been a year since his father had gone off in that ambulance? A year since he and Em and their mum had rolled back home in a taxi at six in the morning to repeats of euphoric scenes in the States. Obama's victory speech. Jessie Jackson crying. Ben had found himself crying too, but he hadn't been sure why. Booze, codeine, his dad, his mum, his sister, a black president . . . A memorable night indeed.

He laid the little table they'd managed to squeeze into the kitchen, then changed his mind and took everything through to the coffee table. There could be something good on TV. He turned the thermostat up because opening the balcony window had cooled the room. He dug in his pocket and pulled out the lighter again, and went over to the ceramic tray of candles on the floor beside his big palm. The candles stood where a fireplace ought to be, and provided a focal point of sorts.

Back in the kitchen, Ben checked the veg lasagne and bumped up the oven to brown it off. From the fridge, he took a handful of green beans and washed them and got the steamer out. He wondered what they'd be eating tomorrow; what the caterers would come up with. Had Susie ordered the finest, or would it be sausage rolls and vol-au-vents? Of course he had to go. He'd get to see his niece and nephew, and Em. His sister had better behave herself. With the kids there, she wouldn't have much choice.

It was bound to be strained. All of them trying to make small talk without referring to the past and personal. 'Oh, I see. So when Dad missed my rugby final, he was with you guys?' How awkward they'd feel. How especially awkward his father – their father – would feel. Why he'd organised it, Ben couldn't quite grasp, but presumably he had some utopian vision of one big happy family. Either that, or he was a masochist. Having two families could be seen as masochistic. Ben had a feeling he'd hate Sebastian, but was open to being pleasantly surprised. His new brother. Half-brother. How weird it still felt.

The bread was warmed, the lasagne was browned and the soup would over-thicken if left it any longer. Ben switched everything off and went to the bedroom.

'It's ready,' he whispered at Julia, who was just as he'd left her: naked, head propped on pillows, *Jake the Fake* in her hand. Only now she was asleep. 'May I see one of your stories?' she'd asked. 'I read all the *Harry Potter*s, do you remember?' He'd chosen his favourite Jake, but could see she hadn't been gripped. Either it was bad, or sex had left her incapable of reading. Since it was Julia, she'd let him know.

Her eyes opened up and she smiled. 'Good,' she said. 'I'm starving.' She put Jake to one side, got up off the bed and kissed him, as passionately as she had an hour and a half ago, after arriving with bags of food, letting herself in and shocking him as much as he had her.

She'd said then that she'd forgotten how gorgeous he was, but Ben thought it was the mention of his job that got her all hot and tactile. She'd looked pretty gorgeous herself, turning up in that sexy little business suit. Sometimes she needed her space, she'd explained, away from Simeon, who could be *so* overbearing. So roughly once a week – or in recent weeks twice or three times – she'd have a night in the flat.

There was more humility about Julia, he noticed, as though Simeon had knocked some of the stuffing out of her. Or perhaps she was being nice because Simeon was an arsehole who made Ben seem saintly. Whatever it was, when they'd tried passing in the gap between the cupboards and the table, he'd suddenly found Julia's tongue in his mouth. It was a very nice tongue on a very pretty face. And since he'd spent a year in a sensual wildernesss, he could hardly resist.

'Oh, Ben,' she'd said, without following it up and then they'd worked their way to the bed and fallen on it. It had been lovely: the act, the closeness, just reconnecting with someone so familiar. And Rampant Rabbit hadn't made an appearance, which was encouraging.

'Mmm,' Julia was saying now, standing before him, all dreamy, all naked. She was undoing his shirt buttons again, her tongue rotating his. She really did love a man with a job.

THIRTY-NINE

1 November 2009

They landed at 7.20 a.m. and splashed out on a taxi. She'd slept briefly on the plane from Vienna, but Carl hadn't, and he'd been up all night too, worrying about his brother, phoning his sister-in-law. Following a motorway pile-up, Stefan was in a critical condition in Manchester. They'd always been close, and Carl had talked so much about him over the past year. That he was devastated came as no surprise to Fran.

'If I lose Stefan, there'll just be me,' he'd said on the plane. He'd cried, as though he'd already lost him. It all had an unreal quality, this drama, coming out of the blue after months of fun and travel, and for Carl, work.

But here she was, unexpectedly back in overcast England, exhausted from disturbed sleep and the early morning flight and worried for Carl, but such a different person from the one who'd flown off the previous November.

He finally slept, his head against a rolled-up jacket on the window, as the car jerked and stopped, jerked and stopped in M25 traffic. She carefully took the holdall from his lap and placed it on the floor at her feet. She knew every item in his bag, every entry in his diary. She knew all about Carl, she realised, in a way she never had about Duncan.

It hadn't occurred to her at the time, but she should have gone through her husband's cases, briefcase, pockets. She'd seen no reason to, but had that been horribly naïve of her? Any wife whose husband travelled that much would have wondered, more than occasionally, just what he'd been up to. Early on, she'd asked him once or twice, accepted his denials, and never asked again. She was bright. She'd had lots of clients whose partners were unfaithful, or they'd been. She knew the statistics. Could it have been that on some unconscious level she hadn't cared?

Fran looked over at Carl. He was balding and definitely over-weight, but the thought of him sleeping with another woman filled her with dread. She conjured up the image and was affected physically: a painful sexual jealousy. But it ran deeper than that, this bond they had, and was probably far too complicated to analyse or explain.

Being back in the UK was bringing up more thoughts of Duncan than she'd like. It was easy to block a person out when you were travelling, helping set up exhibitions, sightseeing, enjoying the company of another man, and enjoying it a lot. The slow journey to Buckinghamshire wasn't helping, and for some reason she was in London, back then, in a hotel they'd booked under false names because she lived at home and Duncan had a room in a religious woman's house and wasn't allowed female guests after seven, and preferably never at all.

After a year and a half of going out together, they were finally about to do it. Duncan wasn't a virgin but he was nervous, he'd said, because it would be her first time. She'd probably blushed and turned her head away, but she couldn't remember. What she did remember was the event itself, and the disappointment. Faking passion because she wasn't really feeling it; not the way she had with Carl. Duncan telling her how beautiful she was but his words not thrilling her, his touch not making her tingle and yearn and all those things that were supposed to happen. He was the handsomest person she could hope to be making love with but something was missing.

Fran looked at the sleeping, quietly snoring Carl and smiled. She reached across and tucked her hand between his thighs. It was all about priorities, she supposed. Having a steady boyfriend you'd most likely marry had been top of girls' lists. Girls like her, at least. And she and Duncan had got on really well. He'd liked football and had sometimes taken her to matches, and he was never reluctant to visit her family, or his in Lincolnshire. In fact, he'd enjoyed those family get-togethers; the Sunday roasts and so on. He'd been perfect partner material, and so she'd married him; young and contented, but hardly ecstatic. It was just what you did. Her parents had helped with the deposit on their first home, and in due course, and to both families' delight, she'd become pregnant with Ben.

She must email Em, Fran thought, to let her know she was back. Later, perhaps, once they'd slept. She'd so been looking forward to Paris before Christmas; seeing Martha and George, especially. They'd Skyped a few times, but seeing their little faces there on the screen, while they chatted and fidgeted, and in George's case, slipped off to play, had made her miss them all the more. She'd go to Paris anyway. Or try to, depending on what happened with Stefan.

Then there was Ben, who, as far as she knew, was still in the house. He'd either be appalled or delighted by their appearance this morning. So far, Fran had kept quiet about Carl, letting her family think she'd been travelling alone. As if she could have afforded that! Explaining who Carl was and why she'd flown off to join him had felt too big and arduous a job. On top of that, she hadn't wanted Duncan to find out; to have the satisfaction of knowing his wife too hadn't been an angel over the years. Was that vindictive? Just easier, really, and a bit cowardly.

But it wouldn't be a secret for much longer. 'Ben, this is Carl,' she pictured herself saying, as they lifted cases from the taxi. 'An old friend.' The explaining would come later, if needed. Em would pry, that was for sure.

Where they'd go from here she didn't know. They'd talked about living together, either at Tudor House, Tavistock or in Hackney, the places Carl divided his time between. She'd asked, 'Why Hackney?' and he'd said because it wasn't comfortable and he needed that. His work wasn't comfortable, that was why: a combination of handwritten stories of loss and abandonment, photographs, drawings and paintings of the individuals involved; videos too. And carefully arranged piles of relevant belongings. When she'd seen the exhibition for the first time, after flying to Chicago, Fran had been moved to tears. He hadn't included his own story of being abandoned by his father, then losing his mother to cancer, but that was what the exhibition was about, really.

Then there was her work to consider. A year's sabbatical had left her unsure of the direction she'd like to go in, which was actually quite refreshing. A year ago, her 'direction' had been retirement, followed by the odd bit of counselling. But after travelling with Carl, witnessing his late success and seeing the world and its possibilities, the idea of settling back into her room at the centre didn't excite her.

They'd sort something out. Having believed they'd be on the road another month, this abrupt ending had left no time for life-altering decisions. One day at a time, beginning with Stefan. Another loss for Carl? One final family abandonment? She prayed not. He'd travel up to Manchester tomorrow, his birthday – and she may or may not go with him, depending on Ben and the state of the house. She could join him there later, maybe on Wednesday, her own birthday. Tudor House was the last place she wanted to be that day.

They were off the motorway at last and driving through familiar scenery. Carl slept on, while Fran grew increasingly tense. Was Ben still hooked on those painkillers, she wondered. She'd almost asked in her emails and calls, but really hadn't wanted to know. Shutting it all out, everything connected with that night, was her way of coping. Or had been. Now she'd have to face things, but from a stronger, calmer perspective. Carl had been instrumental, with all the emotional nourishment, but the great healer, time, had played its part too. And just keeping busy.

Where would she be now, if she'd stayed in the house, with or without Duncan? The thought left her feeling miserable, and she sat herself upright and focused on the positive. She had Carl, that was the positive. If she'd got together with him all those years ago, she wouldn't have him now, that was for certain, and that made it a double positive. He was the glass of wine and cigarette at night that would have wrecked her day if she'd had them first thing. Not that she smoked any longer. At Carl's insistence, a hypnotherapist in Chicago had seen to it that she didn't.

'Carl, we're here,' she said, gently shaking him. 'Have you got that sterling, love?'

She tried not to look at the house because merely driving through the village had made her feel sick. Memories came back, totally uninvited. Walking Duncan up and down the landing with Alex, waiting for an ambulance. Martha waking and asking what was wrong with Grandpa. That horrible brightly lit waiting room, where Em filled her and Ben in on what her father had said. That he had this other family. None of them believing it until they checked his mobile. Susie, Alexa, Seb. He hadn't even disguised their names. Em had called Susie, who confirmed Duncan's story and said she was coming to the hospital.

The three of them left because none of them had wanted to see her. Not then. Not ever, in Fran's case. She'd be happy never to see Duncan again, and she certainly didn't want to meet his lifelong lover, the mother of his other children. She'd heard she was blonde but had asked Em to spare her any more details. She had to be attractive for Duncan to have taken such a risk. No, she never wanted to meet Susie. The humiliation would be unbearable.

Carl came to and unbelted himself, then rolled to one side and pulled his wallet from his back pocket. 'Hey,' he said, bobbing down and peering through the taxi windows. 'Great house.' His voice sounded thick, his mouth dry.

'Thanks.' She'd make them breakfast, if Ben had stuff in. If not, the village shop would be open for another hour and a half, until eleven. Sunday in Long Bellingham meant getting up early, getting in quick.

Carl paid the driver, who took the cases out of the boot and checked his sleepy passengers hadn't left anything inside. All the while, Fran waited for the front door of Tudor House to swing open. But since it wasn't going to, she rummaged for the old familiar keys, and dragging the trusty case that had seen endless hotels and planes, went up the three steps and let them in.

She knew instantly it was empty. It was funny, she thought, the way a place could feel humanless. In this case, though, the supreme tidiness, as she wandered through to the sitting room and the kitchen, added to that instinct. Surfaces gleamed and windows twinkled. Nothing was out of place. What on earth had happened? It crossed her mind that Duncan had spruced it up and had it on the market. But he couldn't have done that without her permission, surely?

'Ben?' she called out, just in case. There was a slight echo that made her shiver. 'I'll put the heating on,' she told Carl, who was busy examining an old photo on the wall. He'd always be drawn to the visual, she realised. Which was nice. She tended to be more aural, as in remembering, word for word, conversations from decades ago. 'And the kettle.'

'Great. Need a hand?'

'No,' she said laughing. 'You have a wander.'

Fran found bread in the freezer and took out four slices. Over at the toaster she pushed down the lever and an image came to her of Duncan hovering and waiting and complaining. She automatically looked over at the long table. Perhaps expecting a pile of birthday cards? But for the first time she could recall, the table was completely clear, apart from a vase of white lilies. Fresh flowers. Someone had been here recently, then. The toast popped up and she put the other two slices in, then buttered the first two and bit hungrily into one.

'Carl!' she called out, and he appeared from the garden, wiping his feet on the doormat before stepping on to sparkling floor tiles.

'I do love your house,' he said, and then he yawned loudly and reminded her of Duncan and how tired he'd always been. Was everything going to remind her of her husband? Maybe the idea of staying here was a hopeless one. Too many memories, and none of them that nice.

Fran yawned as well. Emotionally drained from coming back home, and sleep deprived from Carl pacing all night, exhaustion had suddenly hit her. They finished their toast, drank their tea and went upstairs.

'Are you OK,' Carl said, 'with sleeping . . . you know, here?'

They were just inside the master bedroom, a room that was as immaculate as every other. Was she OK? Fran didn't actually know, and she didn't want to stop and think about it. 'Yes,' she said, already peeling off her jumper, her top. 'Let's just sleep.'

They got under the tightly tucked-in duvet and cover and snuggled up, as they always did, this time spoon-fashioned. Before long, Carl was snoring again and Fran's eyes were growing heavier. If Ben didn't make an appearance, she'd go up to Manchester with Carl . . . it would be his birthday, after all . . . and he was bound to appreciate the support.

'Did you hear something?' he asked.

Startled out of sleep, she took a sharp breath in and rolled towards him. A bang came from downstairs, then another and a cupboard door slamming. Ben, she thought, struggling to wake up, tempted to go back to sleep. But then she heard humming. A woman humming. Perhaps Ben had a friend with him. She rolled back the way she'd been and Carl reverted to a heavy-breathing state. What if Ben came up and found his mother in bed with a stranger? That probably wouldn't be good. She needed to prepare him. Wake up, she told herself, and with all the will she could muster she forced her eyes open.

There was a lot of gravel crunching going on. Fran pushed the duvet back, put her glasses on and went to the window. Hooking back the curtain, she looked down on the drive. There was a woman of around her own age taking things from the back of a van and tramping into the house. Ben must have arranged for some work to be carried out, or perhaps she was the cleaner. The one keeping the house so spruce.

Aware of being almost naked, she went over to the en suite door and unhooked the robe. She put it on and suddenly felt enormous. Never mind, she thought. Since her hair was a mess and she'd not bothered with makeup since Vienna, what did it matter? Leaving Carl to sleep, she went to investigate.

* * *

The woman was taking glasses from a box. Large wine glasses – holding each one up and examining it before placing it on the counter. She was humming something familiar. Simon and Garfunkel, perhaps.

'Hello?' Fran said.

The two things seemed to happen at once; the woman turning around and the glass smashing on the tiles. Or perhaps there was a second or two between the events.

'Heavens! It is Fran, isn't it?' The woman wiggled a finger beside her head. 'Only the hair is . . .'

'Yes.' With a horrible jolt, Fran realised who this must be. God, how awful. Was Duncan about to charge in?

'We thought you were in Japan.' She gave Fran a big friendly smile, and seemed to regain composure with impressive speed. 'I'm Susie.'

Fran was still reeling. If all strength hadn't left her legs, she'd have disappeared back upstairs, woken Carl and told him to get dressed because they must leave. They'd been sleeping in Duncan and Susie's bed. How embarrassing, and appalling. No one had told her they'd moved in. That was why the place was so pristine, it was all down to Susie. The lilies, everything. Or maybe it was their weekend retreat. It was Duncan's home too, and he was entitled to make use of it. But somebody should have told her. Ben, for one.

'Oh, gosh,' said Susie. 'Look at the mess.' She tiptoed on sensible shoes and opened a cupboard, then closed it. 'Where do you keep the dustpan?'

For a moment, Fran forgot. Susie couldn't be spending much time here if she didn't know where things were. So what was she doing here, and why the wine glasses?

'In the tall cupboard at the end,' Fran said. 'On the shelf.' She'd have gone and helped but her feet were bare. Were they throwing a party? Would people turn up any second and catch her looking fat and bedraggled? 'Excuse me,' she said, pointing back towards the stairs. 'I just have to . . .'

She showered in the en suite, her mind galloping through so many scenarios that she wished she'd just asked Susie why she was there, and what was going on.

Carl appeared deeply asleep, as Fran dressed in her least creased clothes and found her old noisy hairdryer, which didn't wake him either. She was glad. He needed to rest and had suffered enough drama for one day. A touch of lipstick and mascara went on, and two squirts of perfume, and then she took a sheet of paper and a pen from Carl's bag and wrote, 'Person sleeping. Please do not disturb.'

Closing the door behind her, she placed the note on the floor, straightened up and seriously considered turning right at the bottom of the stairs and heading out for a walk. But three steps from the bottom a little voice shouted, 'Grandma!' and before she knew it, Martha was hugging her leg, then George ran up, and behind the children, coming through the front door, Em went, 'Aargh!' and dropped a bag of wrapped presents.

'Oh dear,' Fran said. 'I'm beginning to feel like a ghost.' She gave the children and Em a hug and helped pick up the exquisitely wrapped gifts. 'Tell me what's happening,' she whispered to Em. 'I've just arrived home, and that woman's in my kitchen, and—'

Em pulled a face. 'Dad's throwing a lunch party. Wants us all to get to know one another. Us. Her kids. He'll die when he sees you're here.'

'Good!'

Em laughed. 'Now, now, Mother.' They stood up, presents back in their bag. 'How are you, anyway? Why have you come back early?'

'Oh, I'll explain later. Look at you! You all look so French, so ooh la la.'

'I can speak French, Grandma. It's really easy. Even George can.'

'No! I don't believe you!' She listened to her granddaughter spouting something she couldn't quite follow or respond to, then George chipped in, and all the while her daughter was giving her an odd look.

'You're pretty radiant, yourself,' Em said, when the chatter died down. 'It isn't a man, is it, *Maman*?'

Fran smiled at the children. 'Let's get you two a drink, shall we?'

'Yes!'

'Yes!'

'*Please*,' said Em. 'Listen, Mum, I just have to get something else from the car.'

'Alex?'

'Er, no.'

She saw a change in Em's expression, and said, 'What?'

'Later.'

'OK.' Fran hoped they hadn't split up, that Alex hadn't in the end, decided he couldn't forgive Em for the affair. On the other hand, it could mean she'd have her grandchildren back in England.

With Martha and George as a kind of shield, Fran guided them into her kitchen, where she'd spotted an old bottle of

Ribena earlier and hoped it was still good. How wonderful it was, seeing them in the flesh. She could almost forgive Duncan for this absurd party.

Em must have phoned Ben and warned him because he didn't drop anything on seeing her. He arrived in a taxi and before they reached the house, began telling her about the amazing job he'd got and that he was sort of back with Julia.

'You should have asked if I'd like the good or the bad news,' Fran said, and he promised her Julia had changed for the better.

'At least I won't be under your feet here,' he added. 'Anyway, why *are* you back early?'

It was a question Fran was beginning to tire of, and it felt slightly rude – as in, why are you back early and ruining Dad's party?

'Long story,' she said, because it was. She and Carl were a very long story.

Susie was bubbly and natural. With her height and her big bones and a voice straight out of a Coward play, she oozed confidence, but at the same time made whoever she was talking to feel relaxed. Even Ben, who'd been jittery as anything on arriving, was now chuckling at something his father's mistress was saying.

Earlier, Susie had taken Fran to one side and apologised. 'For everything,' she'd said. 'I take full responsibility, absolutely. The trouble is, I've never loved anyone the way I loved Duncan. Still love him. I don't expect you to understand, only I simply couldn't give him up. But, really, I am most dreadfully sorry, Fran.' Her eyes were tearing up and Fran imagined she wasn't someone who cried easily. She knew she should have said she forgave her and that it was OK, but she didn't and it wasn't. Not really. It had been a relief, though, discovering this other woman wasn't horrible, or bitchy; that they all might come out of the nightmare amicably, and with dignity.

Two young caterers were spreading quiches and couscous and little tartlets on one end of the kitchen table, while Fran and Martha played a French version of snap at the other. Em was keeping George away from the food by kicking a ball around the garden with him; both of them in smart new coats. Fran's grandson had grown so much in a year and resembled Alex even more now.

'*Mamie*,' Martha was saying, and Fran realised she meant her. 'You're not concentrating.'

'No. Sorry, sweetie.' It was impossible, though, knowing Duncan could arrive any minute, or that Carl might stagger down. She ought to go and wake him up soon, tell him what was going on. If he wanted to head off to Manchester that would be fine. A taxi to the station, then he could sleep on the trains. 'Grandma's a bit tired,' she told Martha.

'Why?'

'Well, because I've been travelling this morning. All the way from Austria. Do you know where that is?'

'Snap!'

'Oh. So it is.'

'Grandma, you've only got two cards left. Shall we say I beated you and start again?'

'All right.' Was learning French impeding her English, Fran wondered. 'I'll shuffle, shall I?'

'*Bien sûr*,' said her granddaughter.

The food was getting closer and closer to them. Masses of it. How many people were coming? Seven adults – eight, if she included Carl – and two children. But perhaps Susie's kids would bring partners.

It was beginning to overwhelm her, this growing crowd, the inevitable pressure to small talk. She'd love to disappear; go up to Manchester, or something. But it would be hard to tear herself away from Martha and George, and also, very gradually, despite her exhaustion, a curiosity was creeping in. The most feared meeting of her life was over and done with. Susie. And, in fact, she'd experienced no more than passing shock, confusion and a touch of nausea.

Duncan had, apparently, gone to pick up Alexa and Sebastian, or Seb, as she always thought of him, since that was how he'd been listed in Duncan's mobile. Had he and Susie sat and discussed baby names, the way she and Duncan had? How he'd coped with the duplicity, she'd never understand. In the end it had caught up with him, of course. She'd tried many times to imagine the strain of it all; not getting names or events or birthdays mixed up. It would take a special type of person to manage two families well, and Duncan had done it. Although having two capable 'wives' must have helped, and of course one family had known, all along, about the other. It was all pretty tacky, and through a combination of charm and vulnerability, her husband had got off lightly.

He'd have been told by now that she was here, and Fran could picture him clammy-handed as he drove; chewing on a nail. Between herself and Duncan, she was probably the calmer.

FORTY

She'd had Hadi on her mind since arriving in the UK, but here at Tudor House it was worse. That ghastly night a year ago, when it had all come out and Alex had been so bloody serene about it was haunting her. So much so, that when kicking a ball around with George, she'd tried phoning Nigel. Just to find out more; even where Hadi was. But she'd got voicemail. It was Sunday and possibly half term for teachers here. She didn't know.

It was the Alex situation and his lack of communication that was making her insecure. He hadn't arrived when he should have, and he wasn't answering any phones and hadn't emailed or called to say why he hadn't come, and it was driving her nuts, not knowing if she still had a marriage. It was all so out of character, which made it extra worrying. What a mess, she kept thinking, and on top of that the kids had been asking about Daddy and why they weren't going to Grammy and Gramps', Alex's parents. They could still go, she guessed. She'd put on a brave face for them, telling them their son was very busy working.

In her current wobbly state, the last thing she wanted was to meet her cool confident and totally together half-brother and -sister. But Cat had had enough of them, and Martha and George had been desperate to see Grandma and Grandpa. In the car today, she'd finally told them Grandma might not be at the house because she'd had to go somewhere else, only to discover her mother on the stairs, like someone back from the dead. What a relief that had been, and although she hadn't opened up to her yet, Em felt more supported than she had since leaving Paris.

'I'm *hungry*,' George said again.

'I know. But we have to wait for Grandpa and . . . his friends to arrive before we eat.'

'Why?'

'Because it's polite.'

'Why is it polite?'

'Because it is. Here, let's see how high we can throw the ball. You first, OK?'

'OK.'

For all she knew, Alex had moved out in their absence and shacked up with Maxine, or whoever that had been. And she could hardly blame him, after the way he'd been treated by his wife. Had he guessed about Florian? Followed her, followed him? She'd known he was capable of it, but had somehow fallen into a state of false security in Paris.

Susie appeared at the back door and asked if she'd like a glass of wine. Em didn't know if she did. Were they staying the night, or would she be driving somewhere? Her mum's appearance had muddied things somewhat. But then, if she had a drink or two and couldn't drive, they'd have to stay.

'Yes, please,' she called back. 'White would be nice.'

'Right you are!'

Susie was a right-you-are sort of person, and actually rather nice. She'd met her only once before, when she'd stormed over to Belsize Park, bellowed at her and her father, accusing them of forcing her mum to run away, and promptly left. She'd tried to feel bad about that, but it had been a therapeutic bit of venting, so what the hell. And Susie seemed not to have taken it personally.

Em threw the ball in the air, quite low, so as not to intimidate George, then when it was his turn she tried Nigel again and got his message.

Oh, well, not meant to be, she thought miserably, and she put the phone back in her coat pocket, vaguely aware of more voices in the kitchen. They were here, most likely. The brats, as she and Ben had coined them. Christ, this was going to be hell. But with a bit of luck, interesting and dramatic. At least then it would take her mind off everything else.

'Come on, George,' she said. 'Let's go and see if Grandpa and . . .' What would they be to Martha and George – half-aunt and half-uncle? '. . . and the others are here.'

'Hooray, I can have food now.'

'Yes,' Em told him, 'you can have food.'

He raced ahead of her and by the time she got to the kitchen, George had been lifted up by his beaming grandfather.

'Hello, Em,' said her dad.

'Hi, Dad.' She went over and kissed him, then quickly looked around for her mum. She was at the table, stacking Martha's

306

playing cards and throwing the odd glance at the new arrivals. In an act of solidarity, Em went and sat beside her.

Alexa and Seb were introduced to Ben and themselves. They were tall and blond like their mother, and they resembled her too. For one blissful moment, Em decided they weren't her dad's children at all; that Susie had conned him. But then Seb said, 'We weren't sure what to bring,' and sounded just like her father but younger. She could see Ben scrutinising him, as he leaned oh so casually against the fridge freezer. But it was Alexa who walked over to Ben and held out a hand.

'Lovely to meet you at last,' she said, with her mother's self-assurance. 'Although I have to own up to seeing you once before.'

'Really?'

Suddenly, Alexa and Ben were deep in conversation, and Ben was laughing at a photo and saying, 'Look at my hair!'

Em piled bits on a plate for George, who wriggled out of his grandfather's hold and carried his lunch off to the corner where a dinky table and two chairs had once been. Martha helped herself and joined her brother. After days of junk food at Cat's, Em hoped they'd fill up on healthy stuff.

It took him a while, but her father finally came over and kissed her mum on the cheek. 'Hello, Fran,' he said, and Em didn't know if she was imagining it, but there was something in his eyes, like longing, or regret, or maybe just love. She hoped it was love. She wanted her dad to still love her mum, just as she wanted Alex to still love her.

After half an hour, the wine was flowing and people had loosened up, even her mum, who was asking Alexa about her job at the hospital and grinning manically, like someone who'd had three large Chenin Blancs and, as far as Em knew, nothing to eat.

Beside Em, her dad looked on with pride, as his double family chatted loudly and animatedly. 'You wouldn't believe how happy this makes me. What a shame Alex had to stay in Paris and work. I rather miss him, you know.'

Me too, she wanted to say. You could come and visit, she wanted to say too. But she couldn't say anything, because her marriage was in limbo. If Alex had left her, would she stay in Paris? She poured herself another glass of wine and went to talk to Seb, who'd been doing an ancient jigsaw with Martha at the table.

'There!' he said, letting Martha put the last piece in. 'Aren't we brilliant?' He was younger than the rest of them – mid-twenties or so – and had a lovely open face, floppy blond hair and dark blue eyes. He looked a lot better in real life than on his chambers' website.

'You know, I used to do this jigsaw when I was Martha's age.'

'Did you?' he asked and quite quickly his face changed; became sadder, or just pensive. 'With your father, no doubt?'

'Oh, uh.' Em hadn't been expecting that, and there was a sharpness in the question she didn't like.

Seeing her expression, he slumped and said, 'Sorry, that came out badly.'

'It's OK. I was trying to remember if he ever did a jigsaw with me, and I'm not sure he did.'

'No?' Suddenly, he was all open-faced and smiley again.

'As you must know, he was away a lot.'

'But not as much.'

Martha had slipped away, thank goodness. This was becoming

a bit heavy for little ears, or even big ones. But maybe there were things that needed to come out. 'You mean, not as much as he was away from you?'

Seb nodded. He picked up his glass and stared into it.

'There were genuine business trips too,' she added. 'I mean, he wasn't always with us, when he wasn't with you.'

'No. No, of course not.' He looked over at her father, his father. 'What a great guy, eh? Look at him. Jesus.'

'Um, I suppose . . .' Em was shocked by his outburst, and although she wanted to defend her dad, she had to admit she was with Seb in a way.

The smile was back. 'I bet he made it to all your birthdays?'

'Huh!' she said. 'If only. I could write you a long list of important things he missed. Ben and me in school plays, my recorder solo one Christmas. And yes, several of our birthdays.'

This time he knocked back his wine. 'This may sound harsh,' he said, 'but I'm so pleased to hear that. Thank you.'

Em shrugged. 'You're welcome.'

Seb smiled at her. 'Maybe I'm being too hard on him. Alexa's his favourite. I mean, out of the two of us. But . . . well, he did start making an effort with me. Later, when we could have proper conversations, I always had the feeling I grew on him. You know? He even cried when I got called to the Bar. Amazing.'

'Not really,' Em said. 'He must have been very proud.' She laughed. 'I expect I've made Dad cry a few times, but never for anything good.'

'Mummy, Mummy!' Martha screamed from the doorway, stopping all conversation as she often did. 'Come and see George! Quick! He's in bed with a man with no clothes on!'

'Don't be silly,' Em said, and she laughed loudly, as did the others, while her mother bolted across the room, pushed Martha aside, and disappeared.

'It's true!' Martha said with a stamp of her foot.

FORTY-ONE

They'd followed her, as she'd prayed they wouldn't. And there, indeed, was George, lying where she'd been earlier beside a bare-chested Carl, the duvet having been kicked down by George. Incredibly, he was still asleep. Fran heard her daughter gasp and more people plodding heavily up the stairs.

'Person sleeping,' Ben read. 'Please do not disturb. What the—'

'It's OK,' Fran said. 'Everyone calm down. George, come here, sweetie.'

George tried standing and immediately keeled over on top of Carl, who couldn't help but finally wake up. With eyes half open, he sat up and to Fran's horror, Em screamed. Yes, he was over-weight and pretty bald, and he hadn't shaved for a while . . . but really.

Fran looked over her shoulder and there were Duncan and Susie, wide-eyed, and in Duncan's case, mouth open. 'Who . . . ?' he asked, and Fran puffed herself up and strode into the room.

She turned to face the audience. 'Everybody, this is Carl. My partner. Carl, this is everybody.'

'Is that right?' Carl asked. He'd gone from half asleep to a kind of wild stare. He pushed back the duvet to reveal boxers and socks, and Fran willed her daughter not to scream again. 'So, does that mean one of you is Duncan?' He walked unsteadily past Fran and towards the door, looking bigger than he ever had.

'That would be me,' Duncan said, now between Ben and Em and tentatively holding up a hand.

There were more steps on the stairs, and Fran's powers of deduction told her it must be Seb and Alexa. Not Martha, she hoped because she had a bad feeling. Em must have had the same feeling because she rushed over and grabbed her son.

'It would be you, would it?' Carl said, and in a flash he'd punched Duncan's face. He'd probably aimed for the nose but having just woken up, got the cheek. 'If it hadn't been for you, Fran would have married me – the one she really loved, incidentally – and had a happy life. And all the time, you were . . . God, you're a selfish bastard!'

'Yes!' came a cry from the back. It could have been Seb.

Duncan was holding his cheek and walking backwards. 'Fran?' he asked. 'What's he saying?'

The look he gave her would have melted her heart, if she hadn't been so proud of Carl, and so sorry for him too, standing there all chubby in pants and socks and wondering who these people were, and why a little boy had jumped on his chest.

Fran met Duncan's gaze and held it, and all she could do was nod and say, 'It's true.'

Em said, '*Mum?*'

Ben said, 'What is it with this house?'

And Fran went up to the door, ushered everyone away, and shut herself and Carl in.

'Let's go to Manchester,' she said.

Fran explained about Stefan and how he was Carl's only family now, then said her goodbyes quickly and emotionally.

'I'll be back in a few days,' she told Ben and Em and the children.

Em looked the most distraught, and Fran said she'd phone her later.

'Promise?'

'I promise.'

Carl was outside waiting for the taxi, reluctant to be properly introduced, since he'd just bopped the host. 'Another time,' he'd said.

He called her when it arrived and Fran hurried from the gathering without glancing back. They'd have a better party without her, especially now she'd given them something juicy to discuss. While cases were heaved into the vast boot, the two of them buckled up inside and sighed heavily at the same time. They laughed and grabbed hands and Fran flopped her head back. The driver got in and started the engine, and they pulled away over the noisy gravel. Fran knew no one was seeing them off because she'd asked them not to, so she closed her eyes to avoid the village again.

'Who's that?' Carl asked, and her lids popped open as another taxi slowly squeezed past at the entrance to the drive.

Fran unbuckled herself, stretched across Carl and squinted

through the windows of both cars. The man in the back saw her and looked startled. 'Alex!' she said. She quickly waved and he disappeared from view. 'Thank God for that.'

'Do you want to stop and—'

'No. No need.' She kissed the tip of his nose and sat back. 'Let's just go.'

They'd be in Manchester by the late afternoon. Then, depending on Stefan, they'd either stay around for a while or return to . . . where? Long Bellingham? Hackney? Back to the European leg of the tour? The future was uncertain, but there was something rather nice about that.